Stance

HARRIS M. BERGER

Stance

IDEAS ABOUT EMOTION, STYLE,
AND MEANING FOR THE STUDY
OF EXPRESSIVE CULTURE

WESLEYAN UNIVERSITY PRESS

Middletown, Connecticut

Published by Wesleyan University Press, Middletown, CT 06459
www.wesleyan.edu/wespress
2009 © Harris M. Berger
All rights reserved
Printed in the United States of America
5 4 3 2 1

Library of Congress Cataloging-in-Publication Data
Berger, Harris M., 1966–
Stance : ideas about emotion, style, and meaning for the study
of expressive culture / Harris M. Berger.
  p. cm. — (Music/culture)
Includes bibliographical references and index.
ISBN 978–0–8195–6877–9 (cloth : alk. paper) —
ISBN 978–0–8195–6878–6 (pbk. : alk. paper)
  1. Music—Philosophy and aesthetics. 2. Phenomenology and
music. 3. Music—Social aspects. I. Title.
ML3800.B49 2009
781'.1—dc22   2009006593

 Wesleyan University Press is a member of the
Green Press Initiative. The paper used in this book
meets their minimum requirement for recycled paper.

Contents

Preface
What Phenomenology Can Do for the Study of Expressive Culture

Phenomenology is a broad and complex scholarly tradition that has the capacity to transform the ways in which scholars in the humanities and humanistic social sciences do their work. While recent years have seen an increasing interest in phenomenology in a number of fields outside philosophy, the tradition still does not enjoy the profile that other approaches do in the North American academy. A number of factors contribute to this, including the inaccessibility of its fundamental texts and the diversity of strands within the tradition. This book has two goals: to use ideas from phenomenology to shed new light on the interpretation of affect, style, and meaning in expressive culture,[1] and to make clear how phenomenological perspectives can be useful to scholars in the humanities and humanistic social sciences. As a first step in this project, this preface will sketch in straightforward terms why phenomenology matters and how it can be useful to scholars today.

One of the main things that scholars in the humanities and humanistic social sciences do is interpret the meaning of expressive culture. When the provenance of archival evidence is established, the interviews conducted, the field notes organized in a practical fashion, and the work of the bibliographer is completed, the primary task for many people that study expressive culture is to try to figure out what this narrative, this song, this image—this text—means. In the fields in which I work (ethnomusicology, folklore, popular music studies, and performance studies), the interpretation of meaning is largely about understanding what a body of texts means for particular groups of people in particular places at particular times—understanding the much-vaunted local or native perspective. While it is well known that this term has a colonialist heritage (as if there ever was a single "native" with only one perspective), scholars in these fields generally recognize that differing people can interpret the same text in differing ways, and that the perspectives that we as scholars care most about are those of the individuals, group, or closely related set of groups who produce and receive the text in question.

This is not to say that scholars in these fields are uniform in their approaches. The political significance that is ascribed to the texts of popular culture, folklore, or, for that matter, so-called high art varies widely among scholars from differing fields. Folklorists are most likely to celebrate the creativity or the capacity for positive social change found in the texts of vernacular or popular culture; in the past, cultural studies scholars were often liable to see such texts as an expression of the ideologies that hold subordinated groups down. Today, many scholars—feeling that both of these perspectives have some truth—hold some kind of complex, hybrid position. Whatever view they hold on these issues, scholars in these fields seek to understand the meanings that texts have for particular groups of people because they know it is those meanings (however full of insight or confused by ideology they may be) that are at play in the lives of their research participants and the larger social world that they inhabit. Certainly, the scholarship on globalization, post-colonialism, and hybridity has in varying ways continued the long-standing traditions of thought that problematize the notion of social groups as sharply bounded entities, as has the methodological work on multi-site ethnography. Revealing social groups to be fluid, negotiated, constructed, emergent, and shaped by relations of power, such bodies of work have, however, rarely argued that texts have only a single, inherent meaning across all times and places, social or physical. For most scholars in all of these fields, understanding the meaning that expressive culture has for those who produce and receive it is very much a fundamental task.

From the author to the text, the context, and the audience, the routes into those meanings are many and varied, and no little amount of theoretical effort has been expended to understand how meanings are constituted. In most studies of specific works, authors, genres, or cultures, it is the text and context that receive the bulk of the attention, particularly in ethnomusicology and folklore. The workaday world of scholarship in such fields is to locate, organize, contextualize, and interpret a collection of texts, and, in so doing, figure out what they mean. In the strain of folklore studies closely aligned with linguistic anthropology, for example, scholars examine texts (either collected in the field, elicited in formal interviews, or discovered in archives) and explore their semiotic details to reveal the processes of social interactions embedded therein and the meanings that they create. A tradition in music studies takes a similar route, seeing the music sound of live performances as a medium through which the members of the ensemble coordinate their activities and create their meanings. Many strands of music scholarship, however, focus on the music as a text itself and look for meaning among its varying dimensions. Exploring everything from the subtle texture of a story's language to the broadest sweep of its characters and plot, scholars of narrative focus on the elements and shapes of their texts and place them in context to get at meaning. And within folklore, cultural studies, and performance studies, a wide range of scholars investigate genres whose primary material seems to be social practices—festival behaviors, tactics in everyday life, the techniques of producing material artifacts. When the question of meaning arises, though, the practices themselves are often treated as texts—that is, clearly bounded units that convey meaning for a person. Across these fields, many scholars use interviews to try to determine authorial intentions or audience reception, but it is still texts that are seen to convey those meanings. Moving to a higher level of abstraction, we can observe that whether or not scholars conceptualize their work as grounded in semiotics, research on expressive culture often operates as the interpretation of text, that is, the reading of a set of contextualized signs, be they linguistic, musical, visual, narrative, or otherwise.

In this context, phenomenology can make a fundamental contribution to the interpretation of meaning in the study of expressive culture. It is certainly the case that signs convey meaning, and most scholars would agree that we need to look at texts to interpret the meaning of expressive culture. But even when placed in social context, texts do not tell the full story—even when we see them as the result of an embodied performance, even when we use interviews or other reception-oriented techniques to try to understand the meanings that audiences bring to them, and even when we richly situate those texts within their many levels of context. When placed before a reader, a viewer, or a listener, the text does not spring whole cloth into his or her (let us say, her) experience. People engage with texts to make them meaningful and must actively bring them into their lived experience. In other words, the meaning that scholars seek to study is *not* the product of texts; it is the product of *texts in experience*.

Among those scholars who are interested in what expressive culture means for its performers and audiences, experience is not always a welcome theoretical concept. For many in these fields, experience—that most difficult and subtle of key words—is seen as such an amorphous and ephemeral substance that rigorously accounting for its role in meaning is viewed as either impossible or unnecessary. Here, experience is sometimes dismissed as the idiosyncratically personal and individual, something opposed to the shared frameworks of culture that make the work of scholarly interpretation possible at all. While some scholars in these fields do embrace this term, it is often used in a loose fashion, and the shape and structure of experience is rarely something that is high on the priority list of contemporary theoretical work. That experience is knowable and has structures we can study is something that a hypothetical example can establish.

Consider the situation of a traditional singer performing ballads (narrative folksongs) for a large group of people. An English literature scholar may interpret the meaning of the ballads' words and place the performance in its social context. A music scholar might explore the melody of the compositions and the performer's treatment of timbre and ornamentation, and a performance studies scholar may attend to the performer's costume, stage demeanor, or the larger meaning of the notion of performance in this culture. Such interpretive work is the basic stuff of scholarship and can get us close to the meaning of the music for its participants. But consider for a moment these additional details about the scenario. The sold-out performance takes place in a busy restaurant. The layout of the tables and the positioning of some unfortunate ferns mean that only one party of patrons can see the performers, and the songs are inaudible above the din of the dinnertime rush. Though this example is intentionally broad, the point should be clear: if no one can see or hear the performance, the meanings that the scholars interpret in the text cannot be found in the audience's experience. Now imagine the same performer and audience in a concert hall with an excellent PA system. Obviously, the meanings that the scholars impute to the text are far more likely to be a description of the audience's experience of the music (especially if the scholars account for the ways in which the meaning of the venue frames the performance).

This example is stark, even crude, but there is a broader point to be gathered, beyond the obvious idea that people can't make texts meaningful if they can't grasp them with their senses and aren't aware of them in any way: moving to a higher level of abstraction, we see clearly that experience is not an interpretive black hole. The raw fact of the presence or absence of the music in the audience's awareness is something scholars can account for. That experience has a shape and structure that can be described and analyzed, and that this shape depends on more than individual caprice, is one of the basic ideas of phenomenology. Consider the slightly more nuanced example of the same ballad performance taking place at the same eating establishment; imagine now, however, that the singer is performing on a slightly raised stage and using a low-quality but serviceable PA system.

Here, the ruckus of the restaurant competes with the sound of the songs, but the music is audible and the performer is visible. Diners can make an effort to hear the music and ignore the conversation around them, listen to their meal companions and blank out the songs, or shift between the two. Clearly, the exact experience that any individual diner has depends on her choice of focus and her ability to shape her attention.

But there is more here: the shaping of experience is not a strictly idiosyncratic and personal affair. We do have partial control over how we shape our attention, but culture also has a profound effect on what we attend to and how we attend to it. These processes can operate in a direct manner: given the monetary values of coins and bank notes and the importance placed on money in the culture of capitalism, a penny, although shiny, is less likely to attract attention than a bill lying on the floor of a train station. The cultural shaping of awareness can operate in more subtle ways, however. For example, most people need music classes to become able to distinguish the individual melody lines in a fugue and hear the relationships among them; one must spend an equal amount of time in the less formal, but no less rigorous, training ground of a heavy metal scene to be able to hear richly the distorted guitar timbres of the music and identify their associations with artists, genres, and historical periods. The focusing of attention—the ability to pick out one item among many and hold it firmly in the center of consciousness—has been the subject of much of my previous scholarship, and it is an important way in which experience is organized. However, the focusing of attention represents only the tip of the iceberg in the study of the structures of experience. By the phrase *structures of experience* I mean something very specific: the relationships between parts in experience and the ways in which awareness is shaped and organized. Exploring such structures is one of the most important tasks that phenomenology sets for itself. Philosophers from the tradition have examined the organization of awareness in time and space, relationships between self and other in experience, the distinctive ways that the body emerges in experience, and a wide range of other experiential structures. Even if they don't agree with any of phenomenology's positions on the basic questions of philosophy, psychologists and philosophers from other intellectual traditions use the term *phenomenology* to describe what is immediately grasped in consciousness and the structures that are found there. In all of this work, it is well understood that experience is no intellectual quagmire, no epistemological black hole, but is something that has a shape and form that is amenable to study.

I can imagine that someone interested in folklore or popular culture may be willing to agree that experience is neither formless nor independent of culture. However, such a researcher might ask why the study of structures of experience is a job for us, rather than those in the fields of psychology, philosophy, or cognitive science. The reason such study should be seen as part of our domain is that structures of experience are directly relevant to meaning. If one is interested in the meaning of music, narrative, or verbal art for a particular group of people, one cannot study just their texts or performances in context; one must understand how such texts and performances, however contextualized, emerge in the experiences of those people. As I suggested above, many scholars (often those who use ethnographic methods) will affirm that they are interested in people's experiences. Sometimes, ethnomusicologists and folklorists will loosely characterize their research as "phenomenological," by which they mean that they are interested in the supernatural or social beliefs of the people with whom they work and that they don't take a stand on whether those beliefs are true or false. And scholars who use reader response or other interview-based approaches are often seen as doing something related to phenomenology, inasmuch as such methods seek to get at their research participants' perspectives on specific texts or issues. While interview techniques can help scholars and their research participants partially share the meaning of an experience, and while participant observation ethnography can provide profound insights into the everyday life of people and their social situations, deeper understandings are possible if we focus not just on texts and their meanings in particular groups, but on the ways in which socially situated people engage with texts and bring them into lived experience. Such inquiry will require us to attend to the culturally specific ways in which structures of experience contribute to the lived meanings of expressive culture. Indeed, if we fail to account for such structures, many of the most powerful elements of artistic behavior become inaccessible or mysterious.

Providing a method for studying the structure of experience and sensitizing us to the richness of the lived world, phenomenology is a key that opens endless doors. It is no esoteric cult, but rather a rational tradition of scholarly inquiry that seeks to systematically study that which is most readily present to us as people. Folklorist Warren Roberts characterized folkloristics as the academic discipline that is engaged in "looking at the overlooked" (1988), and many scholars in cultural studies, popular culture, and everyday life studies would see their work as embracing a related task. If such fields attend to overlooked culture, then phenomenology is a parallel project that operates at a higher level of abstraction. Phenomenology attends to overlooked experience (or more precisely, overlooked structures of experience), and such structures play a key role in the meaning of expressive culture.

Illustrations of the relevance of such structures of experience for the meaning of expressive culture shine out everywhere in our day-to-day scholarly talk, like neglected diamonds on a crowded beach. For example, one person remarks on the pleasure she derives from noticing a subtle, Beatlesesque harmony that is artfully buried in the mix of an alternative rock song. Another says that the elaborate ornamentation in the performance of an Irish folk melody obscures the beauty of the traditional tune and gives the performance a fey, contrived quality, while a third complains that the repetition of the hook in a pop record is heavy-handed and annoyingly commercial. In all of these instances, the musicians have tailored their musical texts and performances to cog into one of the basic structures of experience—the fact that the objects we place in the foreground of our attention don't exist for us by themselves but are always framed by a background of other, more dimly apprehended objects. The meanings and qualities that the alternative rock fan, the Irish traditional music admirer, or the pop listener may find in these pieces ("pleasurable," "fey and contrived," "heavy-handed and annoying") arise directly from the way that the text is situated within the foreground/background structure of experience.

To take another example, consider the significance that the temporal structure of experience has for the meaning of expressive culture. Any meaning that is attributed to *rhythm* emerges as a result of the positioning of the text in the *living present*, the term that phenomenologists give the structure of consciousness in lived time. The text of the novel alone does not make it a page-turner, for example. It is the way in which the language and the series of events in the story set up a specific network of anticipations and retentions in the flow of a reader's temporal experience that makes it a "good read" or a "fast-paced tale." It is not the physical lines in a painting that give it an interesting rhythm; it is the path through which they lead one's eye and the way that this visual choreography fits into one's lived experience of time that give the painting its lyrical flow. And the sense of what has been called groove in music (that the rhythm of a particular piece is stiff or flowing, mechanical, graceful, danceable, or static) isn't a product of the structure of a musical text and performance but of the engagement among the experiences of the musicians and listeners that that performance mediates.

Of course, the relationships among text, experience, and meaning are culturally and historically specific. In the earlier music example, the mixing of the vocal track that alternative rock fans may find to be artfully subtle could be heard as heavy-handed by a devotee of electronic music who is used to more finely focusing her attention in the extremely dense musical textures of electroacoustic compositions. Alternatively, mystery readers and lovers of modernist fiction may agree that a novel is a page-turner but differ over the question of whether this is a good thing or a bad thing. These two cases suggest differing dynamics in the relationship between culture and experience. In the alt rock versus electronic music comparison, two different music cultures lead to two different ways of structuring experience, from which two different meanings emerge. In the mystery novel comparison, both the mystery fan and the modernist reader structure the lived experience of the novel in the same way, and as a result both find the novel to be fast-paced. What differs, though, is the meaning that they give to the experience of a breezy, page-turning read, and it is the organization of experience that is the bone of contention, the arena in which meanings play out. Despite the differences among these examples, there are deeper similarities. In all of these situations, meaning arises, not from the text alone, but from the culturally specific ways in which people grapple with texts and cog them into structures of lived experience.

Here, I have tried to describe examples of situations that we as scholars of expressive culture (and as performers or audiences) are aware of all the time but for which we rarely account in research or explore in a systematic way. The structure of experience is often overlooked in contemporary scholarship and is a domain of knowledge that phenomenological research most richly examines. The utility of this phenomenology, or any type of theory for that matter, is that it sensitizes us to things we might otherwise overlook, shows us possibilities we might otherwise miss, gives us a language to describe things that would otherwise be difficult to talk about, and systematizes a field of research objects and phenomena that would otherwise be chaotic. Guided by such aims, I devote the main part of this book to exploring a phenomenon that I call *stance*—the affective, stylistic, or valual quality with which a person engages with an element of her experience.[2] As I will explain in more detail in the chapters that follow, an audience member's approach to listening to a musician involves a kind of stance, but so does the musician's attitude toward the piece that she is playing and the composer's feelings about the musical materials with which she works. A necessary dimension of our engagement with things, the structure of experience that I am calling stance is a powerful phenomenon that is at play in all forms of expressive culture. While stance is never the sole factor that determines the meaning that a person finds in a text or performance, it is often a crucial one. Indeed, in many cases, stance operates as the pivot of meaning, the factor that orients the person's overall experience of a work or situation. Examining the role of stance in expressive culture is this book's project.

One of my motivations in pursing that project is the native interest of the subject. The structure of experience is a fascinating thing. In reading the works of Edmund Husserl, I came to understand experience as a domain of inquiry with its own rich structures—a universe to be explored. Discovering the works of Husserl, Merleau-Ponty, Sartre, Schutz, and Todes (the phenomenologists who most shaped my thinking) has been one of the great pleasures of my life, and if my own small exploration of this domain can provide others with even a fraction of the delight that those writings have given me, then this book will have served a worthwhile purpose. Further, the dynamics of stance *are* dynamics of expressive culture and thus a direct and immediate part of all the fields within the humanities and humanistic social sciences that study expressive culture. Yielding new insights into the ways that meaning and affect emerge in performance—the way that expressive culture moves us—the phenomenon of stance is at the very heart of the traditional theoretical concerns of ethnomusicology, folklore, and all fields that examine artistic behavior.

But beyond serving these goals, a phenomenology of stance can yield benefits for research on particular works, genres, cultures, or historical periods. In the field situation, the library, or the archive, researchers often have a glancing, peripheral awareness of stance, and one of the main goals of this book is to help researchers bring this phenomenon into sharp focus. A heightened attention to stance and an understanding of its dynamics will allow scholars to make richer interpretations of expressive culture, delve more deeply into their subject matter, and align their own understandings more closely with those of their research participants. In the context of fieldwork, social and cultural theory are much like the materials that a jazz musician practices. When she takes a solo on the stand, the skilled improviser is often unaware of the scales and patterns that she has learned. That does not mean that practicing scales and patterns was a waste of time. The musician's years of careful study made those materials second nature to her and laid the groundwork for performance. Likewise, theory is, among other things, the foundation that informs fieldwork and the interpretation of culture; and as in music, exploring that ground is a lifelong, ongoing activity. Attuned to the dynamics of stance, scholars will be able to more fully engage their research participants in interviews, more sensitively read their texts, more closely approach their lives. Further, an attention to stance can serve the needs of those who are primarily interested in the ways in which expressive culture fits into issues of power and politics. The low-level meanings that people find in works of expressive culture (e.g., "fey," "heavy-handed," or "graceful") are combined with one another to form higher-order representations of identities. By providing a more nuanced understanding of these lower-order meanings, attention to stance can offer insights into gender, race/ethnicity, class, or sexual orientation—insights that would be difficult or impossible to obtain if the fundamental reading of texts were insensitive to the structures of experience.

Having spoken about the utility of the notion of stance for scholars of expressive culture, I will also say a few words about this book's scope and disciplinary foundations, its treatment of examples, and its structure. While this work grew out of my lifelong experience as a musician and music scholar, I hope that it will speak to anyone interested in the study of expressive culture. Like all academics who seek to address this broadly interdisciplinary audience, I am grounded in particular scholarly disciplines. Though I have been influenced by work from a range of fields, the book's primary grounding is in ethnomusicology and folkloristics, particularly folklore's performance studies strain. While phenomenology is central to the book, it is not a work of philosophy per se, but an attempt to take ideas from philosophy, connect them with concepts from ethnomusicology and folklore, and make them speak to broad issues in the study of expressive culture. While these disciplines have long histories—ethnomusicology is usually understood to have its earliest roots in the late nineteenth century and folklore goes back at least as far as the eighteenth-century philosopher Johann Gottfried von Herder—both developed as part of the U.S. academy during the twentieth century, in part as interdisciplinary meeting places for scholars from more established fields such as musicology, anthropology, and literary studies, and in part as critiques of those fields. Over time, some of the critiques made by ethnomusicologists and folklorists have been assimilated by their interlocutors in more established disciplines, and scholars from the larger disciplines have likewise influenced those in the gadfly fields. As a result of these dialectics, disciplinary boundaries have been both blurred and redrawn. As an ethnomusicologist and folklorist, I have been influenced by the new musicology (particularly the important work of Robert Walser and Susan McClary) and the research on verbal art and culture in anthropology. However, ethnomusicology and folklore are my primary intellectual heritage, and they are at the center of this book's disciplinary landscape.

The role of music examples in this book (and, more generally, my treatment of the issues of media and genre) requires special note. Many of the dynamics that I discuss here are illustrated through examples of music performance, including a long discussion, which forms the backbone of chapter one, of the goings-on in a hypothetical music school. I have tried to cast my discussions of music in terms that any educated reader can follow, and no special musical training is needed to understand these passages. Given my years at the fretboard, I cannot help but illustrate my ideas with musical examples, but I do not want to give the impression that stance is operative only in music. Stance plays a role in the meaning of *all* forms of expressive culture. To make clear stance's broad applicability, after the opening chapter I exemplify my ideas by reference to a broader array of genres and situations, including stand-up comedy, movie viewing, festival behavior, and everyday social interaction. This approach is characteristic of folklore studies, which since its inception has understood the complex ways in which meaning emerges in social life, both through and across the boundaries of media and genre. No special knowledge of folklore, anthropology, or sociology is needed to follow these passages, and I hope that my music colleagues will work through these discussions. Ignoring the nineteenth-century cultural typology of high art, folklore, and popular culture, I draw on examples of artistic behavior regardless of the prestige or stigma associated with them in elite canons. Like many scholars these days, I find this typology to be the product of hegemonic discourses and useful only as a subject to be analyzed, not as a scheme for cutting up the cultural pie or as a valid framework for guiding inquiry. Be they from genres exalted or reviled, musical or non-musical, the examples were chosen with one aim first and foremost in mind: clearly illustrating the ideas at hand.

The role of music examples in the text leads to two other issues that require some attention: the use of hypothetical and personal examples in the book, and the broader question of how scholars from differing disciplines illustrate their ideas. In traditions of inquiry like ethnomusicology and folklore, theoretical generalizations are usually exemplified by reference to the author's own fieldwork, data from the ethnographic literature, or, less frequently, archival sources. In contrast, philosophers often construct hypothetical examples to make their arguments, and they sometimes discuss observations from their own lives. I draw on both approaches in this work, citing field data, as well as constructing hypothetical examples and discussing my own everyday experiences. Each approach has its advantages. Examples drawn from fieldwork can help to show the diversity of human experience, the wide range of ways in which expressive culture plays out in differing social contexts. Hypothetical examples, by contrast, are limited by the always culturally situated imagination of the author, but they offer the advantage that they can be crafted and shaped to make clear exactly the point under discussion. Perhaps more importantly, hypothetical examples, at least the ones in this book, are never fictional in the sense of entailing fabulous situations. To the contrary, all of them emerge in some way from their author's experiences. For instance, the situations in the music school example are, in one form or another, all ones that I have experienced or observed at some point in my career as a musician, while the account of distraction in chapter 2 is drawn directly from the events of a specific afternoon several years ago. Of course, isolated experiences never speak for themselves, and rigorous approaches to these kinds of materials, such as those developed in phenomenology, are necessary to make the particulars of one's own existence be of value for social research. But understood in this way, the utility of hypothetical or personal examples can itself illustrate some of the fundamental principles of existential phenomenology and related traditions: that the scholar is not separate from the social world but is a part of it; that theory does not exist in some independent domain but is theory about our lives; and that to be of use, theory must ultimately return to our lives by informing our interpretations of things and our actions in the world. If this were not the case, theory, it seems to me, would serve no purpose.

Tacking back and forth between the philosophical and the ethnomusicological or folkloristic, the book proceeds on a specific course. Written in an accessible fashion, the first chapter introduces the notion of stance and connects it to features of performance that students of expressive culture will find familiar. The next two chapters tease out the dynamics of stance, both in situated practice and in the long scale of a person's life, and they become increasingly philosophical in their style. The writing in the final chapter steers away from the phenomenological and examines the place of stance in the politics of culture and in politics in general.

In conference settings, I have sometimes heard phenomenology dismissively represented as a religion. While some professional philosophers in the tradition have been interested in studying mysticism, and while some of its foundational texts can be dense and difficult reading, phenomenology is a school of rational inquiry like any other. It requires no faith and certainly no god. In fact, it is a measure of how misunderstood the word *experience* has become that a branch of philosophy devoted to rational inquiry into structures of lived experience could be thought to be based on faith. Perhaps motivated by similar concerns, others sometimes ask how (or even if) phenomenological ideas can be applied to fieldwork and if some unique research technique is implied by this approach. While the study of fieldwork methodology will continue to yield new ways of doing ethnography, the phenomenological ideas I lay out in this book are not meant to offer some new form of access to the experiences of others. They offer no methodological telepathy, no miraculous or supernatural ability to get inside the heads of one's research participants. As I have suggested, ideas from phenomenology are relevant to ethnography in the same way that most bodies of theory are: by revealing the shapes and forms in a domain of knowledge, positing study objects, and sensitizing researchers to phenomena that they may find in the field. On the level of research technique, phenomenological ethnographers may ask their research participants questions that explicitly focus on the structure of their experience or employ feedback interviews to get at the same kind of information. But like ideas from other bodies of theory, concepts from phenomenology may also impact research methods in more subtle ways—framing the ethnographer's assumptions and observations, contextualizing the ways in which interview questions are phrased, and informing the researcher's interpretation of her interviews and texts. The results of such seemingly mundane forms of inquiry can bear real fruit for scholars in the humanities and humanistic social sciences. Interest in phenomenology has been increasing in recent years. Ideas from this tradition can offer powerful new insights into the study of expressive culture, and I hope that this book will suggest some of the dimensions of phenomenology's still untapped potential.

Acknowledgments

In writing this book, I have benefited from the stimulating conversation and friendship of more than a few good colleagues. First, I must thank Chris Menzel, a philosopher whose kindness, keen mind, and open-hearted spirit have never failed to inspire me. While we do not always see eye to eye on questions of metaphysics, the philosophy of mind, or culture, I have greatly profited from his diamond-sharp arguments and endless patience for discourse. My ideas and writing were always improved when I imagined him as my reader. In the early stages of the project, lunches with John Fenn helped to stimulate my thinking about the political and aesthetic implications of my evolving ideas about stance.

Conversations with Philip Auslander during his residency at the Glasscock Center for Humanities Research at Texas A&M University and at our joint panels on music and performance studies at the conferences of the Society for Ethnomusicology and Performance Studies International helped me to develop my thinking about music, performance, and expressive culture.

Deborah Kapchan read a draft of the manuscript, and her penetrating mind challenged me to engage new ideas and sharpen my thinking; this book is far better for it. Discussing ideas, probing concepts, reflecting, chatting, jawing, and otherwise hanging out with Brenda Bethman, Patrick Burkart, Wesley Dean, Rola el-Husseini, Susan Fast, Paul Greene, Judith Hamera, Fabian Holt, Joseph Jewell, Jimmie Killingsworth, Larson Powell, Annie J. Randall, Kati Szego, and Jeremy Wallach has always been enlightening, and I thank them for their kindness.

I am grateful to the College of Liberal Arts at Texas A&M University for their support of this book.

Of course, my greatest debt is to Giovanna P. Del Negro, whose unerring social theoretic instincts and deep sensitivity to the aesthetics of everyday life continually inspire me. This book is for her.

Stance

CHAPTER ONE

Locating Stance

✦

This book grew out of my long-standing dissatisfaction with a certain type of aesthetic explanation that is common in the humanities and humanistic social sciences. In a wide range of fields, scholars frequently explain the meanings or expressive effects associated with a particular text, performance, item, or practice by pointing to its formal techniques, devices, or features. Such an explanation has its merits, of course. It is unquestionably the case that the musical, literary, visual, or performative details matter a great deal in expressive culture,[1] and much of the lives of musicians, writers, artists, and performers is spent in training the body and mind to provide fine and precise control of their expressions. But no matter how sophisticated such explanations may be, they have, I have always felt, left out something important. A wide variety of books and articles could be used to illustrate the problem with such analyses, but an example from my own recent experience will serve the purpose as well.

Recently, I was writing a lecture on the Beatles for a class in rock music history. Casually checking to see how other scholars had taught about issues of music and meaning in that band's songs, I read the passage on "Yesterday" in Larry Starr and Christopher Waterman's valuable textbook *American Popular Music: From Minstrelsy to MTV* (2003). Starr and Waterman identified a range of features in the piece that contribute to the sense of wistfulness and despair that the song evokes, but one bit of the analysis struck me as something my students would find particularly compelling. "The ascending gestures in the melody," they write, "always depict the receding past ('all my trouble seemed so far away,' 'I'm not half the man I used to be,' and so forth), while the immediately following descending gestures always bring us back down to earth in the present ('Now it looks as though they're here to stay,' 'There's a shadow hanging over me,' etc.)" (257). Clearly, the tight correspondence of the meanings of the words with the shape of the melody contributes to the song's evocative power. I was pleased to discover this neat observation and planned to emphasize it in my lecture. A songwriter as well as a scholar, I have not used text/tune relationships in my own songs as much as I would like, and finding this passage got me thinking that I should take fuller advantage of them in my own music. But as I began to think more fully about this analysis, a skeptical voice started its familiar nagging. "Yes, that feature clearly matters in the music," it said, "but something is wrong. You could use that same device in a similar context in one of your songs, but it wouldn't produce quite the same effect. Do formal techniques simply *evoke* meanings or effects? You are missing something important."

Well-known theoretical themes in folklore scholarship from the second half of the twentieth century have been driven by such doubts. The standard ethnographic critique in folklore studies would question if the meaning imputed to the text is present in the experiences of the people in the community that make and listen to it and (among folklorists who study music as well as ethnomusicologists) if the imputed formal technique is present in their local music theory. The related contextualist critique would argue that formal techniques, devices, or features have their meanings only when placed in textual, situated, or cultural contexts. The familiar performance critique would argue that to understand meaning we must attend, not to abstracted texts, but to their distinctive enactment in performance.[2]

Such perspectives are valid, even foundational, for contemporary scholarship; indeed, I have often pursued such lines of criticism in my own work (e.g., Berger 1999). Expanding on Starr and Waterman's discussion to address these concerns, however, did not assuage my sense of dissatisfaction. In this instance, for example, I wasn't concerned with the ethnographic critique. I grew up with "Yesterday." I knew that the meanings ascribed to the tune fit with my experience and that I was a reasonably typical member of this music culture. I also knew that this kind of text/tune relationship was often used by songwriters in British and American popular music. Addressing the contextual critique, I observed how the themes spoke to issues of gender in post-war culture and the history of themes of romantic loss in popular song, and I highlighted these links in my lecture notes. To speak to performance-oriented concerns, I returned to the recording and transcribed and analyzed the ways in which Paul McCartney's phrasing and timbre contributed to the distinctive blend of sadness and wistful despair in the piece. If I could have quickly acquired a live performance of the tune, I would have tried to examine how the interactions among the members of the ensemble or between the band and the audience might have contributed to its evocative power.

But even as I was including these ideas in my notes, the skeptical voice returned. "By transcribing additional performative details," it said, "you have enriched the text that you are analyzing. This is a good thing, but you haven't solved the problem. Would any performance that entailed these features be guaranteed to evoke the meaning that you are after? If not, don't tell me you need to transcribe even more details, because I will come back with the same critique. Interpreting the details of performance is a valid response to performance theory's criticism of textualism (text-oriented research),[3] but it doesn't respond to my charge. It only results in a reductio ad absurdum. You can keep accounting for performative details till the cows come home and still have no guarantee that the devices and techniques you have identified will produce the experienced meanings and aesthetic effects that you imputed to them." I thought I could see where this was going—a reception-centered critique. Scholars who do reception-oriented research very rightly hold that texts never fully specify their meanings and that processes of reception inevitably contribute to the experienced meaning of expressive culture.[4] There is no response to this critique, beyond the valid point that interpretations are always interpretations of texts, and therefore the analysis of form must be a necessary part of interpretation if we are to understand how expressive culture achieves its effects. But my skeptical inner voice never said that the analysis of formal techniques, devices, or features wasn't important; it only said that such an analysis was missing something important.

That hard-to-identify, important thing always seemed to me to be missing from many types of analysis across a range of disciplines and intellectual traditions. Speaking in impressionistic terms, one might say that many analyses of expressive culture seem like they have more to do with features than people. But this can't be the problem, it would seem, because form is one of the main things (though certainly not the only thing) that people love in expressive culture. Musicians and listeners revel in sonic textures, painters and their audiences bathe in light, and poets and their audiences caress syllable, cadence, and rhythm. This is exactly what is missing: not form, but form as it is taken up by producers or receivers of expressive culture; not just light, sound, or word, but light, sound, or word as it is grasped by the brush, bow, or pen, by the eye or ear, by the social person in a social world—the way that the eye of the painter or viewer of the painting "palpates" the landscape or canvas, to use Maurice Merleau-Ponty's arresting, almost disturbingly accurate terminology ([1964] 1968:131). No matter how formally sophisticated, any analysis that neglects such palpations will produce oversimplified and unsatisfying readings of expressive culture. To address this problem, I believe, we need to carry forward the ethnographic, performative, contextual, and audience-centered critiques that have ani-mated scholarship since the 1950s. Such a project must attend to the irredu-cible stratum of practice that is deposited in products of expressive culture even as that practice constitutes them, and is retained in those products even after the producer's hand has left her object. As phenomenological thinkers have long argued, such a project must likewise understand recep-tion, not merely as a bestowing of meaning upon texts, performances, items, or practices of expressive culture, but as a process of grappling with texts, performances, items, or practices—an engagement with them that produces meaning and experience even as it is an openness to what is al-ready there.[5]

The core problem with explanations of meaning or aesthetic effect based solely or primarily on the analysis of formal techniques, devices, or features is that they treat the form/meaning connection as causal and de-finitive and that they view the reception of expressive culture as a mere registering of what is there. Often unintentionally, such work represents expressive culture as a piece of textual or performative machinery that evokes or produces meanings or effects for anyone properly enculturated to understand its code. Here cultural context may be seen as doing the work of enculturation and processes of reception as receiving or decoding the meanings that are there in the text, but the operation of the expressive machinery is still a thing itself whose mechanics exist in their own domain. Indeed, it is that domain that formal analysis sets out to explore, and in the constitution of that domain, the caress of the hand and the palpations of the eye are excluded.

Even when the scholar is able to identify particular formal techniques that everyone would agree play some role in the evocation of meaning, such features never exist by themselves. On the contrary, they must be applied by the producer of the text, and that application can be clumsy or smooth, sub-tle or obvious, done with a wholehearted enthusiasm or with the fingers pinched firmly over the nose. Likewise, those engaged in reception may grasp the technique easily or with difficulty, with an eye keen on finding flaws or with a generous heart, with pleasure at a well-loved technique or annoyance at a tired cliché. Such qualities of production or reception inflect the meaning of the underlying technique, even—or especially—when the presence and rough meaning of that technique are unquestionable. In other words, even when formal techniques, devices, or features do produce agreed upon effects of aesthetics or meaning for those in a particular social world, the connection between technique and effect is never a mechanical and causal one. On the contrary, subjects have complex *relationships* with items of expressive culture and their techniques, devices, and features; such relationships are both social and agentive, and, most importantly, they inflect the subject's overall experience of meaning. Accounting for such relationships is crucial if we are to come to terms with the complex reality of experiences of expressive culture. Such phenomena as facility or clumsiness, subtlety or obviousness, enthusiasm or reluctance have, of course, been noted by scholars in the past. What is needed is to see these qualities, not as free-floating meanings or unproblematic features of the text, but as products of the relationship between the person and the text, performance, practice, or item of expressive culture.

Using ideas from phenomenology, the semiotics of Charles Sanders Peirce, or the anthropology of emotions, scholars from a range of fields have taken up the issues raised by these relationships. This book seeks to offer a distinctive approach to this topic by examining an element of lived experience that I will refer to as *stance*. I will provide a formal definition of the term later, but in a strictly preliminarily fashion we can understand stance as the valual qualities of the relationship that a person has to a text, performance, practice, or item of expressive culture. Stance, I hope to show, is frequently the pivot of meaning, the point around which turn the interpretations of expressive culture. This book is grounded in the fields of ethnomusicology and folklore studies. Though it is not a work of philosophy, this book draws on ideas from key thinkers from the phenomenological tradition of continental European philosophy—primarily Edmund Husserl (the founder of the movement), Maurice Merleau-Ponty (a pathbreaking mid-century thinker best known for his work on embodiment), and Samuel Todes (a more recent philosopher who has profoundly advanced Merleau-Ponty's approach)—and I hope to show one way in which phenomenology can be useful to those interested in music, folklore, and expressive culture in general.[6] A number of scholars in anthropology have employed ideas from phenomenology to get at issues of meaning, and those in the subfield of the anthropology of emotions have used other intellectual apparatuses to explore related topics, particularly the cultural basis of affect.[7] Though I am not an anthropologist, I see myself as a fellow traveler with them. In examining stance, my focus here is on structures of lived experience and the culturally specific ways in which people make meaning by fitting expressive forms into the context of those structures.[8]

This chapter provides an initial sketch of the notion of stance. The next two chapters deepen the discussion, examining in close detail some of the ways in which stance shapes meaning in the production and reception of expressive culture. Chapter 2 explores some basic structures of stance and takes a first look at the way stance is maintained in time. Chapter 3 focuses on the expression of stance in social interaction. In addition, it furthers the analysis of stance and time to show how stance ties the immediate situation of events and performances to the broadest scale of a person's life. Turning to even wider contexts, the last chapter shows the relevance of stance for the politics of expressive culture and issues of power in social life. The ideas of Husserl, Merleau-Ponty, and Todes animate the entire text, and explicit discussions of particular concepts from their work are threaded throughout. Husserl's notion of intentionality is discussed in this chapter. Merleau-Ponty's work is examined in chapter 3; while Todes's ideas inspired some of the discussion in this chapter, they are explored most fully in the final chapter. Less important to this book than phenomenology but still crucial, the classical formulations of practice theory (particularly as found in Giddens [1976] 1993, 1979, 1984; Bourdieu 1977) have shaped the entire text; explicit treatment of those ideas takes place mostly in chapter 4.

Stance Illustrated through an Extended Example

In the music cultures with which I am most familiar, the form of stance that is easiest to see is the stance that a musician has on the piece that he or she (let us say, she) is performing. While the notion is applicable to genres quite different from music and to cultures far beyond the United States, I will begin this chapter with a hypothetical example set in an American conservatory. Starting with a discussion of a performance by a fictional undergraduate pianist, my plan, here, is to introduce stance in its most familiar form, broaden the analysis by illustrating how stance applies to practices of music composition and listening, and conclude with a discussion of Husserl that suggests why stance is a necessary feature of all experiences of expressive culture. That discussion will also allow a formal definition of stance to replace the preliminary one touched on above.

Before we can get a fix on stance in musical performance, we need to get perspective on the thing that is being performed—the musical composition. In a wide range of Western music cultures, the musical piece is conceived of as a preexisting compositional entity that is enacted in performance. Of course, if we compare Western art music from the common practice period with that of the contemporary avant-garde or musics in the rock and jazz traditions, it is clear that there are a wide variety of ways in which dimensions of sonic form are fixed in advance or left open in performance. Likewise memory, written notation, or forms of technology are used in differing ways to store the composition, and the line between composition and performance can be drawn in differing ways as well. This has been illustrated by Bruno Nettl's groundbreaking study of improvisation (1974) and more recent research by scholars such as Deena Weinstein

(1993), R. Keith Sawyer (1996), myself (1999), and many others. For all of their differences, however, many Western music cultures share a notion of the "composition" or "piece of music" as a preexisting entity. Inquiring into the nature of the composition would immediately launch us into the most complex terrain: Is the composition an ideal object as a Platonist would suggest? A conceptual or data structure, as cognitive scientists imagine it? A text in the Derridean sense? A set of embodied practices, as Maurice Merleau-Ponty or David Sudnow (1978) might hold? A supernatural agent, as understood by the belief systems of varying cultures and religious communities? Though the question of the being of the composition is a fascinating and profound one, I will set this topic aside for now and simply observe that, for traditions that understand the composition as an entity existing before the performance, the musician will clearly have a relationship to that composition as she plays it—whatever its ontological status. This relationship is the most straightforward form of the notion of stance.

In a performance of a Chopin piano piece by an undergraduate piano major, for example, those familiar with the Western art tradition hear the notes and their durations as "the composition" and hear the timbre and the fine details of dynamic and rhythm as "the interpretation."[9] Audiences familiar with this tradition literally *hear* the performer's facility or clumsiness with the work's technical demands, literally hear a loving attention to detail, a misunderstanding of nineteenth-century harmony, or a creative approach to traditional material. In such a context, the performer's approach to the performance of the piece is a form of stance. Indeed, if stance were nothing more than the style of performance, it would not be a new idea, although even conceptualized in the most traditional fashion there is great complexity in this form of stance, and its dynamics are crucial for meaning and expressive effects. For example, because the notion of interpretation is so fundamental to Western art music, listeners familiar with a performer can distinguish between her typical style of interpretation and her enactment of that interpretation at a specific concert. Indeed, when a particular interpretation is carefully worked out in advance—for example, "I always employ a dramatic crescendo in bar 56, add a rhythmic accent on the second note of each of the ascending arpeggios in the sequence, and play the cadential chord in such a way that I get a rich, ringing tone"—that interpretation takes on a composition-like status for those who know the performer well.[10] As a result, in any individual performance, the performer will have a relationship to both the composition and her customary interpretation, that is, a stance on the composition and a stance on the interpretation. Before a solo concert, for example, our pianist might think, "I usually use a rhythmic accent on the second note of each arpeggio, but tonight I will use a dynamic accent in order to emphasize my ongoing exploration of Chopin."[11]

Such stances need not always take the form of a plan worked out ahead of time, and even when they do, they take their fullest form only when enacted in performance. For example, after the concert the pianist may realize, "I was off my game. Those dynamic accents were too weak to be heard." That stance plays a key role in the interplay between the musician and the audience and is often crucial in their experiences of meaning should also be clear, as should the complexity of these dynamics. Between the performer and the audience, there may be deception (the performer: "I am sick of Chopin, but no one could tell because of my subtle use of accents"), penetrating interpretation (a professional critic: "She clearly hates this piece; her dynamics are so flat tonight"), or naive misinterpretation (another professional critic: "What an exquisitely loving performance"). It is worth emphasizing here that because the performer's stance is a stance *on* the composition, and because, as we have seen, the idea of what counts as a composition is dependent on culture, what counts as stance will always be dependent on culture as well. In Western art music, stance will be manifest in timbre, dynamic, and rhythm.[12] In a performance of Javanese gamelan music, for example, where the skeletal melody is often articulated only in variation, stance may be manifest in note choice as well. However the composition/performance line is drawn, though, it should be clear that the performer of preexisting compositions has a relationship with the piece that she plays and that this relationship has a complex role in the performer's and audience's experiences of meaning. Throughout, I will refer to the performer's relationship with any entity understood as a preexisting composition as *performative stance*. The term applies to genres well outside of music, as storytellers, actors, those who take part in rituals, and anyone who enacts a preexisting course of action will have a performative stance on the steps that have been laid out for them.

The notion of "relationships" alluded to above needs a firmer theoretical grounding than I have developed in the discussion so far, but for the moment I want to take performative stance as a starting point and suggest that there is also a stance relationship between the composer and the piece, the listener and the piece, indeed between every person in every role in the production or reception of any form of expressive culture. To illustrate this strong claim, I will explore a hypothetical example of a very particular assignment in an undergraduate music class. This example brings up an issue that I mentioned earlier, the ontological status of the composition, a fascinating topic that I do not pretend to consider fully here.[13] Rather, my goal is to conjure up a set of situations that will be familiar to many readers and easily accessible to those with no formal background in music; in so doing, I hope to help readers locate stance in their own experience and prepare the way for a more formal definition.

Imagine a music theory or composition course in which a professor asks her students to compose a short piece of music with a very specific set of restrictions: use four voices and diatonic harmony, do not employ parallel perfect motion, use pivot chords for key changes, and so forth.[14] Let's call these requirements the assignment's "formal rules." To these limitations, the professor adds what we might call a "procedural rule," specifically the stipulation that the student must compose the piece in her head. She can have no access to either an instrument or manuscript paper as she composes; she may commit the piece to the page only when it is complete, and she can make no revisions during the transcription process. Such a pedagogical technique isn't omnipresent in introductory level classes, but it certainly isn't inconceivable. (My reasons for adding the procedural rules will become apparent shortly.) Now in a class of forty students, ten or fifteen may hand in scores that completely conform to all of the professor's rules and therefore receive an A+. There is no doubt that the professor, when reading the assignments, will be able to tell if each student's piece has followed the formal rules of the assignment. But even when considering only those students who have handed in perfect assignments, an experienced professor can tell the difference between those A+ students who have assimilated the formal rules with ease and produced smooth, fluid compositions and those who have colored within the lines, so to speak, but have had to resort to clumsy moves to prevent a transgression of the assignment's formal restrictions. Imagine that for the A+ students, the professor not only gives a letter grade but also provides prose comments describing her reading of the piece. "Clever; I like the way you handle the key change in bar five." Or, "A bit too clever, we didn't need three key changes in bar eight, and the large leaps in the tenor are awkward; don't try to show off until you have the basics." Or, "In your piece entitled 'Composition Study 5,' you are really in control of the voicing leading, but the differing sections of the piece don't really hang together; they feel disjointed and distracted. I wonder if you would rather be in some other class."

While this example is not a typically folkloristic one, its elements conform nicely to the analytic tools of folklore studies. The ideas about melodic contour, harmonic rules, tropes of musical rhetoric, even the equal-tempered tuning system assumed but never specified by the professor can be understood as expressive resources. As the student imagines the melody and the bass line and starts to fill in the inner voices, she grapples with these resources—sustaining the sounds in imagination well or poorly, finding smooth and clever ways of avoiding parallel perfect fifths, or resorting to awkward but legal leaps to keep the music within the rules. She borrows a pretty harmonic move from Chopin and another from the Beatles and wonders if her professor will catch the reference. The point here is that while the embodied performance in the pianist example seems to be very different from the example of seemingly disembodied composition, they share a common *structure of experience*: in both situations, we have a person engaged in a complex relationship with an item of expressive culture, and the quality of that relationship is crucial for experiences of meaning. We can refer to the form of stance suggested in this part of the example as *compositional stance*.

But what does it mean, exactly, to say that a composer has a relationship with a piece of music? When we considered the example of our performer, the composition was understood as a preexisting entity, reified in the score and having a mind-independent reality. But when we speak of composition, and particularly mental composition, we may seem to posit an entity of such pure fantasy, an entity so completely dependent on the work of a sustaining mind, that it is hard to understand how a person could have a relationship to it. Clearly, the composition is dependent on the mind of the composer: if she were to drop dead, the composition would die with her.[15] But the composition, while dependent on the composer to sustain its existence, has a limited and partial autonomy. If this were not the case, composition students would not have to struggle to solve problems in voice leading, mystery writers would not worry about writing themselves into a corner, and playwrights would not have to rely on deus ex machina to solve their plot problems. None of this is to say, of course, that musical compositions have inherent meanings or to deny that perception plays a fundamental role in shaping the form of the composition in experience. Nor is this to say that that partial autonomy is an autonomy from social life. It is to say, though, that entities in imagination have a limited autonomy from the imaginer, and that limited autonomy, though sustained by her acts of imagination, serves to both constrain and enable the ultimate shape of the imagined experience.[16]

Giving a level of autonomy to compositions might seem to run counter to the ethnographic, performative, and audience-centered perspectives alluded to above. With their emphasis on the importance of culture, embodied practice, and interpretation, scholars in these traditions tend to be suspicious of any theory that seems to impart a Platonic or ideal quality to items of expressive culture, because such qualities sever expressive culture from its basis in practice and social life. The intuitions behind these suspicions are valid, but they shouldn't force us to miss the opportunity for new insights that are there if we proceed carefully. On a basic level, we should consider accepting this claim about the partial autonomy of entities in imagination because the claim accurately describes our experience. Composing a verse or visualizing a figure I want to draw, I experience the imagined words or figure as a thing; I experience it as something in "my imagination" and perhaps as mine. I do not, however, experience it as "me" or as possessing a total flexibility.[17] If every day in January I spend five minutes visualizing a blue apple, and then every day in July I visualize a green apple, it would be a lie to say that I experienced green apples in January.

Perhaps more importantly, acknowledging the limited autonomy of entities in imagination does not deny the social and bodily ground of imagination; indeed, it allows us to better account for that grounding. My discussion here is inspired by the insights of Samuel Todes's *Body and World* ([1990] 2001). Advancing Merleau-Ponty's ideas on embodiment and subjectivity ([1945] 1981), Todes shows how our constant need to balance in the earth's gravitational field and our negotiation with physical objects are the fundamental, preconceptual bodily processes that allow the physical world to present itself to us. Todes refers to these basic forms of bodily grappling as "poise" and shows that parallel processes of poised constitution operate in imagination as well. Our experience of imagined sounds, images, or ideas emerges through a kind of mental poise that both constructs and sustains them. Of course, unlike physical objects, imagined entities are dependent for their being on the person who imagines them. Given that dependence, however, imagined entities take on a limited autonomy, and Todes presents a sophisticated argument to show that imagination and conceptual thought in general arise from our preconceptual, bodily engagement with the world.

I will return to a more detailed discussion of Todes's phenomenology at the end of chapter 4, but for now we can use the example that we have been exploring to see the bodily and social nature of imagination. Considering our composition class once again, it is evident that the musical rules and rhetorical tropes are historical artifacts and that the references to Chopin and the Beatles come from a culturally specific repertoire. The orientation toward the future audience of the professor illustrates the embedding of these imaginative processes in a social world. Likewise, the time-scale of the tempo, the very notion of harmonic and melodic interval, and the strictures of overtone, timbre, sonority, and blend all emerge, not from a realm of free-floating imagination, but from an imagination rooted in a body that interacts with a sonic world. And even if the composer imagined high notes that no singer could sing or timbres that even no synthesizer could produce, these very auditory impossibilities would be impossibilities arising out of and in relationship to a contingent physical reality. Far from denying the social and practice-based components of composition, acknowledging the partial autonomy of entities in imagination puts those components in sharp relief. If entities in imagination were completely mind-dependent quicksilver, then there would be no way that we could work *on* them or have a relationship *to* them. We would simply *be* them. But when we acknowledge these entities' partial autonomy, an autonomy derived secondhand from the world and from our consistent efforts to sustain them, then there is something there to have a relationship with and a stance on.

In our composition example, the composer initially has a stance on the expressive resources, generic restrictions, and compositional procedures of her community and the rules set down by the professor's assignment. They are what precede composition and allow it to take place. But as the composition is emerging, every note stipulated develops a partial autonomy, and the composer develops a relationship to that piece as it is being created. In our example, this is attested to by the professor's comments on the piece. What the professor is describing is her reading of the student's relationship to the expressive resources that she employs ("You are really in control of the voicing leading rules we worked on this semester . . .") and the piece as a whole (". . . but the differing sections don't really hang together; they feel disjointed and distracted. I wonder if you would prefer to be in some other class"). Later, we will need to explore in more detail the issue of the communication of stance between differing actors. For now, the key point is that the complex unity of the text and the stance, rather than the text alone, is the fullest source of experiences of meaning.

Comparing the student composer and the Chopin performer, we can start to become more explicit about this notion of relationships. In both examples, the relationship that the hypothetical person has to an item of expressive culture results from her grappling with that item. That grappling is a form of social practice (in the sense of activity, not practice in the sense of rehearsal), and it works in two different ways. On the one hand, that grappling is a production of music in the sense that the composer creates a new piece where none had been before (specifying a series of notes and their durations) and that the performer creates a new performance where none had been before (embodying that composition in movement and sound). On the other hand, that grappling is also a constitution of the music in experience. Producers of expressive culture never fly blind, merely producing their creations without experiencing them; on the contrary, they bring their creations into experience even as they are creating them, and these processes of production and constitution are locked in a complex and very intimate dialectic.

This is obviously true for the composer in our example; merely "hearing" the piece in imagination, keeping the fantasized notes and chords in her head as she writes, is part of the fundamental challenge of the assignment. However, this is also true for composers who write with instrument at hand. To compose a piece at the keyboard or fretboard is as much a question of careful listening—is as much an attempt to hear, keep track of, and judge each new melody or chord—as it is an attempt simply to fix a series of notes. Likewise for the performer, auditory perception is intimately enmeshed with bodily action. Only in the most extreme situation is the feedback loop of bodily motion and auditory perception severed, and then only partially; when a performer can't actually hear what she is playing (as is the case, for example, in certain situations in which American popular musicians perform), she will typically replace the sound in perception with imagined sounds in order to keep herself on track.[18] *Most importantly, qualities of emotion, style, and (speaking most generally) value in this productive and constitutive grappling inflect the meaning of the music.* Such qualities are the central theme of this book. In the composition example, the teacher's comments to the A+ student are not oriented to just the techniques that the student employs, but to the quality of her grappling with those techniques, the expressive resources she has received from her culture, and the strictures imposed by the piece as it emerges. Likewise, when the performer plays the Chopin piece with smooth facility or awkward clumsiness, we see a similar grappling to produce and constitute the music, and the quality of that grappling inflects its meaning or aesthetic effects for both the performer and the audience.

One final example will round out this initial sketch of stance and point us toward its broadest dimensions. Imagine an end-of-the-semester concert in which student pianists play pieces from the composition class. The meaning of the music for any audience member on that evening in early May certainly depends on the formal devices of the piece and its performance. But because perception is not merely a registering of what exists in the world but is an agentive process (a process actively carried out), the listener, like the composer and the performer, will have a relationship to the music. In other words, while the listener in the Western art tradition does not produce the music in the sense that the composer and performer do, her role is like theirs inasmuch as she actively constitutes the music in her experience through perceptual practices. I will refer to the affective, stylistic, and valual qualities of these practices, as performed by audience members, as *stance in the practice of reception,* or *audience stance.*[19] Listening at the concert, our hypothetical audience member follows the melody or gets lost; she feels uncomfortable with the material because it is from another tradition or proudly identifies with it because she thinks of it as her music; she highlights the missed notes because she is jealous of her sister the pianist or attends to the clever key changes because she is proud of her roommate the composer. These qualities of audience stance obviously inflect experiences of meaning. If unable to follow the melody, the listener may simply experience the piece as tedious and uninteresting, or as exciting and challenging, a spur to explore new musical possibilities and an icon of the world's limitless horizons. Hearing the piece as the music of the other, she may experience the careful voice leading as typical of the pretentious convolutions of Western culture or as an exotic pleasure to be savored. In any case, it is not the techniques or features themselves that bear meaning in our listener's experience of the music but a complex gestalt of form and stance.

It is worth emphasizing here that, as with performative stance and compositional stance, stance in the practice of reception is deeply shaped by culture. The foregoing passage may have led the reader to see audience stance as a strictly individual affair. It is true that listeners have a measure of control over their ability to follow a melody or hear a piece of music as foreign or familiar; however, social context clearly plays a key role here as well. For example, one's ability to follow a particular dimension of musical structure depends to a great extent on one's past experiences with musics that employ such structures and one's musical training, both formal and informal. Likewise, whether one hears music as foreign or familiar—and the kinds of valences one attaches to such foreignness or familiarity—depends deeply on one's past social experiences, the ideas about music and identity in one's social world, and the larger political discourses within which one's thought is embedded. Both the production and reception of expressive culture can be understood as forms of *social practice* in the sense of that term elaborated in the classical formulations of practice theory—an activity that is actively achieved by the person and at the same time fundamentally informed by situated and larger-scale social context (Giddens [1976] 1993, 1979, 1984; Bourdieu 1977). I will explore ideas from practice theory more fully in chapter 4, but for now it is important to see that acts of production and reception are practice in the sense that they always have both agentive and social dimensions.

The social nature of listening runs deep, and this becomes apparent in new ways when we recognize that listeners frequently grapple with what they believe to be the composer's and performer's stances. Thus, our audience member may actively focus her attention on the voice leading to hear critically the composer's skillful or clumsy handling of the style's restrictions, or attend to the dynamics and rhythm so that she can experience more fully the performer's loving or disaffected embrace of the composition. For a listener familiar enough with the tradition to make these distinctions, her overall experience of meaning will emerge as a rich, multilayered unity of meanings, a gestalt of gestalts. This includes a gestalt composed of the listener's experience of what she hears as the valual and affective qualities of the composition (the expressive resources it involves, the piece as a whole) combined with her interpretation of the composer's stance on the piece; that unity is synthesized with the listener's experience of the performer's stance on this composition in general and this particular performance; finally, that complex is synthesized with the listener's own stance on the piece in general and this particular listening event. As I suggested in the earlier discussion of deception, penetrating interpretation, and miscommunication in the Chopin performance example, the composer's and performer's stances are not un-problematically registered in the listener's experience. On the contrary, they must be grasped by the listener to play a part in her experience, and the attempt to grasp those stances is part of the relationship with the music that the listener constitutes. Indeed, in many music cultures, much of the composer's or performer's work comes in crafting and enacting stances that she anticipates will be heard by the listener, and much of the listener's experience is oriented toward finding those stances in perception.

Of course, listeners unfamiliar with the Western art tradition may not be able to identify the expressive resources/composition/interpretation/performance boundaries as they occurred in this particular, culturally specific production process, thus misunderstanding or completely failing to recognize the stances of the composer or performer. But whether or not the audience member's interpretation of those stances is an accurate reading of what happened in earlier stages of the production process, and whether or not she listens for anyone else's stance at all, one thing is certain: listening to music isn't merely a registering of what is there. On the contrary, the listener always has a relationship to that music. She grapples with its sound and constitutes it in experience, and the valual and affective quality of her grappling—that is, her stance—plays a key role in the overall experience of the meaning of the music for her.

While various phases of this example involve dynamics specific to the tradition of Western art music, I hope that there has been enough variety in these situations to point toward underlying commonalties that may have broad relevance. Certainly, the differences among these examples are great: composition as production in imagination, performance as embodied enactment of a preexisting composition, and listening as perceptual practice. But if we look closely, the commonalties are equally striking. In all three cases, we see a person actively grappling with an entity that is independent from her and bringing that entity into experience. Whether the person is engaging in perception or imagination, that grappling is social and bodily, and the style with which the person grapples with that entity shapes and inflects her experience of its meaning. Further, that grappling often looks back and forward across the production process to anticipate or recover the grappling of others: the composer emerges from a social context and orients her compositional process to the anticipated probing ear of the teacher; the performer looks back at the composer and forward to the listener; the listener looks back to the composer and the performer, and perhaps forward to the possibilities of future music events. Comparing the Western art music example with other types of expressive culture (e.g., Newfoundland balladry, Turkish rug weaving, the African American dozens, the central Italian *passeggiata*), we can begin to appreciate the range of expressive media and production processes that may exist. Fundamental commonalties, however, remain. All forms of expressive culture involve some material (words, sounds, material objects, practices) that is shaped and formed. Whatever the person's role in that shaping or forming, the person's experience of that material never comes about through a mere registering of shape and form, but involves a social and agentive relationship with that material that emerges when she grapples with that form and brings it into her experience. The affective and valual quality of the person's engagement with such material is stance. Meaning is always more than even an interpretation of shaped materials, but is a gestalt of such materials with stance.

Intentionality of Consciousness as the Ground of Stance; A Formal Definition of Stance

The discussion so far has, I hope, provided a general sense of what is involved in stance. We can give a firmer grounding to this idea if we explore Husserl's notion of the intentionality of consciousness. Before we do so, however, we need to understand some of phenomenology's basic premises. In the interest of brevity, my discussion will elide some of the differences that exist among the various strands in the phenomenological tradition and will somewhat simplify a few of the difficult issues that these thinkers explore. I hope, though, that I can illustrate the fundamental insights that are widely agreed upon in the tradition and, if not prove that stance is a necessary feature of experiences of expressive culture, at least suggest why that contention might be supportable.

The phenomenological tradition begins with the work of Edmund Husserl (1859–1938) and his desire to find an absolutely certain grounding for knowledge. Seeking a radically fresh start to traditional philosophical problems such as the relationship of the subject to the world and of appearance to reality, Husserl argued that we must begin our inquiries by taking an unprejudiced look at the only material we can bring to bear upon such questions—our experience. Setting our philosophical assumptions about the ontological status of experience within an "epoché" (set of brackets), we must, he argued, return anew to experience and describe in a rigorous and unprejudiced manner what we find there.[20] In everyday talk, we often use the word *experience* to refer to something flimsy, personal, and subjective, something standing against the real physical world; however, when we suspend that assumption and return to lived experience, we find that experiences of the physical world, strictly as experience, retain their objective character. I do not experience the table before me as a mental construct that I must later judge in an act of thinking as a valid representation of the real object in the physical world; to the contrary, I directly experience the table as a mind-independent entity. Discovering that the realm of objective reality retains its objectivity strictly as lived experience, Husserl's phenomenology sees the epoché's brackets, not as a temporary thought experiment that comes before the real philosophical work, but as a stripping away of philosophical misunderstandings that allows us to see the nature of experience for what it is. As a result, the epoché's brackets are never to be removed.[21]

The notion of the epoché clears the way for the description of experience, but scholars in the phenomenological tradition are not content to only describe specific, individual phenomena. To the contrary, phenomenologists seek broad insights and fundamental structures of experience that might be the ground upon which secure knowledge can be anchored. The primary structure that phenomenology discovered is referred to as the "intentionality of consciousness." First introduced by Franz Brentano and given a radical new interpretation by Husserl, *intentionality* is at the very heart of the tradition. The term has a different meaning in phenomenology than it does in everyday usage. It does not refer to having a goal or plan and then later enacting it in behavior (though, as we shall see, the phenomenological notion of intentionality is connected to meaning). On the contrary, to say that consciousness is intentional is to say that consciousness never exists by itself. Consciousness, Husserl showed, is always "consciousness *of* something," ([1913] 1962:223). Even a small amount of reflection will reveal the truth of this observation. No matter how hard we look, we can never find an experience of consciousness by itself. Whatever type of experience we seek to examine, we always find that it is an experience of something—an idea, a feeling, a judgment, the body, an object in the world. The very certainty of the intentionality of consciousness may at first glance lead us to regard this discovery as trivial, but its significance is enormous. Rather than seeing consciousness as an entity outside the world that bestows meaning upon it, as idealism does, or as a mental copy of the real physical world, as in realism, phenomenology's intentionalist perspective understands consciousness to be in the world and in direct contact with the world.[22]

At this point, introducing two of Husserl's specialized terms, which he took up from ancient Greek, will help to further the discussion. The term *noesis* refers to the acts by which consciousness engages with its objects and constitutes them in experience (e.g., perception or imagination), and *noema* refers to the objects thus engaged (such as physical objects or fantasies). Noesis is carried out in different "noetic modes," and each mode corresponds to a different type of noema. Perception, imagination, memory, judgment, and anticipation are examples of noetic modes, while things in the world, fantasies, memories, judgments, and anticipations are their corresponding objects.

As is frequently the case in philosophy, the most powerful insights emerge when considering the problem of perception, and by exploring the rich interplay of noesis and noema here, we can begin to see the relevance of these themes for the notion of stance. Discussing Husserl's description of intentionality in *Ideas 1*, Erazim Kohák emphasizes that the importance of intentionality is not just "*that* experience has an object, but, so to speak, *how* it has an object. In an earlier work [*Logical Investigations*], Husserl describes intentionality as the 'act character' of perception" (1978:121). This act character is the critical issue here. Perception is not a mere registering of what is there in the world; it is an active engagement with that world. It is fundamentally a form of practice in the practice theory sense of the term and is shaped by the practitioner's goals and social experiences.

The act character of experience is directly tied to meaning. Wherever one turns within the epoché, one does not find brute things but, to use the phenomenological language, things as meant—entities that present themselves to one as already experienced in types and categories. The thing before me is not a desk per se until I constitute it as a desk in my act of resting objects on it, or, in Kohák's example (51–53), a sailboat is not an entity completely independent of any subject; it is constituted as a sailboat by acts of sailing—by the pulling of ropes, the adjustment of the mast, and the tacking of the bow into the wind. This view likewise differs from forms of philosophy that see perception as a pure bestowing of meaning. On the contrary, I cannot sail a desk or write on a billowing sail. Perception is an openness to what is there in the world, a revelation of both its mind-independent qualities and its possibilities for engagement and use by the subject. This is directly implicit in the notion of intentionality and was suggested in the earlier discussion of imagination in the music composition example.[23] As we saw there, if noema (even fantasies) were nothing but mental quicksilver, they would simply dissolve in the godlike meaning-bestowing act of the noesis. Likewise, if perceptual noesis was only a registering of what is there in the world, qualities of objects like "to-be-written-upon" and "to-be-sailed" would disappear, because these qualities are only qualities *for* a subject. Indeed, to-be-written-upon or to-be-sailed make sense only as to-be-written-upon *by a subject* or to-be-sailed *by a subject*.[24] Beginning with the discovery of the intentionality of consciousness, phenomenology ultimately reveals the mutually constitutive relationship between the person and the world.[25]

These ideas speak directly to the earlier example and lay the groundwork for the notion of stance, though one final piece of terminology needs to be introduced at this point. In the earlier music class example, composition, performance, and listening can easily be understood as forms of intentional engagement with a piece of music. Since they are ways of bringing a piece of music into experience, we therefore might be tempted to think of them as noetic modes. The problem here is that noetic modes are understood in phenomenology to be universal modalities of experience, universal ways in which a person engages her object. As I suggested in the passages preceding the music conservatory example, contemporary scholarship has clearly shown that the stages in the production process of music making are nothing if not culturally variable. What counts as composition, performance, and listening varies substantially across cultures. As a result, I suggest that composition, performance, and listening in the world of Western art music (or any other stage or role in the production process of any expressive form) should be thought of as *noetic sub-modes,* culturally specific forms of intentional engagement.[26] The corresponding noema of these noeses would the object of expressive culture thus engaged (in the music school example, "Composition Study 5").

Beyond the fact of their cultural specificity, noetic sub-modes differ from noetic modes in two important ways. First, noetic sub-modes often combine two or more noetic modes. As we have seen, the performance of American popular music in a nightclub setting often involves not just perception of the music that is being made, but also imagination of those parts that are inaudible in performance. Many forms of composition span perception and imagination as well, with the composer both imagining new parts in her mind's ear and creating new parts on an instrument. Second, noetic sub-modes overlay their noetic acts with valences, usually ones that serve broader ends. In the music appreciation classes of traditional Western music departments, focused listening is prized, and individuals are encouraged to actively disattend to all but the music sound before them. In contrast, composers in the tradition of John Cage and adherents of certain cultures of meditation disdain the focused attention on isolated musical sounds and encourage an openness to the complete auditory environment.

To say that noetic sub-modes are culturally specific is not to posit a world of discrete cultures, each with a fixed repertoire of ways of engaging with expressive forms. Cultures are, of course, reifications, mental short-hand for describing the partial sharing of practices among or between groups of social actors, and as such they are internally heterogeneous, porous at their boundaries, variable over time, and always at least poten-tially open to reinterpretation by the agency of their practitioners. Thus, while actors do receive repertoires of noetic sub-modes from their social surroundings, an individual actor will often employ multiple noetic sub-modes (multiple ways, for example, of composing, performing, or listen-ing to music), and that actor may choose to experiment with the boun-daries and strictures of the noetic sub-modes that she has received. However varied, emergent, and subject to agency such practices are, though, they will always emerge in response to a particular cultural con-text, and in this sense are "culturally specific." For all these differences, noetic sub-modes share one thing in common with noetic modes: both are ways of engaging with objects or other subjects and making them emerge in experience.

Grounded in intentionality, the notion of noetic sub-modes not only applies to music but to experiences of all forms of expressive culture. In our music examples, we have already seen how the noetic sub-modes of an in-dividual genre are culturally specific. Even more differences emerge when we consider genre and culture together.

The genres of the *passeggiata* (Italian ritual promenade) and American improvisational theater, for example, have no noetic sub-mode that cor-responds directly to composition. Consider the passeggiata first. A popu-lar pastime in Italy and other Mediterranean countries, the passeggiata is held on a daily or weekly basis during the temperate months and occurs in both cities and small towns. In the event, children, adults, and senior citi-zens performatively stroll up and down an area designated for the prac-tice, displaying their refinement through clothing, comportment, and gait, and observing the performances of others. While culturally specific and finely crafted styles of walking can be found in the Central Italian passeggiata discussed by folklorist Giovanna P. Del Negro (2004), indi-vidual gaits do not have the sharply bounded, formal identity for pro-menaders in the passeggiata that pieces of music do for conservatory pia-nists. The noetic sub-modes in this genre of performance are "strolling" and "watching the strollers," and the noema of these noetic acts are the individual, specific performances of each particular event. Only in Monty Python's well-known "Ministry of Silly Walks" sketch or in those acting classes where students are asked to create specific gaits for their characters do we see something like the composition of "a walk." Likewise, R. Keith Sawyer's work on American improvisational theater highlights a form of performance whose preexisting units are games and rules, not scripts of words and actions (1997). In the improvisation known as "dubbing," for example, two groups of actors develop a single humorous scene; one group of actors is on the stage, and the other is offstage. The offstage actors improvise dialog based solely on a general situation provided by the audience (such as "two people at a bar"), while the actors on the stage perform the actions for the scene but are not allowed to speak. Unlike composition in Western art music, the preexisting limits on the conduct of the actors in the noetic sub-mode of "improvising a dubbing scene" are only a few general rules, the situation the audience stipulates, and the tacit knowledge of the typical situations of American culture. I will develop my discussion of compositions, rules, and other types of culturally specific objects of attention in the next chapter. For now, though, one point is critical. While one can search out sets of similarities and differences across the various noetic sub-modes of differing cultures and their genres, there is only one structure here that is universal and necessary: the person intentionally engaged with an object in socially informed practices of constituting experience. Within the broad framework of intentionality, modality, and culture, there is an endless space of difference.

This structure provides a secure foundation for the notion of stance. If intentionality refers to the engagement of the subject with her object, then stance is the affective, stylistic, or valual quality of that engagement. Stance is the manner in which the person grapples with a text, performance, practice, or item of expressive culture to bring it into experience—a student composer's bland use of sophisticated formal techniques, an audience member's earnest effort to hear harmonic moves that she imagines speak to the greatness of her tradition, an eager young model's enthusiastic attempt at jaded fashion runway indifference, or a seasoned painter's loving optic caress of the landscape.

Because intentionality is a necessary feature of all lived experience, stance is as well. Indeed, it is the very universality of intentionality that guarantees its relevance to all forms of expressive culture. This is not to say that stance is always the focus of attention or is given the same significance in all cultures. As I will suggest in chapter 4, participants in some cultures of performance may foreground the text and background the stance through which it is constituted, while the opposite may be true in other cultures. At the extreme are situations in which the goal of performance is to obscure or even eradicate stance. In some types of optical, abstract, or conceptual art, for example, the artist seeks not to display her stance on the process of painting or creating sculptures, but to lose her identity and reveal what are understood as objective shapes and forms. Likewise, many types of aleatory music (music that uses chance processes to generate sound) are created by composers who seek to silence their own voice and open their listener to what they see as the power of mathematical randomness, ambient sound, the divine, or the universe in general. Performers from a variety of religious traditions see their actions as a conduit for supernatural or divine entities, and in such situations stance can be given a variety of meanings. It can be seen as an important element of performance, but the agency to whom stance is attributed may be a spirit or ancestor, not the performer; here, the performer may be valued inasmuch as she is able to serve as a gateway for the expression of the perceived supernatural's stance. Alternatively, a performer's stance may be seen as a valuable and unique gift bestowed upon her by the divine. On the audience's side, the energetic individual striving to apprehend the actions of a supernatural entity in performance may be valued in a particular social world, or it may be a self-abnegating openness to the presence of such entities in the performance that is sought in a given culture.

None of these situations involve stanceless experiences. All experience involves the engagement of subject and object, and the valual quality of that engagement is stance. In composing a piece of aleatory music, for example, the composer still defines chance procedures for creating sound, and the very desire to absent herself from the composition process constitutes a stance upon that process. Where such music is understood by the audience as having nothing whatsoever to do with a composer—is understood strictly as an expression of the universe or of God—the listener's experience is not a pure unification with that sound. On the contrary, her experience of the music is constituted in perception, and stance is the affective or valual quality of those constitutive acts. Indeed, a listener's self-abnegating openness to the sound of an aleatory composition is precisely a kind of stance. This is not to say that an openness to the world is impossible or to criticize the ideologies of particular music cultures. One may listen to music with the goal of finding a certain kind of experience or with a more self-effacing openness; likewise, composers may seek to communicate a uniquely personal vision through their music, or they may instead try to create a context that affords listeners the opportunity to discover for themselves the intense power that sound can hold for humanity. But regardless of local ideologies of performance, the intentionality of consciousness assures that stance is always one element in the mix of factors contributing to the texture and meaning of experiences of expressive culture. Founded on the bedrock of intentionality and profoundly shaped by culture, stance is a fundamental part of all experiences, and attention to it will allow scholars to achieve richer and deeper insights into lived meanings.

Stance is related to but distinct from ideas already in our intellectual toolkits like style, sensibility, aesthetic (such as "a Latino aesthetic"), or spirit (such as "the spirit of the German people"). I will refer to such expressions as "traditional style terms" and will conclude this chapter by making clear the differences between them and stance.

The utility and allure of traditional style terms is that they draw our attention to the distinctive affective and valual quality of particular people and their creations. The difficulty with them, however, is that they proceed from undertheorized ideas about the relationships among text, practice, and experience and may thus lead to all manner of confusion. On a basic level, style terms can be used loosely to refer to the properties of objects, the procedures for creating them, the manner in which those procedures are carried out, or the underlying values that they are believed to reflect. When we speak of "a heavy metal style," for example, we might be referring to features of the music sound (passages of power chords; vocal timbres with a rough quality), the performance (the guitarist's use of downstroke picking; a manner of vocal production that holds the vocal folds in a particular position), or the emotional content of the music (aggression and grandeur). Failing to specify where in the chain of production or reception the meanings associated with particular "styles" or "aesthetics" emerge, the boundary between the habitual and the active components of practice becomes blurred and the dialectics of product and process are lost. The result is that questions of agency are implied, but never adequately addressed. Is a Canadian sensibility, for example, something that a writer has or something that she does? Further, traditional style terms encourage us to gloss over questions of interpretive variability. Writers often feel free to debate the meanings of particular genres or works, but when the discourse shifts to that of "sensibility," the linkage between the work and the impulse from which it sprang is assumed to be so direct and the language so totalizing that conversation is shut down and "for whom" questions are excluded. With all of these potential pitfalls, discourses centering on traditional style terms are particularly susceptible to reification—that is, the treatment of texts, meanings, or groups as independent from the concrete reality of people and their actions and experiences. When we allow ourselves to reify expressive culture or meanings, we lose any empirical check on our interpretation, the people about whom we write no longer see themselves in our work, and clarity is lost. At its worst, our writing devolves into little more than an erudite spinning out of our unconsidered personal presumptions.

Reification does not just produce difficulties on the level of theory or argument; it also leads to distortions on the level of the interpretation of meaning. Scholars are certainly susceptible to these problems, but this difficulty is most evident in the work of advertisers and critics, individuals whose stock in trade is describing, evoking, and evaluating the meaning of expressive culture. We may, for example, feel comfortable when a writer refers to *the post-punk style* or *Oscar Wilde's sensibility,* and we may have a clear idea of what those terms mean in the context of particular pieces of music or plays. But the meaning of those terms becomes progressively murkier as they are applied to genres further and further from their initial context or when combined with one another. What might the "post-punk Asian" food at Atlanta's Teaspace Restaurant taste like (Access Atlanta 2004)? What exactly did the reviewer of Stephen Fry's novel *The Liar* mean when he referred to that writer as a "post-punk Oscar Wilde"? And when applied to ethnic groups, countries, or even historical periods, style terms become more vague and more problematic, even as they become more seductive and resonant.

In criticizing traditional style terms, I do not dispute the fact that individuals have affective, valual, or aesthetic predispositions and that these predispositions can be partially shared. However, by highlighting the problems with this kind of discourse, I want to suggest that we are prone to confusion about both the meanings they claim to describe and the broader issues in culture and society to which they are tied if we treat reified meanings as a fundamental, underlying reality that is only contingently enacted in practice. Research framed in terms of stance takes as its object the same kinds of phenomena that have been the traditional focus of terms like *style* or *sensibility,* but charts the ground of practice and experience on which they are established. Requiring us to tease apart the twisted threads of meaning that spool out from expressive resources, texts, and practices of production and reception, a stance-oriented approach calls us to specify the objects to which meanings are ascribed, make clear the role of agency in performance, illuminate the interpretive variability between actors in or across production processes, and show how all of this plays out in their lived experiences; such lived meanings are the reality from which generalizations about cultural styles, approaches, or sensibilities are abstracted. Thinking about performance events in terms of the stances of composers, performers, and audience members encourages us to attend, not to reified styles, but to the specific ways in which the differing participants in a performance actively and socially shape their actions and make them meaningful. Viewing expressive culture in terms of intentionality, we take lived experience as our study object, place people at the center of our analysis, and focus on the social processes with which they engage with texts. Assimilating phenomenological terminology, we gain a vocabulary for talking about that engagement.

This last point is important. The profusion of terms in phenomenology has sometimes served to make the tradition less accessible than it might be, but such terms give us a language for talking about the structure of experience and therefore help us to get closer to the concrete world of people and their relationships to expressive culture. Thinking in the abstract terms of noesis and noema, we gain the clarity that comes from taking a high vantage point and see such seemingly diverse phenomena as perception, imagination, and thinking all as ways of forming experience. Understanding the endless variety of expressive practices (composing a piece of music in a formally defined genre, strolling on a passeggiata, improvising a scene according to the rules of an improv comedy game, or critically listening to a student recital in a concert hall) as noetic sub-modes, we see that such practices are united by an underlying structure: all involve a person grappling with a work of expressive culture and bringing it into experience, a process that is shaped as much by a person's social life as it is by her agency. Taking such an approach paves the way to new understandings of topics fundamental to contemporary scholarship: the ways in which texts evoke powerful meanings for people, the partial sharing of meaning between participants in a performance, the interplay of culture and agency in practices of production and reception, the role of artistic behavior in the long span of a person's life, and the place of expressive culture in power and politics. Using a more philosophical style of writing and argument, the next two chapters illustrate the significance of stance for these topics.

The notion of stance is not only relevant for broad theoretical issues such as these, it can also contribute directly to the interpretation of individual works, genres, or cultures. The music school example that I have elaborated above is a fictional one, but the processes described there are real: composers—and, in the broadest sense, writers—do have stances on the expressive resources that they deal with; performers have stances on the pieces that they perform, and audiences have stances on the works and performances that they engage. Such stances play a key role in the meaning that people find in expressive culture, and attending to the play of stance in performance can help ethnographers interpret such performances more richly. As I observed in the preface, phenomenology offers the fieldworker no telepathic access to the experience of the other, but that does not mean that such structures of experience are inaccessible. As I suggested above and will show in greater detail below, our actions and the fact of our common nature as subjects in the world enable us to partially share our experiences with others; indeed, all people routinely make interpretations of others' experiences, including their stances. Watching for stance in performance gets us closer to the people around us, puts us in touch with their most intimate practices—their engagement with their texts and their worlds—and helps us understand their lives more richly.

The ethnography of the dynamics of stance in particular cultures is a rich topic for fieldwork, and an enormous amount of research remains to be done in this area. Even when it is not explicitly invoked, theory influences research, and the notion of stance can serve the interests of those ethnographers who do not wish to adopt whole cloth the theoretical apparatus of phenomenology. As I suggested in the preface, theory serves a sensitizing function, awakening the field-worker to dynamics that she may find in her field site and helping those involved in historical inquiry to find the actors behind their archival documents or published texts. The theoretical writings that we read shape our empirical research, framing our assumptions, placing data into contexts, and informing our interpretations. By highlighting dynamics of experience that would otherwise be grasped in a peripheral fashion, the notion of stance can get us closer to the people and things we care about. This is the goal that many ethnographers and historians in the humanities and humanistic social sciences have for their work. By orienting our thinking to concrete actors and their engagement with the world, the notion of stance can bear real fruit for contemporary scholarship.

CHAPTER TWO

Structures of Stance in Lived Experience

When we think of interpretation, the paradigm case we use is often one

At first glance, applying the notion of stance to particular research situations might seem to be a straightforward proposition. To attend to stance would be to attend to the styles with which composers compose, arrangers arrange, listeners listen, painters paint, and viewers view. However, unforeseen complexity arises from the fact that the production of expressive culture is not merely the creation of physical objects, and reception is not merely registering preexisting forms and bestowing meaning upon them. To the contrary, the production of expressive forms always involves a constituting of those forms in experience, and reception is always an active grappling that influences, not just the experienced meaning of those forms, but the audience's perception of their very shape.[1] As a result, understanding stance requires additional theoretical work. We need to explore the differing forms that stance can take, the ways in which stance interacts with other dimensions of experience, and the question of stance and time. These issues are the focus of this chapter.

Fundamental Dynamics of Stance

When we think of interpretation, the paradigm case we use is often one of judgment or decision. A prosecutor presents her evidence to a jury, and the twelve citizens sit in a room, think about the facts, discuss them, and, in a self-conscious act of judging, render a verdict. A similar model may seem to fit our most naive understanding of language learning. There is certainly no inherent relationship between the sounds "c-a-t" and the furry creature that sits on my lap at the end of the afternoon, and in our everyday theorizing we suppose that a child learns the meaning of "cat" by associating those sounds with the species *Felis domesticus*. Here, processes of thinking and judging are seen to attach meanings to things as a hat is attached to a head. Of course, such processes do take place in experience and are part of the overall interpretive dynamics of expressive culture; they are, however, only one part of that dynamic, and there are situations in which they do not occur at all. I will refer to any situation in which a meaning is bestowed through an active, self-conscious process as one of *active valuation*.

Active valuation can certainly play a role in experiences of expressive culture, but it is very different from stance, and understanding the relationship between the two is important. As the valual component of the pre-reflexive (though not pre-conscious or unconscious) constitution of lived experience, stance is a necessary part of all experience, while active valuation is optional. For example, the luxuriant pleasure (or moderate enjoyment or crushing tedium) of releasing oneself into the flow of downtempo electronic dance music can be accompanied by distanced acts of critically judging the choice of samples and use of sequencers. But such active valuation need not occur for the music to be meaningful, and it is the manner of engaging with the track in acts of listening and bodily movement that is the source of much of its meaning. When we conflate meaning making with active valuation, we sometimes assume that all situations without active valuation are meaningless and thus turn a blind eye to the rich continuum of meaning that exists in all of our experiences. Such a flawed perspective spawns an equally flawed opposite, a romantic reaction against the scholarly study of expressive culture and ardent claims for the ineffability of "spirit" or "soul" in music or other forms of artistic behavior. The notion of stance can serve as a corrective here by drawing our attention to the chronic nature of value and meaning making in every domain of experience, not just those instances where we bestow meaning through an active and self-conscious process.

The types of qualities invested in stance are as diverse as the forms of meaning in experience. It would be impossible to construct a typology here, but we can suggest landmarks in this territory and perhaps sketch at least one possible way of mapping it. For example, one nearly universal quality of stance is *facility*, the ease or difficulty with which a practice is carried out. In his landmark study *Verbal Art as Performance*, Richard Bauman placed facility of production at the center of his definition of performance: "performance as a mode of spoken verbal communication consists in the assumption of responsibility to an audience for a display of communicative competence" (1977:11).[2] We can build on these observations by noting that it is not only in the performance of expressive culture that this facility is important, but also in reception and composition, and that facility doesn't merely refer to the physical production of expressive forms or the real-time composition of text but to the constitution of experience. Our earlier example was deeply concerned with facility—the composer's smooth or clumsy handling of the rules of voice leading, the performer's deft or awkward articulation of the chords and melodies at the keyboard, the listener's effortless or struggling attempt to follow the key changes and form. Facility is broadly present as a quality of intentional engagement because it stems from the very actuality of our constitution of experience, our ability to have formed an experience at all.

While it is hard to imagine situations in which facility is not present, the meaning of facility and its importance are constructed differently in varying social worlds. The instrumental guitar rock of the 1980s and certain branches of punk music are two straightforward examples of contrasting traditions where facility or infacility, respectively, are valued, but the interpretation of facility is actually a complex issue. In competitive figure skating, it is not raw facility (the mere ability to execute moves) that is valued, but the more fine-grained stance quality of *effortless* facility (the ability to execute moves with no apparent difficulty) that skaters, judges, and fans care about. This contrasts with professional wrestling, which also values the ability to execute complex moves but prizes displays of straining exertion, rather than ease. Further, in those genres of expressive culture for which virtuosity is not a key issue, facility beyond basic competence may be of secondary or even negligible importance. Like other stance qualities, facility can be threaded through lived experience in a rich and complex manner. For example, fans new to jazz may marvel at John Coltrane's effortlessly flowing production of musical lines (i.e., they may hear the facility of his performance) but may at the same time be frustrated at their own inability to follow the fast-moving chord changes implied by those lines (i.e., at their inability to hear the music with a felicitous stance).

Beyond facility there are no universally necessary types of stance qualities or universally applicable typologies that I can discern. However, it will be useful to hazard a list of typical categories, with the full awareness that they are historically contingent, culturally specific, and porous.

Affect, for example, is a broad class of stance qualities. I compose a piece of music with frantic anger or mild annoyance; the art critic views paintings with her heart hardened against them, predisposed to disliking them and intent on revealing their tiniest flaws; the congregant lights the candles with awe and reverence, or distraction and doubt. Affective qualities mix with facility to create *timbres of attention and action*: the theatergoer who watches the play with rapt engagement or the Theater 101 student who reluctantly follows the play's plot to prepare for her test; the professional potter whose distraction is palpable in the tiny cracks in the glaze and the uninspired pattern, or the first timer who eagerly digs her fingers into the clay.

Style is a particularly complex category of stance qualities, mixing the affective timbre of social relationships with qualities of attention and facility. Cool, down home, geeky, solid, flighty, and sophisticated are a tiny collection of possible stance qualities that might fit into the category of style, and teasing out the components of even one of these would be a substantial project. For example, to say that the singing of Canadian vocalist Carol Pope is cool is at least partially to say that the valual quality with which she articulated Rough Trade's songs involved a very specific approach—articulating her melodies with a sure-footed confidence, directing them at her audience with a haughty regard, constituting them in her lived experience with what at least appears to be an intense attention, and all of these qualities of engagement in production and constitution overlain with a thinly disguised rage. When particular styles of intentionality become connected to social groups or social individuals, we have what might be referred to as *stance qualities of identity*—a Neapolitan approach to imagining a line or a heavy metal style of listening.[3]

A possible misreading of these examples can serve as an opportunity to clarify key features of stance and introduce an important concept—*sedimented quasi-stances*. In culturally specific ways of engaging with an object of attention (what I referred to in the previous chapter as noetic sub-modes, such as the composition of a formal study in a music class or playing that study at a recital), stance may seem to be equivalent to style, and, as I suggested above, there is certainly a partial connection between these ideas. Stance refers to the valual quality of intentional engagement, and as the term is commonly employed, style covers some of that terrain. However, the reason that stance and style may seem identical in the previous examples is the high level of abstraction that plays out there. When stripped of its details, stance may seem to be nothing more than "a way or mode of doing something" (as in Dell Hymes's classic formulation of style, 1974:434). The gerund "doing" in this construction points toward action, but the full phrase is a noun phrase, and this is the crux of the matter: when conceptualized as style, stance loses its "act character," a phrase that, as we saw in the last chapter, Husserl used to refer to the agentive and practice component of intentionality. Style is an important concept in its own right, but it is different from stance.[4]

Consider the genre of proverbs. Here, the proverb is the noemata, "telling proverbs" and "listening to proverbs" are noetic sub-modes, and one might be tempted to refer to a particularly parental style of performance as a common performative stance. At first glance, all of this seems relatively straightforward, and the now familiar performance-studies approaches to verbal art in folkloristics—attention to timbre, prosody, and contour— would seem to capture the phenomena that we are interested in here.

In fact, they do tell part of the story. The difficulty is that, *by focusing on regularized features at high levels of abstraction, such analyses capture only the cultural resources that situated practices draw on and deploy, not the performances themselves or their fundamental agentive qualities.* Thus, for example, the chiding tone and singsong rhythm with which a parent intones "a penny saved is a penny earned" are nearly as much a cultural commonplace as are the words of the proverb. Evidence of this can be found in the *Peanuts* animated television cartoons, where the characters of teachers and parents never speak in words but instead use nonsense syllables intoned with a nasal, singsong character; here, the prosody, contour, and timbre of the adults' "dialog" not only communicates meanings but, even in the absence of actual words, also references and evokes the cultural tropes of proverb telling. The *generalized* features of timbre, prosody, and contour in proverb telling here are not performative stance; to the contrary, the chiding tone and singsong rhythm are preexisting cultural resources, and performative stance is the particular way in which they are handled and engaged in a specific situation. Subtle control of stance is exactly what sets apart the high school actress and her over-the-top, clichéd performance of a teacher from a finely trained thespian who puts just the right amount of spin on the words, calibrating this particular performance on this night to those of the other actors and creating a meaning that works with this very specific context. It likewise separates the performance of the annoyed but indulgent father of one from that of the exhausted and long-suffering father of six. While generalized performative features of style are a first approximation of stance, further reflection shows them to be something that the person *has a stance upon* and reveals that stance is the irreducible practice component that inevitably takes up style and adapts it to a given situation. As a result we can think of styles as *sedimented quasi-stances*—abstract and generalized ways of approaching a noema that lack the reality in lived practice (and the attendant three-dimensional complexity) that stances have. In addition, as we saw above, stance doesn't only operate in performance; it also operates in reception and composition, which are less frequently interpreted in terms of style and which also involve an irreducibly practice-based component.[5]

The distinctions between stance and sedimented quasi-stance are basic to a stance-oriented approach to research. Looking at performance in terms of cultures and their styles, we see people and the affective cast of their performances as articulating or exemplifying a preexisting pattern. Looking at performance in terms of stance encourages us to see people in all of their concreteness. Following this approach, we of course understand that all expressive behavior is shaped by its social context and attend to the cultural resources at play in any given situation; however, we see those resources as sedimented quasi-stances, things that people bring to bear on performance. Further, we go beyond attention to sedimented quasi-stances and seek out stance itself. In doing so, we see the ways in which such resources are taken up in performance, viewing action in all of its inevitable concreteness and the processes by which that full concreteness shapes the meaning of a performance or situation.

Though the stance-quality categories of facility, affect, timbres-of-attention-and-action, style, and identity are admittedly ad hoc and porous, we can be specific and precise about the ways in which stance-laden intentional practices plug in, so to speak, to the differing phenomena of the immediate field of experience. So far I have discussed stance as a relatively unitary phenomenon. But when we consider the immediate lived situation before us, it is clear that we do not relate to it as an undifferentiated, monolithic block. On the contrary, we engage with differing facets of the lived situation in differing ways, and the valual quality of our engagement with those facets could be referred to as *facet stances*. Return once again to our original example of music performance. Our student pianist has always been an "expressive" player; her dynamics are subtle and varied, and her teachers have always said that her phrasing is very musical. At the same time, however, she has small hands and has a hard time remembering long pieces. In her performance of "Composition Study 5" on that evening in early May, her playing is particularly ebullient, with a sprightly tempo and sensitive dynamics in the left-hand accompaniment. Though she plays all of the notes in the piece, there is the slightest hesitation in grabbing the more difficult, spread chords that appear occasionally there, and similar hesitations appear in transitions between the sections. Her relationship to the various elements of the piece—the notated dynamics, the spread chords, the overall form—constitute facet stances. The valual quality of the first facet stance is confident and sensitive, while that of the latter two is awkward and uncertain.

Distinct from facet stance is *meta-stance*—not the stance that one has on one's primary object of attention (noema) itself, but the stance that one has on one's *stance* on that noema.[6] For example, the problems that the pianist had with the spread chords and form were something she could never completely overcome this semester. When she played "Composition Study 5" in January during her lessons for her teacher, every near fumble was followed by a bar or two of very dynamically and timbrally flat performance that lasted until she had controlled her frustration and regained her focus. Her teacher worked with her on this, explaining that even the best performer makes mistakes and that she can't let herself become distracted by an error when she's in front of an audience. Assimilating this advice took time. In March, near fumbles were often followed by aggressive overcompensation, passages with exaggerated dynamic and timbral shifts. At the May concert, the student pianist still wasn't able to grab all the spread chords in section transitions, but she had improved her relationship to this very failing. When the near fumble occurred, she played right through, with no apparent breakdown in the texture of the dynamic and timbral nuances. "Nearly fumbling awkwardness" is a description of the pianist's facet stance on the spread chords and transitions, and, in the May performance, "unflappability" and "self-assured focus" describe her meta-stance. Meta-stance is not uncommon in performance. Where there are sedimented quasi-stances, as in the Chopin performance discussed in the previous chapter and the "penny saved is a penny earned" example, the unique articulation of those quasi-stances in particular performances can rightly be said to have a second-order quality. Similar examples of meta-stance can be found whenever popular musicians perform or record "covers" (songs originally composed and performed by other bands) or in theatrical revivals.

Because the constitution of experience is a coherent actor's social practice even as it engages a multifaceted noema, the various facet-stances and meta-stances relate to one another in a complex way that may be called *total stance*. Using slightly different terminology, I have discussed one aspect of this phenomenon at length in my earlier work (Berger 1999, 2004), and I will only touch on it here. At any given moment, our experience is organized into a complex foreground/background structure, with some phenomena emerging with sharp detail at the focus, others appearing in a blurry fashion in the background, and still others receding into the ever more distant horizon. Drawing one's focus from one noema to the next, fostering certain constitutive processes and diminishing others, allowing oneself to lapse into a state of vague disattention, or spurring oneself on to an active and alert engagement would all be differing ways in which total stance is manipulated. Such processes of organizing attention are rightly called stances because the intensity with which particular phenomena appear in experience and their place in the overall field of attention unquestionably have a valual quality. When I foreground the melody and background the accompaniment, or foreground the music and background the performer's body language, I don't just move them around in the experiential field; those positions entail differing valences and meanings, and the overall tenor of the experience thus formed is a meaningful whole composed of those valences. This is not to say that phenomena in the foreground are always considered to be the most important or that those in the background are insignificant.

As my previous work has suggested, backgrounded phenomena color and shape those in the foreground, and the meanings attached to differing positions in the experiential field are culturally specific. The point here is that the organization of attention draws the various constitutive processes into a complex whole, and as a result, constitutes the person's relationship to the immediate situation, forming a total stance.

Total stance is a result of direct and immediate relationships among stances. But indirect relationships among stances also contribute to meaning, and in many ways these are the most important of interpretive dynamics. As we have seen, the objects of consciousness are not unitary and undifferentiated; they involve multiple facets. As we have also seen, lived experiences of meaning depend on both the particular object that the subject engages and the stance with which that engagement occurs. Drawing these ideas together, we can observe that the experienced meaning of any given facet is a synthesis of the meaning found in the facet and the facet stance that engages it; if we call this a facet/facet-stance complex, then the overall experience of the meaning of the object is a synthesis of all of the facet/facet-stance complexes.

The language here is cumbersome, but the situation to which it points is intuitive, and an example with somewhat exaggerated contours will make the idea clear. Consider an emeritus professor of piano pedagogy in attendance at the student concert discussed above. Simply out of habit, the professor may listen with a focused and critical ear to the performer's agility on the keyboard, but she may be more forgiving in her partial attention to the composer's treatment of expressive resources. Sharply aware of the sensitive dynamics and the play-them-as-they-lay approach to the difficult chords, and more dimly aware of (and more generous toward) the composition, she finds herself inspired by the music. Describing her experience at the reception after the concert, she tells a colleague that what she heard was energetic youthfulness. "Our tradition has a promising future," she tells her friend. Noting the errors in performance, she admits that there were some rough edges, but she says that these were more than made up for by the composer's smooth control of voice leading and the performer's sensitive dynamics. The impression of energetic youthfulness that the professor experiences is not merely a function of the music sound, even if we consider the sound as a unity of heterogeneous elements made meaningful in a cultural context. To the contrary, her impression is a product of heterogeneous elements heterogeneously grasped, and a meaningful unity brought to that gestalt of gestalts by constitutive practice. If, for example, our pedagogue were to focus with a more critical ear on the composer's bland themes and their indistinct treatment, she might have been less inspired by the piece's promise of a vibrant future for her musical tradition. However, by paying less attention to the composition and judging it by a lower standard, the main thing that she notices about "Composition Study 5" is the smooth control the composer has over her materials. Here, the relationships among the facet stances and meta-stances contribute to meaning in an indirect fashion, as routed through the facets of the object of her experience.

The notions of facet stance, meta-stance, and total stance are the basic tools of stance-oriented research. Observing events and reading texts in these terms helps us to see the varied elements of meaning that emerge in a person's experience and to make richer and more nuanced interpretations. Moreover, such an approach helps us to understand the meaning of a work or performance, not just as the sum of its semiotic parts—or even as a whole that is greater than the sum of its semiotic parts—but as the result of a person's differentiated and yet holistic engagement with those many parts. In so doing, we get a fuller view of basic interpretive processes.

Exploring the multifacetedness of our engagement with the world leads to a related issue: the multifacetedness of the things in the world themselves. As we have seen, the intentionality of consciousness ensures that stance engages with its objects, and because of the intimacy of that connection, the forms that stances may take are as varied and shaped by culture as the full breadth of experience itself. One cannot, of course, construct a typology of all possible objects of attention or even construct a scheme of categories for describing the types of objects that emerge in experiences of expressive culture. The term *object of attention* can be a misleading one, making us think of experience as populated by nothing but stable, material things; if our phenomenology of stance is to be as rich as it needs to be, it is important to get a sense of the great diversity of such objects. Exploring rules, gestures, and other types of noema, the following series of examples is intended to point toward the variety of objects that people might confront in experiences of expressive culture and to suggest the differing ways in which stance might engage them.

First, consider a game of chess-by-mail. The first player, Trinna, types her opening move on the piece of paper and mails it to her opponent. When the second player, Helena, receives Trinna's letter, she has one day to choose a move, type a response, and mail it off. As in the composition class example, the rules of the game stipulate that the players must not set up a chessboard but must sustain the game strictly "in their heads." In this context, the objects of attention are ideas—actually enacted moves, the current chess position sustained in imagination, and possible next moves.

In thinking about her next move, Trinna paces her apartment, reflecting on her options with aggression or delight, smooth precision or distraction. What constitutes "making a move" here is highly subtle. It may occur only as the letters are typed on the keyboard or the envelope is released into the mailbox. Alternatively, one might argue that such acts constitute only the transcription and communication of the move, and that the actual move making occurs at the moment of decision on the commute to work, when the player has irrevocably committed herself to a course of action. Acts of thought or gesture such as these may be made with certainty or hesitation, resignation or joy. It is worth emphasizing that the complex dynamics of media and expression referred to earlier play out in this example as well. If Trinna and Helena are experienced players, they may have a clear sense of the stance of the other, rightly doping out the intensity or caution of the other player's thinking as expressed in a move that is bold and creative or traditional and timid. If either player is unfamiliar with the game or her partner's style, the other's stance may be harder to ascertain. Here, the objects of attention are positions and moves in the conceptual space of the chessboard (i.e., they are ideas), and stance engages itself with its object, emerging as the valual quality of acts of thinking and imagining. Contrast this with the situation of a musician sight-reading a piece of music. Here, the objects of attention are the score, the instrument, the sound, and the performer's own body; stance in this context refers to the valual quality of acts of reading, playing, and listening. Philosophers in the tradition of Merleau-Ponty and Todes would suggest that both examples involve embodied activity in the sense that there is no thought without a brain to think and in the sense that, as Hubert Dreyfus has argued in his discussion of chess-playing computers (1992), the seemingly disembodied relations of logic such as those among the pieces in a mental game of chess gain their structure and sense from our primary embodiment and engagement with the world. Whatever position one takes on the relationship between mind and body, one can agree that the objects of attention in these two examples are experienced differently and that the noetic processes that engage these objects differ correspondingly.

Many of the examples I have explored so far involve situations in which a performer engages with a pre-composed text. This is not always the case, though, and we can get a richer understanding of the ways in which the objects of experience differ and of the corresponding diversity of stances by returning to an earlier example, inspired by R. Keith Sawyer's work on improvised comedy (1997). In this genre, the pre-composed entity is not a text or a static set of instructions to perform a series of actions, but a more abstract entity—a set of rules. The various subgenres of improvised comedy are often referred to as "games," so it will be convenient to refer to the most immediate object of noesis in improvised comedy as the move.

Consider a game with the following rules: two actors take the stage and improvise a scene. They can portray any characters that they like, but their roles must be of differing statuses (e.g., a teacher and student, or a worker and a boss); the audience gives the actors a line, and however the scene develops, the actors have to end the scene with that line. If an actor were to take the stage and indicate that she was driving a limousine, that action would constitute a move, in that it sets up the situation and requires all of the other actors to respond to it. The stance would be the affective or valual quality with which the move is made: quickly leaping in to mime steering-wheel gestures or waiting for the other player to make a move; accompanying the driving gestures with the phrase "Where are we off to today, buddy?" (thus defining the setting as a taxi cab), or merely doing the mime, which could indicate a bus scenario, a family trip scenario, or a child driving her Big Wheel. Each one of these differing options indicates a differing stance on the move. Because the predefined elements of the genre specify rules rather than bodily or verbal gestures, there is a second level of noemata here, the *improvised text,* which includes the specific words, gestures, or blocking enacted by the players. Because the improvised text is a key element of the participants' experiences, the participants will have a stance on it as well; for example, the actual words an improviser utters can be said with certainty or fumbled insecurity, the gestures made aggressively or weakly.

For anyone who knows the rules of the game, the moves and the improvised text are distinct levels of experience, and stance in both contexts can play a key role in meaning. Sawyer reports that it is bad form to try to control the direction of a game and not be open to the definitions that other actors bring to an emerging scene. Imagine an inexpert actor entering a scene, immediately miming steering-wheel gestures, and saying to the other actor, "Come on, President Jones, you better not be late for your inauguration"; his mime gestures are crude and sloppy, and his working-class Brooklyn accent is broad. Here, his move is "miming a car and becoming a chauffeur to the president on inauguration day." Angry that he doesn't get enough respect in the troupe, his stance on the move is aggressive, quickly defining not only his role but the scene and the other actors as well. His text is the line "Come on, President Jones, you better not be late for your inauguration" and his miming gesture. As an inexpert actor, he defines the steering wheel poorly and mumbles the words. Here, his stance on the text is the opposite of his stance on the move—uncertain and stumbling, rather than clear and specific. Picking up the earlier terminology, we can observe further layers. His broad accent is a sedimented quasi-stance; indeed, as an element defining the scene, it might be clearer to call it a *quasi-text* upon which his stance is clumsy and broad. In this example, rules, moves, improvised texts, and actions are the noemata (objects of attention); comedy improvisation is the noetic sub-mode; and the uniquely layered structure of experience is the surface around which the tendrils of stance, so to speak, wrap themselves.

Indeed, stance engages with its object so intimately that even fuzzy and ill-defined noemata engender corresponding stances. Consider the example of Carl, an amateur dancer reluctantly dragged onto the dance floor at a disco by his friends. Carl doesn't like to dance and doesn't know any specific dance moves. In an ill-defined manner, he shifts his arms and legs roughly in time with the music. To the surveillance camera at the club, nothing in his movement is ill-defined. At time X his arm is exactly 2.3 inches from his torso, and by time Y he has lowered his arm by exactly 0.125 inches. However, this gesture is not a dance move per se, to either his partner or to Carl himself. One could call his precise movements a movement text and his listlessness a stance upon that text, but his experience of his movements is not specific enough for that interpretation to be phenomenally salient for him or the other participants. Of course, a choreographer might compose a piece that depicts a reluctant and uncertain movement, and the gestures the choreographer specifies might be the same as the ones that Carl made. Interpreting a performance of the choreographer's piece by a professional dancer, an interpretation of the choreography-as-text and the dancer's stance upon the choreography might be warranted. This, however, is a very different scenario from the one of Carl at the disco. Where the object of attention emerges in a fuzzy manner, the stance will by definition engage itself with that fuzziness. At best we can say that the object is a "generalized dance movement" and the stance is "apprehensiveness and reluctance." It should be emphasized that the fuzziness does *not* come about through an absence of intention, in the everyday, non-phenomenological sense of that term as a preexisting plan set out in words or images. Indeed, dancers can make crisp and well-defined gestures without such explicitly formed, before-the-fact plans. What make Carl's gestures fuzzy are his imprecise proprioceptive self-awareness of the position of his limbs, a vague experience of how those positions might be changing in time, and little coherent connection among the differing moments in his awareness—in other words, a lived experience of both the actual movement and the relationships among its parts that consistently lacks detail or clarity.

Considering phenomena such as these, one might be tempted to suggest that the boundary between the object of attention and one's stance upon it begins to blur. Even here, though, stance does not collapse into its object. The same reluctant dancer could make equally fuzzy and ill-defined movements with a clumsy joy or even with annoyance or rage. Consciousness is always intentionally linked with its object, but, as we have seen throughout, it is fundamental to experience that we can distinguish our immediate objects of attention from the manner in which we grasp those objects—that, contrary to the obscurantist implications of Yeats's rhetorical question in "Among School Children," we can, and indeed routinely do, tell the dancer from the dance. The larger point here is to highlight the intimacy with which stance engages and envelops its objects, even ones that are defined in a loose and fuzzy manner.[7] Taken together, the chess, improvised comedy, and dance examples highlight the diversity of objects of attention that people confront and find meaningful in experiences of expressive culture. An awareness of stance not only sharpens our observations in the field and our interpretation of texts, it also reveals the unity that underlies seemingly disparate phenomena. A chess player's intense attention to a series of moves, a comic's clumsy handling of the rules of an improvisational game, a dancer's tentative relationship to his gestures, or a student pianist's smooth facility with a composition and keyboard: all are forms of stance.

Stance and the Expansive Quality of Meaning

We have now seen some of the basic dynamics of stance. While stance is a fundamental element of meaning in expressive culture, it is by no means the only element, and the next logical step in our discussion would be to explore how stance is related to other modes through which meanings emerge in a person's experience. The dynamics involved here are some of the most fascinating in the phenomenology of expressive culture. Meaning is the fungible currency in the economy of our lifeworld, constantly crossing borders between one phenomenon and its neighbors, one location and the next in experience. A woman viewing a play, for example, sees an actor direct a subtle, leering glance at an actress on the stage; the viewer experiences the glance as vile, and feels uncomfortable as painful memories of sexual harassment in the workplace come forth into her awareness unbidden. News that his favorite political candidate has just won an election lightens a music critic's mood, and he finds himself unusually receptive to a CD from a genre that he normally dislikes. Insecurity about her job and a sense of weakening race privilege shape a white music teacher's listening during orchestra auditions, steering her attention to every flaw and weakness in an African-American violinist's performance. Examining the expansive quality of meaning is crucial for placing stance in the context of other modes of experience and seeing its relevance for the study of expressive culture.

Before we can explore this topic, though, we need to double back and take a closer look at an issue that is at the core of stance—the act character of experience. Though this discussion will lead us through some more densely philosophical language and into some examples of mundane situations that may seem to be far afield from expressive culture, it is necessary because it lays the groundwork for later analyses. Having a clearer sense of stance itself, we will then be able to make our first approach to the relationship between stance and other modes through which meaning emerges and to gain a series of concepts crucial for the study of expressive culture.

Consider this slightly fictionalized description of a situation from my own life. For the last six months, I have become more and more angry with a person whom I will call Jeff. I felt that he was treating me badly, and the more time passed, the more frustrated I became. One Saturday afternoon, Jeff called on the phone, and to my mind, his words added insult to my still raw injury. After the conversation, I read a magazine and fumed. I couldn't concentrate on the articles, and tired from a long week, I decided to take a nap. I lay down in the bedroom, closed the door and the light-blocking shades, and curled up in bed. With the house quiet, my eyes closed, and no aches or pains, there was little to my experience besides my thoughts. These were enough, though. My last conversation with Jeff dominated my experience and kept me from sleeping. I thought about what he had said, what I had said, what I should have said, and the way his words contradicted his actions in recent months. Angry and hurt, I couldn't settle down; one after another, ideas sped quickly through my mind as I hunted for some new wrinkle or angle on the situation. After a while, I looked at the glowing digital clock. Ten minutes had passed, and I hadn't gotten a wink of sleep. I started to think about how the conversation was ruining my Saturday afternoon and tried to put it out of my mind. Actively forming the words in my head, I thought, "Get some sleep and stop dwelling on Jeff. Think about the novel you are reading instead of spinning your wheels." I actively thought about the plot and the characters, replayed amusing scenes in my mind, and wondered how the book might end. Almost immediately, my thoughts returned to Jeff, and for the next ten or fifteen minutes, I shifted back and forth between thinking about Jeff and thinking about the novel. Eventually, I focused on the more pleasant thoughts, that train of ideas about Jeff became decreasingly intense and vivid, and sleep overcame me.

Certainly, most people can understand this experience. We have all had times when our thoughts dwelt on topics we would rather set aside. The spoiled nap example presents a situation where thoughts were almost the sole object of experience, where the valences were angry and unpleasant, and the fast and aggressive pacing of thoughts was unwanted. It is the phenomenon of distraction, rather than anger or fast-paced thinking, that I want to explore here. To remove those qualities from consideration, let us turn to an alternative example of a young man shopping for items for his plot in the community garden. He takes his plants very seriously, and for the last three years he has participated in the garden's annual competition. Now it's early spring, and he needs to make very specific decisions about the cost, color, and size of the flowers that he wants to grow, their compatibility with one another, the soil, the light conditions, and the rules of the garden association. Walking through the nursery, he is bombarded with images, sensations, sounds, and smells, and he keeps trying to plan out his beds. In past years, he quickly and efficiently tacked between looking at the botanical offerings, imagining different garden scenarios, and considering his budget. However, on this spring day he is one month into a heady love affair, and thoughts of his beloved distract him from the task at hand. Images and thoughts about his lover drift lazily through his mind, and he realizes that he has been at the garden store for an hour without making any headway. He forces his mind to his plot and plans, and for ten or fifteen minutes thoughts of the garden and thoughts of his lover vie for his attention. Eventually the shopping task takes root in his mind, and he is able to mentally sketch out a scheme and buy his items.

In some ways, the experiences of the hypothetical, love-struck gardener are different from those of my spoiled nap. The gardener had a busy, rich sensorium, while mine was limited largely to my thoughts. For him, the distracting ideas were pleasant ones, not filled with anger, and the desired pacing of his thoughts was quick and businesslike, not slow and dreamy. Despite these differences, the dynamics of distraction operate in the same way in these two examples: a train of thought dominates the person's experience, prevents him from doing what he wants to do, and at least briefly resists his attempts to displace it with another. Should such distraction become chronic and interfere with one's ability to carry on everyday activities, one would call it obsession. While relatively few people experience that type of mental illness, distraction is something that everyone has faced, and its unique dynamics can illustrate the relationship between stance and other forms of meaning in a way that less compelling experiences could not.

On a basic level, the phenomenon of distraction illustrates a point raised earlier: we do not merely "have" thoughts. Rather, we have relationships with our thoughts, and the valual quality of our thoughts is complex and multidimensional. Looking more closely, we see that the phenomenon of thought—distinct auditory forms, or wispy and ephemeral conceptual entities that appear to oneself alone—have affective or valual qualities built into them. The thought "Jeff lied!" is suffused with anger like heat in a glowing coal; pleasure and delight run through "I love Jan!" like the grain in a plank of wood. Further, and this is the situation in which stance can be most clearly seen, the thought does not merely emerge in our experience. We participate in its emergence, and that participation has a valual quality. When I first tried to take a nap, for example, I *embraced* my thoughts about Jeff. I allowed thoughts to tumble forward, grasped them richly, and even scanned what Don Ihde would call the "leading edge" (1976:93) of the living present for each new wrinkle and angle.[8] Later, in an act of reflexive consciousness, I realized that this anger had usurped my original plan to get some sleep. I wanted to have a relaxing nap and get my Saturday afternoon back on track, but the thoughts kept coming nevertheless. Resisting my thoughts of Jeff, I focused on thoughts about my novel and tried to approach my stream of consciousness with less intensity.

Resisting and embracing are, of course, stances in the strict sense of the term I defined in chapter 1 (affective, valual, or stylistic qualities with which a person engages the objects of her attention), and the utility of the distraction examples is that they illustrate the Husserlian "act character" of experience in places where they are deeply intimate. If we consider thoughts only in unproblematic, everyday activities where the flow of ideas from one to the next is unimpeded, it becomes easy to conceptualize thinking as an automatic process and to assume that one's thought and one's engagement with that thought are one and the same. Distraction highlights the act character of both thinking and our stance upon thinking. Resisting or embracing a flow of thoughts, or grappling with or giving into distraction, are the kinds of experiences I want to evoke here, because they offer the most directly lived sense of the act character, not just of thinking and the stances we have upon it, but of stance in general. With everything largely removed from experience but thought, and with anger making those thoughts vividly intense, the napping example highlights stance in its purity and affords a uniquely direct understanding of our topic. Further, these examples illustrate that the valence of thought and the valence of a stance upon that thought are two different things. In the gardening example, there is a clear difference between the valence of dreamy pleasure that inheres in the thoughts of the beloved and the gentle but persistent resistance with which the gardener tries to set those thoughts aside. In the nap example, the distinction is more subtle. The valence of the thoughts is anger, but the stance upon them is frustrated resistance to thinking about Jeff, not anger per se.[9]

At this point, we may seem to have come far from the topic of expressive culture but are close to the heart of stance, and pursing this last topic will lead us to ideas directly relevant to the study of artistic behavior. The distinction between the valence of thoughts in experience and the stances we have upon those thoughts can be made for all objects of experience. Further, valences move smoothly between locations and modalities of lived experience, changing shape and transforming as they go. Indeed, this traffic and transformation of meaning is more than just an interesting phenomenon; it is one of the fundamental features—perhaps the defining feature—of meaning itself.

By its very nature, the meaning content of individual phenomena involves valences that radiate out, richly interacting with the valences of our noetic processes (i.e., our stances), the global valual qualities of the immediate lifeworld, and sometimes even with the broader, more persistent elements of the person, such as dispositions and capacities. To return to the nap example: as I attempt to sleep, I think, "Jeff lied to me. He told me that he would do X, Y, and Z, but he told Mary that he would do just the opposite. When I called him, he denied ever having committed to doing X, Y, and Z. I can't believe he lied to me!" As I suggested above, the thoughts themselves do not appear in my experience only as pure propositional contents; rather, they are suffused with the valual qualities of energy and pain. Further, that complex of meaning radiates outward to other parts of my experience. On a basic level, the valences of each individual thought shape the pacing and intensity of the ones that follow it. Red hot with pain, the thoughts flow quick and fast from one to the next, glowing with intensity. Early in the example, the valence of my stance is in perfect consonance with the valence of my thoughts; I actively and energetically pull the thoughts forward, searching the horizon of the living present and actively holding them in the center of attention. But the expansion of meaning does not stop here. Meanings may radiate outward to interact with the full breadth of my immediately lived experience. Angrily thinking these angry thoughts, my body tenses, my breathing comes faster, my heart races. I toss and turn on the bed and cannot find a comfortable position for my pillow. This example is almost trivial in its straightforwardness, but most situations involve a more complex traffic and transformation of valence among the forms and modalities of experience. Early in the example, my involved stance stoked the affective intensity of my thoughts; later, though the thoughts were still painful, I actively tried to take a more cool and detached stance. I observed the thoughts, allowing them to pass through experience without scanning the temporal horizon of the living present for each new nuance or detail, and my distanced stance took some of the pain and sting out of the thoughts.

Examining this situation, we can specify a range of locations and modalities with which valences may appear in lived experience. Teasing out all of the dynamics would require a full phenomenology of affect and meaning, a task far beyond the scope of this study, but I can sketch here some of the forms that valences may take. Consider mood, for example. As a very rough first approximation, we could say that we experience mood as the global affective character of immediately lived experience. Approaching the issue in the style of Merleau-Ponty, we can observe that mood is a property of the lived body, both something that happens to us and something we do. In everyday life, it is common for us to feel that mood operates in each of these ways. In powerful states like depression, overwhelming affective responses weigh the body down, stop thought in its tracks, and install affects of sadness and pain at the dominating center of experience. At the opposite extreme are times when we can exercise agency in affect, shaking ourselves out of a dreamy mood or actively calming a restless anxiety. Speaking very loosely, we can describe mood as the ensemble or gestalt quality of all valences in our experience, a global affective character of the lived body that appears to us as the environment in which we operate. In this context, meaning and valence radiate out beyond the focal phenomena and one's stance upon them to interact with one's overall mood.

Beyond this global character, valences emerge in a range of other modalities and locations within experience. For example, affects can sometimes appear as discrete, objectlike phenomena. Previously, we saw how valences can be experienced as qualities embedded in some other object. Affects are a kind of valence, and in everyday life, body parts are the phenomena in which affects are often embedded—a fist clenched in anger, eyes brimming with tears, hands shaking with fear. Indeed, the famed James-Lange theory of emotion claims that physiological reactions are the sum and substance of affect, that to feel an emotion is to identify after the fact that a bodily response has occurred (James [1890] 1981). However, at times the affective qualities of specific bodily phenomena are so great that we describe them as affect-things, rather than as the body in affect. The "fear in the pit of my stomach," for example, may be a particular posture of my stomach muscles and nervous system. But because it is rare that I am focally aware of those internal organs, I likely feel the affect, not as a tensed part of my anatomy, but as an objectlike thing. If affect-as-object represents the most intense and sharply bounded modality in which valence may enter into lived experience, then disposition is the opposite extreme. In general, philosophers use the term *disposition* to refer loosely to a tendency to think, act, or feel in a particular way. At their most expansive, valences exceed beyond objectlike things, qualities of focal phenomena, stances, or moods, and function in this way. In unreflexive behavior, the disposition itself is often outside of experience. Here, I simply act in a certain manner and feel that the valual qualities of the immediate phenomena, my stances on them, or my global mood are shaping what I do; in reflexive self-consciousness, however, I theorize that I was disposed toward a certain course of action. Because I do not directly experience the disposition as a thing in itself but only posit it in retrospect, dispositions can be said to exist in a zone beyond the horizon of the immediately lived. Disposition represents the expansive character of meaning operating at its extremity—meaning having trafficked beyond the horizon of qualities, phenomena, stance, or mood.

In a related fashion, we can observe that it is not merely affective qualities or valences that expand beyond themselves in lived experience; the meaning contents themselves operate in this way. The most dramatic examples of this kind of generative process are evident in self-hypnosis or psychotherapeutic affirmation. In self-hypnosis, one enters a relaxed state of mind and, as much as possible, blocks from one's experience any perceptual information. This accomplished, one conjures words in one's mind, and, in theory, the meaning contents expand forward, producing the corresponding state in imagination. One tells oneself, for example, to imagine a red apple sitting on a green table, and the image appears vividly in one's experience. In a related fashion, certain kinds of psychotherapy rely on what are called affirmations. If the patient suffers from anxiety, she is told that before leaving the house each day, she must spend five minutes alone repeating an affirmation to herself, such as "I can handle anything the world throws at me." In theory, the meaning content of the repeatedly imagined words diminishes the predisposition to respond to situations with fear. Whether or not affirmations are effective forms of therapy, it is fundamental to the nature of meaning that its contents should expand beyond themselves. In the nap example, I think, "Jeff wasn't telling the truth!" and that meaning content draws forth thoughts with related contents: "I shouldn't have trusted him!" "What else has he lied about?" "What am I going to do about this?" "Am I really this bad a judge of character?" Further, meaning contents cross sensual modalities. Thinking my angry thoughts about Jeff and his lies, for example, I may visualize a smug expression on his face, hear the taunting, nasty guitar line from Buckethead's "Revenge of the Double," or find the lyrics and vocal melody from the Magnetic Fields's song "I Don't Believe You" running through my head. The traffic of meaning in experience is as multifaceted as it is diverse.

Seeking to identify the expansive quality of meaning, this discussion has operated at a high level of abstraction—at the level of meaning per se, not at the level of particular kinds of meanings in particular spheres of experience. The issue of why and how particular meanings expand is obviously an enormous one, and in any given social situation the power relations of the society in question will play a fundamental role in these processes. Ultimately, a dialectic of social context and agency determines how one set of meanings leads to another for an individual or group, and it is the intellectual tradition of discourse studies that seeks to understand how these factors play out in history to shape connections among ideas. While this kind of research is essential, it does not invalidate phenomenological inquiry into structures of lived experience; indeed, the two complement one another. Attending to the dynamics that I have sketched here, we can more richly interpret the social discourses that play out in particular places and times.

Such an approach is particularly valuable for those who study performance. Thinking about the expansive character of meaning in situated events, we can observe how the meaning of a performance for an individual is not just shaped by her experiences of the elements of the text, but comes about through an interaction among those meanings, the stance quality with which she engages them, and her larger mood and dispositions. In my own fieldwork, for example, I have observed how some commercial hard rock musicians will view the shows of rival bands with a critical and affectively flat stance, listening for any mistake or flaw in the performance; only slowly, across the span of a show, might they allow their affective experience of the text to color their mood. Considering a very different genre, it is precisely the interplay of disposition, mood, performative stance, and text that was in question when the comic Gilbert Gottfried decided to take the chance of doing 9/11 jokes at a Friar's Club Roast in the period shortly after the attacks on the World Trade Center. In considering this material, the question for Gottfried was whether or not the mood of mourning had lifted enough from his audience for them to find the jokes humorous. This is precisely a question about meaning's expansive quality: How would the crowd's disposition and mood affect their stance on the objects of their attention (Gottfried's jokes)? What texts and what performative stance in the telling of the jokes would make the audience grasp the material as funny, rather than as offensive?[10] The concepts that I have introduced in this section provide some language for thinking about issues such as these and suggest areas of research. They are only a starting point, though, and to explore these concerns more deeply, we need to examine the role of time and time perception in the traffic and transformation of meaning, as well as the ways in which meaning expands, not just across differing locations in an person's lifeworld, but between people in performance events. The former concern is taken up in the next section, and the latter is the topic of the next chapter.

Dynamics of the Expansive Quality of Meaning: Time and Practice

Summing up the discussion so far, one might say that experience has been conceptualized as having a number of components: a graded field of phenomena, each of which is embedded with meaning contents and valences; a subject's engagement with those phenomena, which involves a specific affective, stylistic, or valual character (i.e., a stance); a global valual environment of mood; and a horizon beyond which valences exist as dispositions. Likewise, one might speak of all of this as a space and say that meaning traffics and is transformed within this space.

To say that something moves across a space is necessarily to raise the issue of time. Though in many ways mysterious, the temporal dimension of experience is fundamental in our lives and present for us in the most mundane occurrences. I go to the movie theater to watch a comedy, for example, and the images and sounds appear one after the other. Though the film has gotten mixed reviews and I generally don't like the director, I try to approach it with an open mind. In my experience, the first camera shot is intriguing, and I'm amused by the layout of the credits on the screen. The first few lines of dialog strike me as funny; then, however, the lead character delivers a joke that I find to be sexist, and most of the jokes fall flat for me after that. Image after image, line after line unfolds until two hours and ten minutes have passed, and the film is over.

The dynamics of meaning in time are rich and complex.[11] On a basic level, we can observe that, beyond the raw fact that events proceed in succession, the movement of meaning and valences in the space of lived experience is iterative—that what happens at one moment shapes what happens in the next moment.[12] In terms of preliminaries, I enter the theater with a universe of past experiences and capacities that predispose my initial engagement with the images and sounds. The background cultural knowledge I have allows me to make sense of the social roles and situations depicted in the film. This knowledge combines with ideas from my culture about what goes on in movies in general, knowledge of particular films, genres, actors, and directors, reviews, word-of-mouth knowledge about this particular film, and my own highly contingent and situated mood at the particular moment the film starts. All of this shapes my stance on the very first images and sounds that pour forth from the screen and sound system, and my initial experiences come about through a complex interaction of the filmic text and my stance upon it. Amused by the opening shots and layout of the credits, for example, I overcome some of the initial skepticism I had about the film and find myself laughing at the first few lines of dialog. When the main character makes a joke that is blatantly sexist, the fragile goodwill that the film has established evaporates, and my skeptical stance removes some of the pleasure from the lines that follow. This in turn creates a downward spiral, and my stance on the film disposes me against much of what comes next. Clearly, the movement of valences among my experience of the film, my stance, and my mood is an iterative process—a series of steps, each of which influences the one that follows it.

The straightforward, each-event-shapes-the-next processual dynamic of iteration well describes some of the simpler processes in biology or mathematics, but the fullness of lived experience is far more complex. In lived experience, past events do not merely shape future ones; they are retained within experience and accrete to form large-scale variegated phenomena over time. As a result, new iterations do not merely shape future ones but can cause present retentions of past ones to change as well. This process is the complement of iteration, and I will refer to it as *retrospection*. The simplest example of retrospection can be found in what linguists call "garden path sentences" and in the structure that humor scholars have found in certain kinds of jokes. Consider these lines from Judy Tenuta's 1987 live stand-up comedy recording *Buy This, Pigs!*:

How many times have you been walking down the street, and you see someone coming towards you from the past that you don't want to talk to. . . But they recognize you, they recognize you and they try to make you talk to them. And they say "Judy, Judy." They said, "Judy, were you going to walk past me without saying hello?" And I said, [pause] "No, Mom."

Here, the first two sentences of the joke bring up a general type of situation: a person running into someone that he or she does not want to see. The speaker in the first sentence of reported dialog is "they," and we are led to believe that Tenuta is still describing a general situation, not one with particular people. When we hear the word "Mom" in the punch line, however, we must go back and reinterpret the previous sentences, retrospectively seeing that Tenuta is avoiding, not some acquaintance in a generalized situation, but her mother particularly.[13] Following Husserl's fundamental observations on time consciousness ([1929] 1964), we can observe that Tenuta's words from the recent past continue to exist in the temporal thickness of the listener's experience (what Husserl called the "living present"), even as each new moment passes. When Tenuta utters the word "Mom," there emerges in the listener's experience a conflict between, on the one hand, the idea that "Tenuta pretended to ignore someone," which is persisting in what Husserl called "retention" (the present awareness of recently past phenomena, which remain in experience even as new phenomena continuously emerge), and, on the other hand, the new meaning content "Tenuta pretended to ignore her mother," which is forming in what Husserl called the "now-point" of the living present. In other words, the past sentence isn't brought back from mental storage into an infinitely thin moment and actively imbued with a new meaning; on the contrary, the meaning content of the still persisting past utterance changes, even as it remains in the retentional portion of the living present. I will expand my discussion of Husserl's insights into time consciousness in the next chapter. For now, my goal is only to illustrate the interpretive dynamic of retrospection, in which meanings in the now-point shape those in the retentional portion of the living present without an act of memory proper or a process of active valuation.

Examples of retrospection are neither limited to humor nor unusual in expressive culture. Retrospection occurs in large-scale narrative structures, such as in the film *The Crying Game*, when we discover that a character who appears to be of one gender is actually of another, after which the broader sense of the story on the temporal scale of the entire narrative undergoes a shift. Indeed, retrospection is fundamental to entire genres. Much of the pleasure of the classical drawing-room murder mystery is the neatness with which its ending ties together the clues laid out in its early scenes. Likewise, much nineteenth-century symphonic music depends on a narrative structure in which the piece returns, through smooth and clever modulations, back to its home key. Greek tragedy sets up complex crisis situations, the resolution of which brings the narrative to its conclusion. The revelation of the murderer based on clues that were never given to the reader, the clumsy key change back to the original tonal center, or the deus ex machina ending all cause us to invalidate the pleasure of the earlier scenes or movements. When such genres are successful, culminating acts complete the empty anticipations of closure formed and retained in the early scenes, thus producing a sense of satisfaction.

Striking or dramatic examples of retrospection may seem to be little more than isolated literary or narrative devices, but the accretion of meaning and the more subtle cases of retrospection are fundamental to the lived experience of expressive culture. In many traditions of literature and theater, for example, the central point of the work is to depict a complex character. Each of the protagonist's actions shows a different side of her character, and the well-drawn protagonist is one whose personality is complex and multidimensional, possessing varied motivations and feelings that nevertheless hang together in a coherent or at least dialogic manner. Reading a novel that comes from such a tradition, we find that each new scene reveals more and more of the character's personality and causes us to view her past actions in a new light, forming a complex whole that is revealed over time. Where dramatic retrospection involves the sudden inversion of past meaning, subtler forms of retrospection such as these modify the meaning of past scenes merely by virtue of their joining into a long-scale temporal gestalt with the present scene and the emerging meanings of new scenes.[14]

The fact of retrospection does not invalidate iteration; indeed, the two interact in a complex manner that is crucial for experiences of expressive culture. At each point in time, the flow of new experiences and the person's evolving stance upon them bring further new experiences to light. This is the primary iterative quality of experience. But lived events do not merely move forward; past phenomena accrete and events expand in lived time.[15] The past is retained, forming a complex relationship with new phenomena, and as it does so, iteration becomes complemented by retrospection. In the movie theater example discussed previously, positive valences radiate forward from the unexpected clever lines in an early scene to soften my hardhearted stance; they also radiate backward in retrospection to color the first few scenes with a sunnier hue. When a sexist line turns my stance on the film cold once again, each new scene more deeply entrenches that negative stance in a series of iterations. These also have a retrospective impact: I do not suddenly deny that those early lines were funny, but I experience them as situated within the context of the mass of tedious, humorless passages. Scene after scene piles up to form a relatively long temporal whole, the new episode not only shaping both those that follow and my ongoing stance in iteration, but also reaching backward in retrospection to color those past. Thus, the circulation of valence among various modalities and locations in experience (foreground phenomena, background phenomena, one's stances upon such phenomena, the global contexts of mood and disposition) takes place in a living present that not only moves forward to the future but expands to retain an accreting past.

So far, the discussion of time has focused on the noematic pole of experience (i.e., on objects of consciousness), rather than the processes that constitute them. Reversing that emphasis returns us to the issue of stance and begins to draw us toward our conclusion. Retrospection and iteration are not automatic processes. They are actively achieved, and the manner of that achievement—the stance of a person's temporal engagement with a work or performance of expressive culture—is crucial for the meaning that a person finds in that work or performance. The reader of character-driven novels, for example, maintains a stance on the characters over time, actively bringing them into her experience and making them meaningful. Reading a particular novel, I may follow the machinations of the plot and connect each new action to the character's ongoing history, assembling the large-scale experience of the plot with facility. Alternatively, I may let my attention wander, losing interest in the character and allowing the descriptions of her past actions to slip out of my experience. As I read the early scenes of the novel, it is not clear to me if the author is espousing an elitist view or simply revealing the main character's elitism. When a heavy-handed plot twist makes it clear that the world of the novel is divided between the creative elect and the mundane masses, my primary retrospective constitution reads those ambiguous scenes with a skeptical eye and sees them as elitist, and I attend to the rest of the chapter in a distracted state. Then again, I may read with a more generous eye, a more open stance. Lightly passing over that section and resisting the urge to retrospectively reinterpret those scenes, I may forge ahead, looking for passages more attuned to my sensibility.

The examples of stance that we have explored in this book so far are quite diverse, and it is worthwhile to take a moment to emphasize the conceptual unity that underlies this diversity. The examples from chapter 1 and the first part of this chapter mainly illustrated stances on small temporal scales: the pianist's immediate bodily stance on her piano playing and the phrase that she is currently performing; the listener's stance on the melody being played right now. The examples of iteration and retrospection focus on stance in the large temporal scale of an event: one's stance on the character whose actions unfold for the person across several hours of reading. Despite the difference of temporal scale, both sets of examples involve a person actively engaging an object of attention and making it come alive in her awareness, and the affective quality of that engagement shapes her overall experience of meaning.

Moving to a higher level of abstraction, we can observe that underlying both the iterative process of one event coming after the next and the accretive retention of experiences in the living present is the fundamental fact that experience must be *sustained*. At each moment in the event, the person must attend to newly emerging phenomena and also continue to constitute other elements of the living present on various time-scales. The fact that experience must be sustained may seem obvious, but the point is worth emphasizing because it illustrates the stratum of agency that underlies all experience. Watching a movie, attending a play, or listening to a concert, one may become lost in the narrative or caught up in the sounds, and, reading these events in a naive manner, it may seem that experience simply happens to the person. Comparing such performances with those tedious or uninte-resting events where one struggles to follow the thread, focus on the per-formers, or even keep one's eyes open, we could be tempted to suggest that experience has both active and passive modes. The phenomena of distrac-tion that opened the previous section suggest that this is not the case. Situ-ations of being absorbed in a performance illustrate the pull that the world can have on our experience and the effortlessness with which processes of engagement can occur. What is obscured in such situations, and what the phenomena of distraction reveal, is the acts of sustaining experience that—whether they involve an affirmative quality of work or not—are the sus-tained, ongoing achievement of the subject. Mihaly Csikszentmihalyi ([1975] 2000) has argued that the person's absorption in the immediate task before her takes place when her capacity to carry out action is evenly matched with the demands of the situation. This is certainly true, but ab-sorption also depends on our ability to hold at bay the deep well of irrele-vant capacities, dispositions, memories, and thoughts, and to allow our-selves to be open to a world that beckons us forward. Holding-at-bay is a phenomenon that requires much deeper exploration, but here the point is that openness-to-the-world is a property of the subject, not the environ-ment around her; more precisely, it is a property of the subject's dialectical engagement with the world. Whether the acts of constituting experience occur smoothly or with great work, they are the doing of the person and must be sustained.

Beyond its native interest, the fundamental stratum of agency in experi-ence is important for research into expressive culture because it highlights dynamics that are essential to meaning. Understanding how the moments of a performance are shaped by iteration and retrospection, and attending to the ways in which such moments add up to form complex, long-scale events of one of many possible configurations can help us interpret expressive cul-ture more richly. When conducting interviews, observing events, or inter-preting texts, scholars can gain fuller and more nuanced readings by sensitiz-ing ourselves to such dynamics. Valences and meanings move among phenomena, stance, and mood; this movement exists within a temporal space that evolves forward in an iterative fashion, expands in accretion, and even rewrites its own history in retrospection. The complex experiences that result are neither the simple aggregate of isolated events occurring in a series nor an unbroken unity welded together among various events in a manner that overcomes time, but rather are a particular set of what William James ([1904] 1967b) would call "conjunctive relationships" and "disjunctive rela-tionships" between experiences actually lived by a person.

These ideas may seem abstract, but they describe in general terms the dynamics of experience that are intimate and directly grasped. I catch a stand-up comic at a local club. I listen to the first few jokes with a skeptical ear, find myself seduced by a couple of fast lines, begin to feel that the material is repetitive, am almost drawn back in by some serious remarks, find myself brought up short by a homophobic line that retrospectively invalidates some of the earlier material, and lose interest at the finish. I remark that the comic is homophobic and lacking in creativity, but it is the pacing of these elements and my stance upon them, not the elements alone, which shape my experience. I don't merely see the individual jokes as homophobic; in retrospection, they color my overall long-scale sense of the comic's character as a swaggering, dominating bully. Alternatively, a line at the end of the act that is both hilariously funny and politically progressive wins back my heart, and I see the swagger as resistant, rather than dominating. It is the subtle dance of valence among phenomena, stance, and mood—a dance that takes place on the expanding stage of the living present—that gives experience its rich texture, and interpretive work can only be enhanced by increasing our sensitivity to these movements.

CHAPTER THREE

Stance and Others, Stance and Lives

Examining the basic dynamics of stance, the previous chapter revealed some specific ways in which stance is tied to its social context. For example, the act character of stance, the emergence of facet stances, meta-stances, and total stance, and the movement of meaning and valence among differing modalities and locations in lived time are all social inasmuch as they all are constituted through *social practice* (in the sense of that term elaborated in practice theory): that is, they are actively accomplished by the agent and at the same time fundamentally shaped by the agent's culture and history. I will discuss ideas from practice theory more fully in the next chapter, but for now I will observe that experience is not social only because past interactions shape present behavior; it is also social because it unfolds in the lived give-and-take between the experiences of differing actors in face-to-face or more highly mediated interactions. The music theory class and piano recital examples alluded to these social dimensions of stance, and this chapter explores this topic systematically. I begin by examining the relationship between stance and its expression and the ways in which stance is partially shared across the experiences of individual actors. From there, I will explore the phenomenon of stance on the other and suggest how stance ties immediate situations to the largest temporal scales of a person's life.

Stance and Its Expression

As we have seen, an audience's interpretation of a performer's stance has a large impact on the meaning that the audience finds in the performance. But how might I come to experience your stance? In considering this issue, it is easy to confuse stance with the media that we interpret as a reflection of it. Making that distinction clear is the first step to seeing the complex relationships among stance, the body, and media. This in turn will lay the groundwork for understanding how the possibility of an in-principle awareness of media as an expression of stance can enable the partial sharing of meaning between people. From this abstract discussion, we will be able to examine the particulars of how specific stance qualities are shared in expressive culture.

To get our first fix on the question, we return again to our hypothetical conservatory. What, exactly, does it mean to describe a stance—to say, for example, that our pianist's dynamics are "sensitive" or that the way that she fingers a chord is "awkward and uncertain"? While descriptions such as these can be contested or misunderstood, within the confines of particular social worlds it is often the case that such descriptions are unproblematically understood and agreed upon among a group of actors. In this situation, the term "sensitivity" refers to fine-grained and varied changes in tempo and dynamics that make sense with respect to the formal structures of the preexisting composition. The ease with which such terminology communicates its meaning within a social group obscures the complexity involved in judging a musician's playing as sensitive. Certainly, when a performer in the Western art tradition has a sensitive stance, the amplitude of the sound waves varies in a way that that description explains. However, the first point to see here is that there is nothing inherently sensitive in the physical sound waves that would be captured by a microphone at our May student concert. Sensitivity is a function of the intentional subject engaged with an instrument and the sound produced by it. In the noetic sub-mode of Western conservatory recital performance, sensitivity requires a musician enculturated to know what counts as a composition and how that composition works, a moving body that can enact the composition with dynamics relative to that shape, and a hearing body that monitors that ongoing action. In the noetic sub-mode of recital listening, hearing the performer's sensitivity requires a listener with an auditory apparatus relative to which the dynamics are "fine-grained" and a familiarity with the tradition such that she can, in intentional engagement, distinguish the composition from the performance and make sense of the relationship between them. Thus, while stance qualities of performers may be partially understood by audiences, and while research can uncover how particular media in particular social worlds embody and partially mediate the stances of their producers, the physical media of communication never contain stance qualities. Further, there can be no universal interpretive scheme that could extract such qualities from the media. Stance is, by definition, the valual quality of a type of action, not the shape of the thing acted upon, though the former is often richly, though never fully, marked on the latter.

This is true for all forms of expressive culture, even those in genres where the body and the media it works upon are one and the same. Consider a dancer whose stance on the movement is one we find to be sprightly and alert. There is nothing inherent in a particular path through three-dimensional space that a physical body (like an arm or torso) might travel that involves those qualities. On a most basic level, a viewer's perception of the sprightliness of a motion depends on her understanding of the time-scale and forms of movement that human bodies are capable of achieving. Further, to articulate a movement in a sprightly fashion or to see a movement as sprightly requires us to distinguish the choreography (or the dancer's intended gesture) from this particular enactment of it; the manner with which the line between the two is drawn, of course, is always influenced by culture. In addition, the positive valence attached to sprightliness will depend on the culture in which such expressions are given meaning and the typical palette of movements in which they are contextualized. And even with these points excepted, it is never the movement per se that is sprightly; as stance, sprightliness is the act character of the moving body, a quality of an agent, not a physical mass passing through a route.

The distinction between stance and its expression is true even in those situations where the two seem most intimate, and exploring related examples will be necessary if we are to see the full implications of this point. Doing so will take us once again into a more philosophical style of discourse and illustrations that might not seem to involve expressive culture, but they are essential to the larger discussion. In the genre we have been discussing, dance, bodies are critical, but they are not the sole mediator that connects the performer and the audience; rather, the light reflecting off the dancer's body mediates between the dancer and her audience. For genres like massage, however, the collapsing of the medium of interaction into the bodies of the participants is even more complete; here, the medium is the body of the client as directly worked by the body of the masseuse. But even in this situation, there exists a distinction between the stance and the media that expresses it. For example, the masseuse seeks to work her client's paraspinal muscles with a gentle touch, but the spot that she rubs is sore and the gesture ends up being harsh. Likewise, the client has a stance on the massage she receives, even as its medium is her own body. Here, as always, perception is not just a registering of what is there, a purely passive reception of the masseuse's gestures. On the contrary, it involves a stance on the massage: the client warily tightens her muscles in response to the heavy-handed gesture of a novice masseuse or trustingly relaxes, even when a deep pressure results in some discomfort; the client times her breath with the masseuse's gestures to get the most out of her hour on the table, or she distracts herself with thoughts about her sister the pianist so as to better endure a painful therapeutic session. The furthest extreme of the trajectory we have been tracing occurs when the masseuse works on herself. But even here production, medium, and reception do not collapse in on one another. As both masseuse and client, the individual deploys thumb and fingers in massaging gestures, relaxes or tenses her spinal muscles to receive the gestures, and alternates between foregrounding the awareness of rubbing and of being rubbed.

The dynamic suggested by this last example was richly explored by Maurice Merleau-Ponty in *Phenomenology of Perception* ([1945] 1981) and then reworked and developed further in *The Visible and the Invisible* ([1964] 1968), where he discussed it as a kind of a chiasm.[1] In Western rhetoric, a chiasm is a rhetorical trope in which the terms of a two-part construction are presented and then presented again in reversed order (e.g., the philosophy of history and the history of philosophy). In Merleau-Ponty's language, the situation of a person touching one of her hands with her other one is a kind of physical chiasm, and across his career Merleau-Ponty repeatedly explored this example to reveal the embodied nature of subjectivity. When grasping an object (such as a pen or a rock, I might suggest) with one's right hand, a person may try to palpate that right hand with the left one, Merleau-Ponty observes in the *Phenomenology of Perception* (92). As the right hand grasps the object, it reveals that thing through its active, physical exploration. As the right hand engages in this exploration, however, that hand itself disappears (or, I might suggest, perhaps only recedes) in experience. If the left hand then grasps the right hand, the right hand will re-enter experience, but as an object, and the *left* hand then recedes in experience. Comparing these cases, Merleau-Ponty suggests that the body (here, specifically the hand) is not an object, as older schools of philosophy had had it. The body is the ground by which objects appear, the agent of perception; its subjectivity is obscured in the act of perception (thus allowing the illusion that perceptual experience is merely a property of mind) and becomes revealed only when the body is turned back on itself as in situations such as these. In *The Visible and the Invisible,* Merleau-Ponty reinterprets these ideas, emphasizing that, while one can shift from exploring the world with one's right hand to using one's left hand to explore one's right, one can never do both at the same time (147–48). This "reversibility" between being the touching subject and being the touched object, Merleau-Ponty argues, is the essence of the "intertwined," chiasmatic relationship that defines bodily being. In many ways, the bodily chiasm is the clearest illustration of the embodiment of our intentionality, and the point applies to our discussion of the mediated relationship between stance and its objects. Even in self-massage or the composition of music in imagination, noesis never completely dissolves into noema, and the valual quality of that noesis (i.e., stance) is never purely expressed in its object. If it were, consciousness would lose its hallmark quality, that of an entity that always points beyond itself to an other; there would be no experience, only the pure coincidence of the thing with itself, the for-itself become the in-itself.

Though the relationship between stance and its expression may seem esoteric, it is of directly pragmatic importance for anyone involved with expressive culture. Actors switching from film to live theater or from one venue to another in a touring show constantly adjust to make sure that their performance "reads" in the audience. Musicians debate whether an easier fingering sounds as good as a more difficult one, or whether a technically "proper" posture on the instrument makes an audible difference to a person's tone or agility on the fretboard. And anyone who has done detailed transcription from archival recordings in the disciplines of either music or phonetics is aware that the same sound can often be produced by more than one physical gesture.

These examples all involve slippage between stance and its expression, but the structural necessity of mediation in general and of slippage in particular do not relegate stance to an insignificant or optional feature of expressive culture. Contrast, for example, musical performance on a sensitive instrument in a small recital hall with a very different case of real-time communication—instant messaging on computer networks or cell phones. In instant messaging, it matters not if I violently mash the E key or gently caress it with my finger; however I type, my reader will see the identical character. In this case, the richness of my body's performative stance is abstracted to a (literally) digital expression; nevertheless, even in this relatively insensitive and opaque medium, the relationship between stance and its expression is complex. Reading my instant message on her computer screen, my interlocutor may not know if the long pause between her comment and my reply is an indication of my indecision or of network congestion. However, she is probably right in guessing that my speedy responses are indicative of my at least partial attention to our electronic conversation. And even when composing a document on my word processor, an example to which I will return in a moment, my physical engagement with the keyboard will feedback to me my level of involvement with the act of writing, thus potentially shaping my prose style and indirectly being reflected on the page.[2] More extreme examples of sensitivity or insensitivity of media to the body's performative stance during real-time performance may be found, but the larger point should be clear: stance is never fully expressed in the media upon which it works, but neither does the fact of mediation, however opaque and insensitive to the action of the body, obscure the in-principle awareness that performers and audiences have stances, even if by necessity they are partially obscured or imperfectly expressed at any given moment. The possibility of an in-principle awareness of stance is what allows it to be partially shared between people and therefore contribute to the overall meaning of expressive culture.

Turning our attention to genres like written literature or painting, we can see even more clearly the in-principle necessity of the existence of stance and find even more complex dynamics in its expression and interpretation. It is true that one may have a harder time interpreting stance in media that can be edited before they are shared with another or in media that people in the world of computers might call "non-real-time" (media that are created at one time and in one situation but are taken up by the intended audience at another time or in another situation). It is also true that the editing of non-real-time media can partially conceal an individual's embodied, performative stance. But because all editing (and all production processes, even those processes most extended over multiple production events) is itself a kind of practice, such examples do not escape from the fact of stance but instead involve a more complex set of dynamics in its expression.

Considering writing, painting, or a range of other non-real-time genres of expressive culture, we see production as a type of practice that need not be continuous over long stretches of time and that may be interrupted by periods of other types of activity, such as the span of a night's sleep or the weeks spent letting an unfinished piece "sit" while ideas simmer on the back burner. Certainly, productive practice takes place only in the immediate, situated act, but the temporal scale of that act is not bound by the immediate situation; likewise, there is no doubt that editing can obscure immediate situated stance in bodily production. But, as we saw in the end-of-the-semester concert illustration, the phenomena of obfuscation, misunderstanding, or incomplete expression of stance do not invalidate the significance of stance for experiences of meaning but rather represent a further set of its dynamics. Beyond its functioning to obscure or reveal bodily performative stance, editing is itself a form of practice and therefore necessarily has valual, affective, or stylistic qualities. It can be done sloppily or with great skill; it can draw attention to itself as act (as in collages or flashy music videos), or it can seek to hide itself (as in the subtle cutting and pasting that sometimes occurs in studio recordings of American "old-time" music). In reception, audiences may bring editing to the fore, relegate it to the background, or so completely fail to understand the production process that they may miss it entirely. After reading the score of "Composition Study 5," for example, the director of a music festival may compliment our student composer on the way in which her limited editing retained the rawness of the original moment of composition, polishing the initial ideas without overly refining them. Listening to a CD of the piece recorded a few months later, the director may still appreciate the restrained compositional editing but may wish that the performers had spent a little more time in the studio correcting mistakes in the performance. However editing or practices of production on large time-scales may emerge in the experiences of audiences or performers, they involve stance and thus play a role in the larger gestalt of experienced meaning.

Taken as a group, the examples of massage, dance, text messaging, live music, and recorded music sketch some of the terrain in the problem of stance and its expression. Certainly, the ways in which a person's stance is expressed in differing media and genres vary widely. But underlying that diversity is a common situation, a common structure of experience: a person engaged with an object; the affective, stylistic, or valual quality of that engagement; and the possibility that another may have an in-principle awareness that some gesture or media is an expression of the quality of that engagement. Whether found in the quality of one's own actions or dimly sought after when probing the mediated acts of others, stance may become present in the mix of experience and thus serve to frame, inform, or interact with whatever additional meanings people find in a given text, performance, practice, or item.

The discussion so far has laid the groundwork for understanding the relationship between stance and its expression. But beyond the in-principle awareness of the body or media as an indication of the other's stance, how do we get the particulars? Why do we grasp one stance quality rather than another? How do we experience a subtle reference, a fumbled gesture, or a focused gaze as another's stance of loving devotion to a tradition, carelessness in performance, or rapt attention?

This is clearly an enormous topic, and to make our discussion easier, let us narrow the field of phenomena to consider those cases of real-time interaction in which an individual's performative stance is partially grasped by an audience member. While even here the processes that enable the partial sharing of stance are diverse, one set of them stems from a common understanding of production practices. A shared awareness of the body, its possibilities for action, and its relationship to the environment is the most basic commonality. No dancer can run across a stage at 100,000 miles per hour; no singer can sing a pitch whose fundamental is 100,000 hertz; no storyteller can continuously recite a narrative for 100,000 hours. When a performer's behavior approaches the limit of human capacities, an audience member might not grasp the full valual, affective, or stylistic meaning of her action; nevertheless, a shared understanding of the capabilities of bodily action will allow the audience at least to grasp "extremity" as one element of the performer's stance. Of course, we must be careful not to participate in an essentialist humanism here. The body is a product of evolutionary biology, social forces, and technology, not divine fiat, and its parameters have and will continue to change over time.[3] Considering the differing forms of nutrition that exist in world cultures, the phenomena of mutation, disability, and individual variation—as well as culturally specific practices of body modification, gene doping, and human-machine integration—it is clear that the body's form and capacities are far from a universal or transhistorical essence. As such, the common ground that it affords to understanding stance is partial at best. On the side of the physical environment, it is at least within the realm of possibility that, in the longest cosmological view, even the physical constants might be historically variable. However, we need only look to the astronauts on the International Space Station to see that the very environment in which we live cannot be taken as a transhistorical given. However much or little stability there is in the human form and its environment, the larger point is clear: where a common understanding of the body's capacity for action in the environment exists, that understanding can serve as a basis for partially grasping the stance of the other.

Of course, it is not the body or the environment per se, but the social body engaged with culturally specific forms of technology in a situated context that is one parcel of the partially shared ground on which some stance interpretations rest. A second parcel is the resources and rhetoric of expressive traditions, their cultures of pedagogy, and their technologies— factors that shape practice and constrain and enable what actors can do, what they want to do, and what they expect of others. When performer and audience have a common understanding of the possibilities for action, the audience can understand the valual qualities of the manner in which the performer's action is carried out. In the 1980s, some music scholars referred to the culturally specific qualities of music as *code* and understood features of music sound as arbitrary signifiers that represented particular meanings, as when the first notes of a national anthem signify the country with which it is associated. Culture can certainly serve to encode meaning contents in this manner, but my point here is that cultural knowledge can function in another way as well—to allow audiences to understand the valual, affective, or stylistic quality with which the expressive behavior of the performer is engaged. Specific to particular social worlds at particular historical moments, it is nevertheless distinct from the kind of strictly arbitrary relationship of signifier and signified that classical Saussurian linguistics saw as encoding the meaning of words in language.[4]

Consider the audience member who hears the heavy metal guitarist's solo as virtuosic and, to use a more affectively loaded and culturally specific term, *hot*. It is not the raw number of notes per second that the guitarist plays that portrays the qualities of aggression and skill, nor is it even the number of notes contextualized by an awareness of the abstract capabilities of the human body. What is virtuosic in one tradition with its palette of physical techniques and instruments is merely adequate in another tradition and its kinesic and organological palette. Further, it is not merely the case that a listener will have an abstract knowledge of the typical number of notes per second that heavy metal guitarists can play and then hear any solo with denser playing as more virtuosic. While musicians trained in a tradition will be able to discern the easy part that sounds hard to play from the genuinely difficult part, even untrained listeners commonly hear with an awareness of the practice-based realities of the instruments they are hearing. Some of this understanding rests on watching performers, but some of it rests on the more fundamental awareness of the fact of practice, an awareness that is simultaneously cultural and embodied.

Shifting the example slightly, the discussion of distorted guitar timbres in Robert Walser's celebrated study of heavy metal music *Running with the Devil* (1993) will illustrate the point. Walser argues that the distortion devices that heavy metal guitarists use communicate a sense of power by allowing the notes to sustain longer and by boosting the upper harmonics of the guitar's timbre. The distortion of vocal timbre in shouting signifies its meaning in the same way, "by overflowing its channels" (42), and Walser observes that the meaning of distortion is inflected by its social context. Walser is correct in all of this, and it is the way in which the player's timbre communicates that meaning that bears closer inspection. Bright and sustained sounds are neither inherently powerful, nor are they an arbitrary code for power; on the contrary, the listener's sense of the performance as powerful rests on a common understanding of practice. One prerequisite is a pre-reflective awareness of the distinction between impulsive sound sources (which receive an initial burst of energy and then slowly dissipate it in sound, such as when the bar of a xylophone is struck with a mallet) and driven sound sources (which vibrate as long as energy is fed into them, such as when a bow is pulled across a violin string)—a distinction that is there in the physical world and of which any hearing person is aware. Further, to hear the performance as powerful requires an understanding that the sound one is hearing is a guitar, that the guitar is an impulsive instrument, and that in this instance its impulsive physics have been transformed to make the guitar more like a driven instrument. Finally, this physical and practice-based grounding is given meaning by the listener's awareness of the place of distorted guitar timbres in the history of rock and heavy metal musics. As Cornelia Fales and I have discussed (2005), the last thirty-five years have seen a constant increase in the amount of distortion used by metal musicians. To hear a metal guitarist's timbre as an expression of a powerful stance is not only to hear her playing as the sound of an impulsive instrument transformed to the point of being driven, but to hear it as possessing an extremity of sustain and brightness relative to past timbres in the genre and those found today. Audiences unable to hear the sound as an impulsive source transformed into a nearly driven one or audiences whose hearing doesn't contextualize the sound in terms of the genre's timbral history will simply misunderstand the performer's stance. Of course, greater amounts of knowledge of shared context will further deepen the understanding of the stance. The point here is that the stance quality of power in the guitarist's playing is not merely an arbitrary, culturally specific code, nor is it an inherent feature of the sound; it is a quality understood by performer and audience member because of their common awareness of practice—a domain that is always simultaneously physical, bodily, cultural, and agentive. Not merely synthesizing the physical, the bodily, the cultural, and the agentive, social practice is the fundamental experiential reality from which those seemingly a priori spheres are constituted.[5]

The variety of forms of distortion illustrates the complexity with which stance is expressed in its media. Distortion can be produced by many differing elements in the chain of technologies that carry the sound from the guitar to the listener: an effect device that is placed between the guitar and the amplifier, the amplifier itself or its various components (its preamp or power amp), the speakers themselves, signal processing performed by an engineer in editing a recording or feeding it to a live PA system, or some combination of these. Literally hundreds of effect devices, amplifiers, and software packages can generate distortion, and each can be adjusted in a variety of ways to create differing timbres and shape the sound in differing ways. Distorted timbres are often the defining feature of particular genres—the warm, liquid distortion of an overdriven tube amp in the blues, the crushing distortion of a cranked Marshall amplifier in heavy metal, or the in-your-face nasal buzz of a transistor fuzz box in 1960s surf or garage rock. These qualities—smoothness, heaviness, attitude—speak to stance only in the broadest and loosest sense. Inasmuch as audience members are able to listen to a timbre and make it meaningful (as discussed above with regard to the increased sustain and overtones signifying power), timbre is one element in the larger mix that gives a genre its meaning. Inasmuch as timbres become conventionalized signs for genres, it is the genre that makes the timbre meaningful, and the two processes relate to one another in a dialectical fashion. For example, the guitar timbres of the extreme metal genres of the 1990s provide so much sustain that the guitars are nearly indistinguishable from driven instruments. While such timbres do not denote weakness and few guitarists in these styles are returning to acoustic or undistorted sounds, I would suggest that, for metalheads, distorted timbres do not evoke a sense of power with the freshness that they once did. While more than merely conventionalized signs of the genre for devotees of extreme metal, these timbres do not have meanings based solely on their physical qualities, and timbre reflects stance here in a way that ties it to history and culture as much as it does to the acoustics of the media.

The question of "sensitivity" in distortion illuminates another set of issues within the topic of stance and its expression. Guitarists refer to a mechanism for generating distortion as "sensitive" if differences in the player's physical gestures of picking, muting, and even fretting are clearly registered in the sound. A Carvin guitar played through a Mesa Boogie amplifier with the correct settings will produce a loud, sustained, distorted tone; in addition, subtle differences in vibrato, in the angle of the pick on the string, and in the pressure with which the string is struck produce differing tone colors. The player's moment-to-moment stance on the instrument is more or less directly reflected in the sound; in fact, such a rig exaggerates the mapping of gesture to sound and creates new possibilities for timbres. As a result, the technology actually allows the guitarist the opportunity for actions to be meaningful in new ways, in effect allowing new actions, and thus new stances, that were previously impossible. Other combinations of gear erase those differences. For example, if one sends the signal of almost any electric guitar through a Big Muff fuzz box with the gain and distortion turned up all the way, and then one feeds the boosted signal into a cheap practice amp with the volume set low, almost all subtleties will disappear. Here, the guitar becomes like a harpsichord, with all of the musician's gestures resulting in the same timbre and dynamic. The larger point here is that in action, the body engages with its physical environment, including any form of technology that is present. The intimacy of that engagement creates a breadth of ways in which technology may affect the expression of stance, from obscuring stance to opening up new vistas of its expression.

In heavy metal, there is much more to playing with a powerful stance than plugging in a distortion pedal, of course. Regular rhythms in accompanying parts, tight coordination with the rest of the band, crisp pick attack, precise articulations such as hammer-ons and pull-offs, and properly intonated bent notes occur when the performer plays powerfully and sounds powerful. Each of these features comes about because of the quality of the performer's action—a clear and certain auditory image of the part to be played, an ingrained familiarity with the terrain of the fretboard, and an alertness to the rest of the band, their collective sound, and the sound of the player's own instrument. As with timbre, metal audiences will hear these features as an expression of a powerful stance because they hear that sound as the trace of an action and have a common understanding of the type of action that would produce them. This point raises the issue of the performative features of expressive texts, and in returning to this theme, the discussion has come full circle to the critique of the interpretation of features that I discussed at the beginning of chapter 1. In genres dense with information, where multifaceted bodies work on sensitive and continuous media such as light and sound, the scholar can endlessly enumerate features. The interpretation of features is certainly not a futile task, but such work is most fruitful when we understand that the meaning of those features is framed by stance and that such features are often intended and interpreted as traces of stances. Indeed, in social worlds where stances are highlighted in the interpretation of expressive culture, the absence of a feature (a silence when another plays, a failure to respond) may be as important as its presence. In sum, stance is a quality of acts of intentional engagement, and a shared understanding of how those acts are carried out is one means by which an audience member can hear media as a trace of a performer's stance.

There is more to practice than the gross movements of the visible body in the physical world. Less obviously embodied features of experience—the organization of attention, of memory, of affect—are other pieces of the common ground by which audiences understand the performer's stance. Again, the broadest examples illustrate the point. No composer can imagine 100,000,000 simultaneous melodies, nor could any conductor lead them; no sideshow memory artist can memorize 100,000,000 names; no writer can compose a plot that ties together 100,000,000 characters; no verbal artist can simultaneously duel with 100,000,000 competitors. The limits on our ability to imagine, focus, recall, and interact are manifest, and, as with limits on more obviously embodied forms of practice, inching away from the gargantuan places the discussion solidly within a realm constrained and enabled by cultures and their technologies.

In *Outline of a Theory of Practice*, Pierre Bourdieu observed that tempo is fundamental to meaning in all forms of practice (1977), and I would suggest here that tempo reflects traces of stance in both obviously embodied domains of action such as musical performance and in those spheres, such as music listening, television watching, or the reading or composition of prose, in which embodiment is less apparent. In a mundane definition, *tempo* is merely the pacing or the speed with which events transpire, and it is easy to see how the tempo of activity is a trace of facility. The musician may express her skilled stance by taking a difficult piece at a fast tempo or reveal her lack of familiarity with it by slowing down the ensemble to a tedious largo; the stand-up comic may display her verbal skills by firing off fast one-liners or reveal herself as a first timer by employing a clumsy, leaden pacing. Tempo is, however, much more complex than these simple examples may suggest. In music, tempo is measured in terms of the number of underlying beats per minute.[6] In a related fashion, I will define *phenomenal tempo* as the density of phenomena in experience over a given period of time. Understanding tempo in this way requires us to problematize what counts as a meaningful unit of experience for a participant in an interaction, and such an exercise can open up for interpretation subtle and important realms of meaning.[7]

Phenomenal tempo in music is not a question of the number of notes per minute, but the number of meaningful units in a given span, and substantial complexities arise from this seemingly straightforward idea. In the 1980s, for example, heavy metal guitarist Yngwie Malmsteen popularized sweep picking; in this technique, a single-note melody line, usually an arpeggio, is produced by quickly raking the pick across the strings in one fluid unidirectional motion (rather than alternating between upstrokes and downstrokes) and letting the fingers of the other hand alternatively fret and damp notes on the adjacent strings, one after the other. The technique requires a moderate amount of coordination, but it is not extremely difficult to learn, and by using sweeps the guitarist can play blindingly fast arpeggiated runs that otherwise would take years to master. Much of the heavy metal tradition uses modal harmony, and sweep picking was the only context in which many metal guitarists learned to play arpeggios. For the majority, arpeggios were memorized as manual patterns—blocks of coordinated movement, a fixed unit of gesture. Guitar virtuoso and teacher Lou St. Paul has observed to me that while the garden-variety metal guitarists could, by the late 1980s, impressively sweep arpeggios at high tempos, only the better players could play the same parts cleanly at slow or medium tempi. For the mediocre guitarist, the sweep was a riff, a single, indivisible unit of kinesic and auditory experience. Listening to a phrase with a series of four sweeps in rapid succession, an audience member unfamiliar with guitar technique might hear a blinding run of sixteen notes in two beats. In contrast, for the heavy metal guitarist performing on the stage (or for another one listening in the audience), the primary meaningful unit was the sweep, and the phenomenal density was really four phenomena (four sweeps) in two beats. Indeed, after hearing so many guitarists use this technique, many non-guitar-playing metal fans would probably hear the riffs as the basic unit of experience as well. This is not to say that those wise to sweeps would not hear the individual notes, but the primary focus of their attention—and the meaningful entity in their experience—would be the sweep unit, not the individual pitches.[8]

The notion applies equally well in musical examples beyond heavy metal. In a variety of musical traditions, a basic compositional technique is the *melodic sequence*—a pattern of notes moved regularly through a scale or other pitch collection. If we refer to the notes in a C-major scale by number (1, 2, 3, 4, 5, 6, and 7), we could indicate a simple sequence as 1235, 2346, 3457, and so forth. Musicians often find that it is easier to hear (and even sometimes easier to play) complex sequences at fast tempi. This may seem counterintuitive, but examining practices of playing and listening makes this situation easy to understand. When a sequence is delivered slowly, it often becomes more difficult to group the notes together in experience and hear the pattern. When the notes come fast, one after the other, it is easier to group them into units, and the pattern becomes obvious. The larger point to see here is that where audience and performer have a common understanding of the meaningful units of experience, phenomenal density of expressive media can serve as an expression of the performer's facility or of other types of stance.

The same dynamic occurs in all forms of practice that scroll forward in real time. In "The Corporate Veil," a particularly noteworthy episode of the television police drama *Law and Order*, a teenager dies in a car accident; a complex series of events eventually results in the prosecution of the manufacturer of the defective pacemaker that had caused the heart attack that led to the teen's collision. Speaking in non-technical terms, one might say that the action in the show is fast paced. Here, the phenomenal tempo is not merely a function of the number of words uttered per minute or the editing of the shots. A more pedestrian police drama may have the same number of words in its hour and the same number of rapid cuts. What makes the "The Corporate Veil" possess a high phenomenal tempo is the number of plot points that occur in the hour. In a weaker episode, two scenes, six minutes, and a thousand words may be uttered to establish that the detectives suspect that a witness is lying; in "The Corporate Veil," the witness's statement and the police's incredulity are sketched in a quick exchange that takes place in one scene, and the consequences of their disbelief emerge immediately thereafter in a series of further investigations. Discussing the show with my friends, I would probably not be able to recite any of the lines of the episode verbatim, nor could I say exactly how long each scene lasted. What I recall is the outline of the plot and the sensation of overwhelming forward momentum. The breakneck phenomenal tempo comes about through the high number of significant units—here, plot points—in a given period of time. Phenomenal density is an expression of the production team's facility with narrative materials (the story author's ability to weave a plot, the screenwriter's ability to manifest it in dialog, the editor's ability to cut to the heart of the scene, the producer's ability to bring these various parties together), and the fan's enjoyment emerges from her intense engagement with that density, her alert and capable stance in viewing and listening that follows each move in the story and connects each clue with its resolution in the jury trial, the attorney's arguments, and the final conviction of the corrupt factory owner.

This example introduces the issue of stance in expressive forms that involve multiple parties. I will return to this crucial issue below, but for now I want to point out that in narrative, phenomenal density need not correspond solely to plot. In moody character studies, the plot may be summed up in a few phrases and the dialog may be sparse, but the observation of everyday activities and the framing of the images make the seemingly "slow" film dense with subtle cues to the characters' diverse feelings and motivations. None of this is to suggest that the only good expressive products are phenomenally dense ones; in some cultures of music or film, phenomenal sparseness is valued, and changes in phenomenal density are a common technique in all manner of expressive culture. The point, rather, is the way in which phenomenal density serves as a trace of stance and its fundamental importance for many types of expressive culture.

Opening the topic onto wider vistas, we can observe that in those forms of expressive culture that involve complex production chains and multiple participants, the final media that reach the bodies of the audience may bear traces of the stances of a variety of participants, and audiences may grasp these stances with varied levels of accuracy and amounts of intensity. This point has been amply demonstrated in the discussion of the end-of-the-semester concert, but it applies equally well to a variety of other genres. Of all expressive forms, film may have the most elaborate and varied production process. From developing the story and script, to casting, to choosing locations and then to designing, building, lighting, and dressing sets, blocking, acting, filming, creating special effects, and editing, an army of individuals engages in the production of a feature film. Here, each individual has a stance on her actions—a stance that may be expressed in greater or lesser degrees in the film that is finally screened or in cuts that are released later. Further, the producers and directors and their subordinates not only shape and guide the actions of others, they coordinate those actions, thus producing layers of phenomena that are the result of such coordinations. Audiences may be more or less aware of the production process for film in general, and in viewing any given film they may be more or less accurate in interpreting any of its images or sounds as evidence of the production process that went into making it or the stance thus involved.

Watching a light comedy, for example, an audience member may find the screenplay to be mundane but may find herself caught up in the fun with which the actors deliver the hackneyed lines. Such an appreciation of the actors' stances may be an accurate interpretation of the quality of their engagement with the script; alternatively, it may be that the film's dialog was improvised, that the clichéd lines were all that the actors could invent in the moment, and that what seemed to the audience to be a stance of vibrant fun was in fact nervous energy. Likewise, viewers of a murder mystery may attend to the meticulous way in which the threads of the plot were woven together and see the unfolding narrative as evidence of the screenwriter's sharp-eyed stance. Such an interpretation may be correct, or the clever, implied motivations and smoothly resolved actions may have been the work of the director or the film editor. No matter how well or poorly any audience member understands the production process of film in general or of any given film in particular, the issue of stance will always play some role in her interpretation, often an important one. This is true for all forms of expressive culture, not just film. At the very least, the audience member's own stance on the process of reception will be part of the mix of meanings in her experience, and often, interpretations of the producers' stances will play a role in the audience member's broader meaning-making processes. These may or may not be veridical, but the importance of such partial sharing can be great, particularly in genres that subscribe to an ideology that prizes authenticity.[9]

Of course it is not only producers of expressive culture and their in-group audiences who interpret the stances of others. Scholars do so as well. In the field or the archive, we constantly read performances and texts as traces of the other's stances. This is one of the main ways in which we make the social world meaningful, and we are no different from the people we study in this regard. For both scholars and our research participants, the effects of our interpretive processes are substantial, but the processes themselves often operate at the periphery of our awareness and their workings seem mysterious. We see that this performer is intense, that that director is clever, but how those impressions are made is not as clear as it could be. But when we attend to the dynamics of stance and its expression—to phenomenal tempo; to the interplay of culture, the body, and practice in revealing our engagement with things—we are better able to see the manner in which those meanings are achieved, thus allowing ourselves to make more nuanced interpretations and get closer to the people whose lives we study.

Like that of anyone else, our sharing is always partial, and our interpretation is a never-ending business. Nevertheless, an increased understanding of meaning-making processes can help us be better interpreters of social life.

Stance on the Other

The counterpart of the expression of stance is the reception of stance. In situations where the person is alone and the focus of her attention is an object (such as the texts or rules that we explored in the previous chapter), the only stance immediately involved will be the valual quality of the person's engagement with that object. However, where the focus of attention is not an inanimate object but another subject (another entity that has experience), the potential exists for both a *stance on the other* and a *stance on the other's stance*. These categories of stance have been suggested above. In the music school example, we saw that the performer had a stance on the composition that she was playing and on her own engagement with the instrument. The audience member had a stance on these things, but she also had a stance on the performer as well. How does this work? How an other can appear in one's experience is a rich and complex issue that goes to the very heart of stance and requires our most careful attention.

While philosophers still debate the problem of other minds, the fifth of Husserl's *Cartesian Meditations* ([1931] 1960) is, to my reading, among the most powerful phenomenological works on this topic. I have discussed the "Fifth Meditation" at length in previous work (2004:96–100), and here I will examine only its main points. Staying completely within the realm of descriptive phenomenology, Husserl showed that in social interaction, we experience the other as a subject per se—an entity that has experience—rather than merely as another physical object in our immediate presence. Saying that one sees the other as a subject is *not* to say that one is directly aware of the other's experience, but neither does it suggest that one looks at another body and deduces from observation that it has experience. Husserl observed that I see the other as a subject in the same way that I see a physical object as an instance of a type; in both cases, I do so in my fundamental, pre-reflexive constitution of experience.

The nature of this pre-reflexive constitution of experience, this "seeing as," is at the heart of the issue here, and one set of examples for discussing this issue, richly examined in Don Ihde's *Experimental Phenomenology* (1986), comes from visual illusions.[10] In the Rubin's Goblet illustration, for example, the person looks at the dark patches and light spots of the figure and can see it either as a pair of faces in silhouette or the outline of a wine glass. Here, one does not inspect the exterior contours of the dark patch, reflect on past shapes that one has seen, and conclude that the dark patch has the same contour as faces in silhouette. To the contrary, in one's pre-reflexive visual engagement with the image, one sees it as a pair of faces, and the intriguing feature of the illustration is that, because it can be seen as either the faces or the goblet, the usually taken-for-granted work of seeing as is itself made an object of attention. Seeing as is not merely a factor in the operation of amusing psychological novelties; it is fundamental to everyday life that, in our pre-reflexive engagement with the world, we see things as instances of types. Husserl's example is of the type "scissors." Looking around my desk, I do not ordinarily glance at the connected strips of sharp-edged metal, reflect on them, and conclude that I could use that object to cut paper. In my pre-reflexive constitution of experience, I see the object as a scissors. I may later judge that I can use the scissors as a paper-weight or even discover that the object is not really a scissors at all but a cleverly painted piece of cardboard. However, just as my pre-reflexive gaze sees the dark patches of ink as faces or goblets, my gaze sees entities in the everyday world as examples of types—scissors or trees, apples or hats.

As the Fifth Meditation makes clear, seeing the body of the other as a subject is a particularly important kind of seeing as. I understand the type "subject" from my direct experience of being a body in the world (of experiencing my body as distinct from other things in the world, of having experiences of the world, of my body's own responsiveness to my intents), and in the pre-reflexive constitution of experience, I see the body of another person as another subject. What I share of the particulars of the other's experiences is always partial; it is constrained and enabled by the vicissitudes of communication and misunderstanding, expression and deceit. Although distinguishing real subjects from what Husserl called "pseudo-organisms" (entities like robots that might appear to be subjects but in fact do not have experience; [1931] 1960:114) contributes additional complexities to the problem of other minds, that issue is not our concern at this juncture. Husserl's phenomenology of the other cogently describes the fundamental dynamic at stake here—the in-principle awareness that the other has experiences—which is the experiential reality of the social from which everything else in interaction flows.

Grounded on this foundation, we are able to define *stance on the other* as the affective, stylistic, or valual quality with which an individual constitutes an entity as an other subject in her experience. Its "meta-" counterpart is *stance on the other's stance*, the quality with which the other's stance is grasped. It is worth emphasizing that stance on the other and stance on the other's stance are subcategories of the general category of stance, which I defined in the first chapter. There, I explained that stance is the affective, valual, or stylistic quality with which a person engages with an entity and brings it into her experience. In chapter 2, we saw how material things and more abstract entities like rules or the moves of a game can be the focus of a person's attention, and here I have suggested how a *person* can become the focus of another's experience. Understood in this way, stance on the other is a particular kind of stance: it is the quality with which one engages a particular kind of entity in experience—other people.

The stance qualities associated with stance on the other and its meta-counterparts are quintessentially social. While they can encompass simple affects (anger, sadness, happiness, etc.), they also involve those complex qualities of social relationships that are crucial to the sophisticated interpretation of expressive culture, including but in no way limited to trust and suspicion, domination and resistance, familiarity and alienation. Indeed, it is just these stance qualities that so often act as the pivot on which broader interpretations turn. Such terms are notoriously fuzzy and difficult to define, and the utility of the notion of stance is its ability to bring back into view the connections between such crucial but difficult-to-define qualities and the media through which they are constituted.

The problem that the concept of stance helps to resolve here is a familiar one. For pragmatically oriented musicians and for music scholars who like to keep their research close to issues of music form and music sound, acts of listening to music involve the listener's awareness of pitch, harmony, rhythm, dynamics, and timbre, the grouping of sounds into units across time, and the hearing of sonic relationships. Where, hardheaded musicians or scholars may ask, are qualities like trust, alienation, or suspicion in music sound? What might it mean to listen with an open heart or to hear the performer's sure-footed confidence? If we treat music performance as nothing but an auditory process, such qualities are nowhere to be found in experience, and the evocatively descriptive writings of music reviewers or humanistic music scholars who rely on such terms may seem to be nothing more than poetic fiction. If, however, we understand such terms as stance qualities, we can reconnect meaning to bodily practice and be specific and clear about what such terms might mean. In our spring concert example, to listen with an open heart and hear the performer's sure-footed confidence is indeed to listen, to hear pitch, rhythm, dynamics, and timbre, to group sounds into units and hear sonic relationships. But it also means something more: hearing those sounds as the sonic actions of an other and thus constituting that other as a subject in one's own experience. Listening is thus listening to an other; here, the valence of one's listening act—the stance on the other—embodies a quality like openheartedness in one's focusing and arranging of that sound in experience, in highlighting the bright tone and the sensitive dynamics, and in back-grounding the nearly fumbled chord.

The fact that we can see the other as a subject enlarges the arena in which meaning might move, and this point allows us to further our exploration of the expansive quality of meaning. As we shall see below, both the significance given to stance and the interpretive processes by which the listener constitutes it in her experience are deeply informed by culture, and there is no guarantee that in any listening situation an audience member will attend to the other as a subject. But in those situations where stance on the other and stance-on-the-other's-stance are treated as an important part of an event, the awareness of the other as a subject broadens the lived space in which valences may circulate. Thus, valence may not merely move from an object in *my* experience, to *my* stance, *my* mood, or *my* disposition; experiencing you as a subject, I may partially share *your* stance, *your* mood, *your* disposition, thus widening the space in which valences may traffic. By acknowledging this vast terrain, we can begin to see some of the complexity with which meaning emerges in expressive culture. Such movement can be extremely complex. Playing guitar with a jazz ensemble, for example, I may hear the bass player's precise intonation as a trace of her alert stance on the ensemble, and this may inspire my more intense engagement with the music, the bracing stance quality of alertness radiating from her to me. With senses sharpened, I may hear the bassist's ahead-of-the-beat playing as a trace of an aggressive stance toward the drummer, and I may find myself playing more straight-ahead and laid-back solo lines to counteract the aggressive tone in the ensemble. The examples that could be developed are endless, and the larger point is that the potential for partial sharing creates the possibility that meanings may circulate not merely between locations in my lived experience but among locations in a space that traverses the experiences of the multiple participants in the event.

Acknowledging the fact that we experience the other as an other subject does not negate the elements of our earlier analysis of the experience of texts, rules, and so forth; to the contrary, the different types of phenomena coexist in our experience. In the conservatory example, the composer had a stance on her composition as it emerged, and later, the performer had a stance on the piece as she performed it. When our audience member listens to the pianist with an open heart, her listening act distinguishes the composition from the performance, marking the notes and their durations as the composition and the fine details of dynamics and timbre as performance. In so doing, the audience member hears the composition as a preexisting and abstract object that is contingently instantiated by the actions in this event, and the performance is grasped as the ongoing actions of an other subject. Further, when the audience member constitutes the other in her experience as a subject and distinguishes composition from performance or script from behavior, those constitutive processes serve a faceting function, making the performance a multi-sided entity even as she experiences it as a single, unified physical reality.

The examples we have explored so far have been of face-to-face situations, but other forms of interaction involve seeing the other as a subject as well. For example, depending on the interpretive ideologies of the music culture in question, the audience member may hear the composition as an object, or she may alternatively hear it as a highly mediated trace of the actions of an other subject. The latter describes the interpretive process of the professor in the music class example, in which the score was read for evidence of the student composer's clumsiness or sure-footedness, disinterest or excitement—qualities of engagement left as traces on the media. There are important continuities between seeing the body of the other in performance as a subject and seeing media as the traces left behind by the actions of a past subject. In the former situation, I see here and now before me the other subject. I don't directly grasp her experiences, but I see her present body as an entity that has them. In the latter case, before me here and now I see the object as medium. Again, I don't directly grasp the other's experience, and in this case her body as a site of her experiences is not even present for me. But if the object is understood as a series of expressive signs, then I may take its meaning contents as, in some sense, a description of her experience. More importantly for our present concern, I may see in the object traces of the other's productive stance, as in the examples of the composition class. Further, my reading the object as the trace of another's action performs the same faceting function on the phenomena for me as seeing the body of the other as a subject did in the examples of face-to-face interaction. Reading a piece of Marxist cultural criticism, for example, I follow the flow of evidence and argument, but I may also feel the keen-minded rage with which the author assembles and displays the elements of her case. Of course, her body is not present for me as the physical site of her affect, and all of the forms of misunderstanding and deceit outlined above may make my interpretation of her stance problematic. Veridical or not, though, I grasp the text as the work of a subject and therefore experience stance qualities as facets of that object, disembodied valences lodged in the object that point to an other no longer present.

Culture profoundly influences the practices of reception through which a person constitutes a phenomenon as an object, a subject, or the traces of a subject's action, and when we consider the possible ways in which stance interpretations may fail to partially share the other's experience, the continuities between real-time, face-to-face interactions and those that are more highly mediated appear to be even greater.

This idea is apparent in several ways. First, in both cases the audience may be incorrect in interpreting media as the result of the actions of a subject. The score that the teacher sees as the product of another subject may, for example, be the work of a computer program; the piano music that I think I hear the pianist perform may be generated by a player piano, a CD, or a piano-playing robot. Further, in a variety of contexts there may be differences of opinion about what counts as a subject. To followers of certain religious or magical traditions, for example, entities that others may find to be merely inanimate objects (grimoires, prayer books, songs, ritual accouterment) may be viewed as having a subjectlike status, experiences, or agency. Informed by culturally specific ideas about the nature of mind, individuals may see varying kinds of non-human animals, plants, or even machines as entities that have experience. Second, in both face-to-face and more highly mediated interactions, the audience may attribute the media to the wrong subject. In the composition example, the composer may have copied the assignment from another student in the class, or it may be the work of several individuals writing in a group. In live performance, the sound emanating from the piano on the stage may be attributed to the musician on the piano bench, but that instrument may actually be triggered by remote control by a performer in a backstage room. Far more subtle illustrations of mistaken attribution in live performance can also be found. In certain kinds of live ensembles, for example, it occasionally becomes difficult to tell which performer in a section played which part, and this is even more common in studio recordings or live performances of very large ensembles. As we have seen in the discussion of filmmaking, the complexity of the production chain can lead to additional problems in attribution, and considering genres of performance that involve what the participants understand as spirit possession or inspiration from the divine, the problem of attribution takes on metaphysical dimensions. Finally, as the previous examples of misreading and deceit have extensively illustrated, the content of particular interpretations of stance may or may not be veridical.

Highlighting the continuity of face-to-face and more highly mediated forms of interaction may seem to reduce the intimacy of face-to-face interaction to mere illusion, downgrade the experience of the other to mere appearance in our minds, and lead us to question our in-principle ability to know other minds. While acknowledging the nature of mediation, we must resist the temptation to skepticism.

It is certainly true that the sharing of experience between persons is never complete and that my experience of an other is always a phenomenon for me, rather than an internalization of the other into my own consciousness. However, it is equally true that the continuities among my own experiences of myself are similarly partial. When I recall my past, for example, I do not transcend my present self to become my past; my past emerges as a phenomenon for me now, and the connection of my presently recalled memory and the experience in the actual past is always partial. Likewise, my experience of my own body is incomplete. It is not a direct apprehension of an essence but rather a flow of perceptual experiences of a body that happens to be mine; it is not a pure intuition of me. For example, I can be sharply or dimly aware of my own movements; while the other does not have a proprioceptive experience of my body, she may see or hear things in my gestures that I myself may miss. A physical therapist may catch a pronation in her patient's walk of which the patient was unaware; a voice teacher may hear the constriction of the student's throat, which the student hadn't noticed; and in everyday conversation, my good friend may observe my sagging shoulders and furrowed brow, which I, absorbed in my own tired and worried state, didn't notice. Even in thought, I do not directly apprehend my intentions and motivations as some pure essence; rather, I interpret the flow of experiences of my ideas. While the other does not have direct access to my thoughts, in conversation with an intimate companion, the other may have insights into the meaning of what I say that I myself lack.

In sum, it is not the case that my experiences of the other and my experiences of my self are made of different metaphysical substances, one being appearance (the other in my mind) and the other reality (the actual other). To the contrary, using the language of William James's later work ([1904] 1967a), one could say that they are made of the same substance, "experience." In other words, while the "appearance" of the other in my experience truly is just my experience of her, her own awareness of herself is also "only experience," and the continuities among her experiences of herself may be as loose or as tight as those between my experiences of her and her own. Using Husserlian intellectual apparatus to further explore these continuities and discontinuities, one could additionally observe that both the self and other are examples of the type "subject," and the possibility of partial sharing is secured by our common nature as bodies that have experience and that inhabit a common world.

If these fundamental structures of experience and embodiment provide some of the basis for partial sharing, then culture adds further layers. Above, I emphasized how cultural difference can reduce partial sharing, making two groups of people see phenomena as subjects or objects in different ways, read the roles of the production chain into musical sound differently, or read the features of expressive products as evidence of differing stance qualities. But culture both constrains and enables partial sharing. Those unfamiliar with production processes in rock music may indeed draw the line between composition, arrangement, and performance in inaccurate ways, thus misreading the stances of the songwriter and the musicians. However, the inverse is also true: familiarity with tradition allows one to more or less correctly read the production chain into the music sound and make more or less accurate stance interpretations. And while culture change and internal variations within a culture provide further space for misunderstanding, it is precisely the phenomenon of learning that makes it possible for individuals to partially bridge the gaps of difference over time and social space. Indeed, one dimension of culture is the emergence of partially shared experience between interacting individuals over time.

Emphasizing continuity across the experiences of individuals over time leads us to a final element in our examination of stance on the other—the phenomena of interaction and reciprocity. It is not always the case that I see the other as another subject or that attention to either the other as a subject or to the other's stance is a prominent element of experience. However, across cultures and in a wide range of domains of social life, the accomplishment of an event depends precisely on the participants' ongoing and mutual awareness of each other as subjects and of their stances. The interactive nature of performance events is something that has long interested scholars of expressive culture (e.g., Stone 1982, 1988; Sugarman 1997; Askew 2002; Danielsen 2006; Goffman 1959; Kirshenblatt-Gimblett 1975; Bauman 1977, 1986; Fine 1984; Cowan 1990; Del Negro 2004), and my own work has explored the ways in which attention to the other is shared in the performance event. What I want to emphasize here is that it is not merely mutual attention to the other or the partial sharing of experience that is critical in music, theater, verbal art, and other forms of expressive culture, but specifically that mutual attention to each other's stances is the key factor. Where the participants in an event seek to coordinate their behaviors in real time, they must attend to both their own stance and the stances of others for the event to be carried out successfully. In situations where the action is firmly regulated beforehand and oriented toward achieving some future goal, such attention is strictly pragmatic. On an assembly line, for example, the workers need to attend to one another only enough to be sure that they are doing their job, not so slowly that the line gets backed up nor so quickly that they have done more work than the next person down the line can handle. In genres of expressive culture where there is more flexibility in action and the coordination itself is aestheticized, mutual attention to the other's stance enables coordination and becomes a key venue through which the event is made meaningful.

Consider the performance of small ensemble jazz. Very rightly, much has been made in the study of jazz of the ongoing and interactive nature of the performance event (e.g., Berliner 1993, Monson 1996, Berger 1999). In a jazz rhythm section, for example, good bass players, drummers, and pianists continuously listen to one another to make sure that they are playing together in time and that the music possesses a sense of rhythmic forward momentum. More than just maintaining temporal cohesion and swing, the players listen to one another for changes in dynamics, phrasing, rhythmic density, harmony, and, more broadly, affect and style; as a result, the constant negotiation and responsiveness of the players among themselves make the performance an ongoing, emergent conversation. I would suggest that the establishment of this conversation depends not merely on attending to sound or even on attending to the other as a subject, but on the mutual and interactive attention of the players to the ongoing maintenance of each other's stances.

Consider only the first few moments of a performance and the interaction of only two musicians, the bass player Beatriz and the drummer Diane. In such a context, Beatriz does not merely hear whether the drummer is keeping regular time or not. Taking all the caveats about possibilities of misunderstanding and deceit as given, we can say that an experienced bass player may hear the drummer's performative stance; further, hearing that stance is fundamental for the event to take place. Beatriz hears Diane as another subject (an experienced drummer) with a particular stance (Diane's a bit edgy tonight and the time is rushing). Beatriz's performative stance on the task of playing a bass line for the piece emerges as a response to her interpretation of Diane's performative stance. Wanting to make the piece work, she sticks to a constant flow of quarter notes and resists her usual desire to play ahead of the beat. While Diane may experience her own edginess as a flow of distracting thoughts or a nervous sensation in her limbs, her most musically salient sense of her own stance will come in a James-Langeian attention to the time-feel of her own drumming—the same phenomenon to which Beatriz attends. Further, hearing Beatriz play four-to-the-bar walking lines right on the beat and knowing her to be an ahead-of-the-beat player who prefers rhythmic ornaments and the occasional contrapuntal line, Diane's attention is alerted to her own edgy stance, and she hears Beatriz's stance as supportive. Buoyed, Diane may relax and lose some of her edginess, thus freeing Beatriz to play with a more aggressive stance. Of course, a range of alternative scenarios abound:

Beatriz may fail to notice Diane's stance; Beatriz may hear Diane's stance but play in her usual fashion, feeling that taking a four-to-the-bar and on-the-beat approach would be patronizing; or she may hear Diane's edginess and take a more aggressive stance, either to spur Diane on to better performance or to show her up for a fool. Focusing on only one pair of participants for only a brief stretch of behavior, the example represents just a fragment of the complexity of situations in which mutual attention to stance is valued. The larger point is that the coordination of behavior does not merely depend on attention to the sound of the other; it depends on attending to sound as an expression of the other's stance, and the collective sound of the band is, among other things, a trace of the participants' mutual attention to each other's stances.

It is not merely in the negotiation of tempo that performers indicate stance on the other. For example, in certain kinds of post-1950s jazz, some details of the harmonic rhythm (e.g., the use of diatonic upper extensions in dominant chords as opposed to non-diatonic, altered tones) are open for negotiation in performance. This flexibility creates a place in which stance on the other can enter the scene. At those moments where there is harmonic flexibility, accompanists may play with a supportive stance by sounding only the third and the seventh of the current chord; those notes are the bare minimum necessary to indicate harmonic function, and sounding only them leaves the soloist free to decide which upper extensions to use (diatonic upper extensions versus altered ones). If the accompanist plays more notes, she limits the soloist's options. Though the soloist is generally seen to be in the driver's seat in post-1950s jazz, she can give more autonomy to the accompanist by playing harmonically ambiguous parts or allowing her phrases to begin after the chords have changed, thus letting the accompanist pick the precise harmonic colors. Of course, what counts as rhythmic or harmonic coordination is defined by the generic and cultural norms of the participants. Generic, and more broadly, culturally specific ideas about how tightly musicians should be synchronized in time or how the note choices of one player may constrain the note choices of another set up a context of meaning that makes stance on another possible. In a traditional bebop context, for example, a soloist would feel precluded from emphasizing an A-flat in her improvised melody if the pianist played a G9 chord (which includes an A, rather than an A-flat) to articulate a G-dominant color. In a free jazz context, that kind of harmonic clash might be allowed or even encouraged.

While partially shared ideas about what counts as coordination are always social, this does not mean that they are arbitrary. If two musicians aren't strictly coordinated, the hocket effect produced when they trade off individual notes to create the impression of a single line does not come off. In the circus arts, a moment's delay in the actions of one trapeze artist will prevent the second artist from being caught and send her plummeting to the nets. In these cases, the goal of the two musicians to trade off individual notes to produce a single line or of the two trapeze artists to link up in mid-air are definitions of what counts as coordination. The mutual attention to the stance of the other enables the hocketing musicians to keep coordinated and the trapeze artists to arrive at the right moment. Further, the smoothness with which the paired performers attend to one another—the effortlessness with which the musicians hocket or the trapeze artists link up—gives those events extra levels of meaning for their audiences. As we have seen previously, it is not always smooth or effortless coordination that is valued in performance. In boxing, for example, the impression of smooth coordination is not at issue. The boxers' goals are antagonistic, so there is no sense in which they might work together to coordinate their behaviors. Boxer A seeks to block Boxer B's blows from striking his face and torso, and vice versa. While the explicit goal of the event is for one boxer's actions to triumph over the other, sportswriters would remind us that stance is still a large part of the pleasure of the event for its audience. Five different boxers may use a roundhouse or an uppercut, but it is the scrappy or dominating or cunning manner in which those moves are deployed that will endear a particular boxer to her fans. Further, the boxers will attend to each other's stances, not to coordinate their actions, but to look for opportunities for what we might refer to as antagonistic counter-coordinations—sniffing out weakness, preparing for an onslaught, and so forth.

The significance of mutual, interactive stance on the other is apparent by comparing face-to-face situations with more highly mediated ones. In the context of solo behaviors such as reading or composing music in one's head, individual compositions are the textual object upon which a person may have a stance, and social and cultural contexts provide the background that allows those texts and the person's stance upon them to be made meaningful. In the context of certain kinds of real-time, face-to-face interactions, the practices of one's self and one's others serve as the object upon which the participants have their stances, and partially shared ideas about what counts as coordination among them is the background that allows those practices and the person's stance upon them to be made meaningful. The larger point here is that mutual, ongoing, and interactive attention to stance is the crucial factor in a wide range of events; further, such interactive arrangements enable the circulation of valences, not only among locations and modalities within a single person's experience, but across the experiences of two or more individuals as well. In exploring these intense forms of partial sharing, I am in no way suggesting a blurring of the boundary between the person and the world or between persons. To the contrary, each person's experience is always concretely lived as her own and each person may always misunderstand or deceive the other. What is revealed by examining situations of the mutual, interactive attention to stance and the flow of valences between persons that such attention enables is the fundamentally social and embodied nature of experience: the common fact that what each of us has is experience, even as our experiences are always our own; the common situation that we apprehend ourselves in the same way that we apprehend others, through our experiences; and the common mode of those experiences, embodied social subjects engaged with a world.

The dynamic of mutual, interactive attention to stance bears upon a key idea in contemporary music studies—groove. In his often cited "theory of participatory discrepancies" ([1966] 1994; [1987] 1994; 1995), Charles Keil argues that for music to be compelling and powerful, its elements must not be coordinated in a precisely metronomic fashion, but must instead be "'out of time' and 'out of tune'" (Keil [1987] 1994:96). When discrepancies of timing or pitch are large, Keil argues, the members of an ensemble are disconnected and the music is ineffective; when they disappear and players perform with absolutely metronomic coordination, the autonomy of the individual is subordinated to a conductor or clock, and thus dehumanized. But when differences in the players' timing, tuning, and timbre—what Keil calls "participatory discrepancies" or "PDs"—are small and continuously negotiated, the players' involvement in the music becomes manifest, a participatory interaction between people is achieved, and the feeling of groove is struck. Keil emphasizes that no two instances of groove are ever alike and that there can be culturally specific traditions of groove, but at a more abstract level he asserts that groove and participatory discrepancy are the universal basis, not just for compelling music, but for humane social life. While scholars have expressed doubts about the universalistic thrust of Keil's arguments and groove's utopian potential (see Cowdery et al. 1995), the notion has been highly productive in ethnomusicology and popular music studies. Keil is undoubtedly correct that a sense of rhythmic forward momentum is crucial for many types of music, and in highlighting the importance of time-feel in music and the interactive nature of performance, Keil has made a major contribution to music studies. Setting aside the difficulties with Keil's broad social speculations and the value judgments he makes about particular types of music, problems remain, I believe, with the notion of participatory discrepancies, and I would like to close this section by suggesting how the concept of stance can contribute to this thread of research.

Because Keil's work comes from a scholarly tradition different from phenomenology, some intellectual work is necessary to make the two sets of ideas commensurate. Except for a passage in which Keil quotes several musicians who argue that focusing attention on groove will hamper one's ability to produce participatory discrepancies (1995:8), the dynamics of lived experience are not discussed at length in his writings on this topic. Building on the work of Owen Barfield and Lucien Lévy-Bruhl, Keil makes clear that, in his view, participation is the means by which discrepancies of rhythm and pitch make music powerful for its listeners: the "'out of time' and 'out of tune'" coordinations between performers, he claims, directly involve the listener and invoke her bodily participation in the music. Further, Keil states that the reception of PDs as joyful or life affirming is a natural response, and his later work suggests that a failure to have the proper reaction to them is an aberration, perhaps even a litmus test of a listener's humanity. "Participatory discrepancies," Keil writes, ". . . appear 'irregular,' 'far out,' and 'wild and crazy' only to the power-tripping, control-over people still trapped inside civilization." For everyone else, they are the source of pleasure in music, and Keil goes on to assert that "PDs are the basis of all musical creation" (1995:4). Groove is clearly a key issue in many music cultures, but what is striking to me in this work is that, in a theory that so strongly champions the participation of music makers and listeners in performance, reception is depicted as uniform, one-dimensional, and automatic. It is true that many listeners across the world enjoy ecstatic musical performances. But can't a listener engage with the PDs of a performance with greater or lesser intensity, read them in differing ways, misinterpret them, or freight them with more than one type of valence? Do PDs *always* "bring people into the sound in a totemic or pre-symbolic mode," as Keil states in a dialog with Steven Feld (Keil and Feld 1994:167), and do they always have a life-affirming quality? Further, the participatory mechanism by which groove evokes emotion itself requires greater elucidation: by what means does the sound of grooving musicians spur the listener into participation?

I would suggest that we can understand the discrepancies of timing and pitch among the performers in an ensemble as the traces that the participants' stances on each other leave in the medium of sound. When a jazz aficionado hears the temporal and timbral coordinations between the drummer's and the bass player's parts in performance, for example, she grasps those Keilian discrepancies as traces of the musicians' stances on one another—as locked together with the stiffness that comes from insecurity about the performance, or trusting in their loose but consistent coordination, or amateurishly disconnected, or any other set of stances on each other that their interactions may co-constitute. In the example of Beatriz and Diane, the issues of micro-timing, tuning, timbre, and texture that Keil calls participatory discrepancies are the means by which stance on the other is negotiated, and by thinking of PDs as traces of stance, we can use the intellectual apparatus of phenomenology to explore the ways in which groove emerges in lived experience.

Taking this approach also allows us to see more clearly the wide range of valences that grooves may invoke. Both an ensemble of competitive young jazz performers seeking to out-play one another and an ensemble of supportive older performers may strike a groove in Keil's sense and forge a performance with compelling rhythmic forward momentum. Nevertheless, both groups differ sharply in the kinds of social relationships by which those grooves are constituted and the affective and social valences with which they are freighted. In the former case, the relationships are aggressive and contestatory, and the valence of the groove is edgy and intense; the latter may also involve dynamic and energetic grooves, but the experience may be comforting and secure, not freighted with the kind of tense energy found among the contestatory younger musicians. While Keil does identify a range of different kinds of time-feel—in jazz: "chunky bass players" grooving with "on-top drummers," as compared with "stringy bassists" grooving with "lay-back drummers" ([1966] 1994:64)—his insistence that effective PDs represent a universal value of humane sociability has the effect of reducing the variety of valual qualities that time-feel can express to a binary of grooving or not grooving. Setting aside this universal thrust and viewing groove as the trace of stance on the other, we can appreciate the range of valences that groove can evoke.

Further, reading Keil's work through a phenomenological lens allows us to problematize the issue of the reception of groove. Keil rightly recognizes that differing musical traditions may value discrepancies in different dimensions of sound—the attack of a sound versus its release, discrepancies in pitch versus those in timbre (1995:7)—and he urges scholars to take a comparative approach to this topic. Such cross-cultural differences raise questions of reception. Far from being a natural response to PDs in music sound, hearing the pleasure of a groove and experiencing the valences of the musicians' stances on each other depend on knowing how auditory elements are coordinated in the musical tradition at hand—where discrepancies are valued in the sound, where they are not, and how much discrepancy is allowed. Clearly, listening for discrepant attacks in a tradition where such musical features are not a valued dimension of ensemble coordination will fail to reveal the stances that the musicians have on each other in performance. And like all forms of perception, the grasping of stance on the other is a kind of practice and is thus shaped by agency and the contingencies of situated activity, as well as by culture. For example, the distracted listener will be partially inhibited from grasping the groove of a performance, even if it is from a tradition with which she is familiar, while the highly motivated listener from another tradition may make the effort to grasp the coordinations of a tradition that she is still learning.

Further dimensions of interpretation complicate the reception of groove. Even in those situations where stances-on-the-other constituted through performers' ensemble coordinations are accurately grasped by the listener, there is no guarantee that that listener will freight them with the same meanings. This was driven home to me sharply in an interaction I had with one of my students. A few years ago, a fan of industrial music took a class from me. Not as familiar with the genre as I wanted to be, I asked him to lend me some discs and educate me about the music. He offered a CD by Ministry that I had never heard and a few days later asked me for my opinion of it. I explained that I favored a certain track, and he responded with a wide, predatory grin. The track I liked was the only one on the disc with a loose, swinging groove, and he explained that he and all of the other industrial fans that he knew agreed that that song was the worst piece on the disc. What he and his friends enjoyed, he explained, was to dim down the lights, turn on an industrial CD, and descend into the absolutely static, absolutely stiff time of the music, a temporal coordination as strict as the clock cycles that timed the drum machines and samplers and as far from jazz swing as possible. While the example confirms that the student and I shared a common understanding of what constitutes a loose groove, we gave that phenomenon completely opposed valences: a Keilian jazz groove was exactly what this devoted music fan did *not* want. The example is anecdotal, but the broader relevance is clear. Differing music cultures prize differing types of coordination, and unless one is willing to give rankings to the musical values of differing cultures—for example, telling industrial fans that they have bad taste or that their music reflects an anti-democratic impulse, which is something I am not prepared to do—the study of groove requires a multi-leveled attention to reception.

Stance, Practice on Long Time-scales, and the Totality of the Person

A certain objection to the notion of stance elaborated so far might arise from the perspective of contemporary psychology. Applying stance to the awareness of oneself, a critic may protest, confuses differing levels of psychological function. For example, most of my earlier examples of music listening seem to involve higher brain functions, as do all of the complex, meaning-making processes that in general I have been associating with stance. However, I also have suggested that we have a stance on motor behaviors. Such behaviors are extremely varied and are controlled in differing ways. One might object that the auditory cognition in music listening and the low-level motor behaviors in some types of musical gestures involve totally different processes. The affective valences that accompany or drive them are different as well, and as a result, stance isn't a single psychological phenomenon but a wide array of unrelated functions. This is not the case, and addressing this concern will enable us to see how individual situations and the stances formed there are connected with the context of a person's life in its broadest dimensions. That discussion will prepare the way for the next chapter, which explores how stance and the meaning of expressive culture fit into large-scale social and historical contexts.

My approach to stance treats the person as a *potentially* coherent source of action. While this potential for coherence of the parts of the person is not always made manifest, it is the fact of that potentiality that unites the differing kinds of stance into a single element of experience and makes it so fundamental to meaning. The fact that this element of experience is enacted through varying psychological mechanisms is indeed true; as I suggested earlier, in any given situation the form of one's stance conforms itself to the type of object on which the stance is held. However, the diversity of bodily mechanisms through which stance is enacted does not invalidate their underlying connections or negate the need to understand them as manifestations of the same kind of experiential process.

Consider an example of low-level motor function. A teenager teaches herself to play rock guitar. After a year of practicing on her own, she starts taking lessons with a classical guitar teacher. This teacher tells her that she must re-train her left (fretting) hand, so that when she raises her fingertips, they will come up only an eighth of an inch or so above the string, rather than the two or three inches that they currently do. To work on this, the teacher assigns the student an exercise in which she is supposed to fret and then play a note on the sixth string with her fourth (pinky) finger. (Her other fingers should be pressed against that string as well.) Next, she is supposed to play the note three frets lower by pressing her first (index) finger just behind that fret and raising her other fingers just slightly off the string. The exercise progresses with the student playing the same descending interval on the fifth string, the fourth string, and so on. When she reaches the first string, she is to repeat the exercise one fret up the neck, until she reaches the body of the guitar. Practicing this fingering exercise at home, the student plays the first note, and then lifts all fingers but her first off the string in order to play the note three frets back. Seemingly out of control, all of her fingers jump a full two inches above the fretboard! The student plays the same melodic interval on the next string, and once again, the fingers leap away from the fretboard. Frustrated, the student continues at a slow metronome tempo for ten minutes, having made no headway whatsoever in assimilating this technique. Only after a week of determined practice does she begin to pick up the new approach and keep her fingers somewhat closer to the fretboard.

Glancing at this example, a psychologist would rightly point out that the fine control of the motions may be the result of neural mechanisms in the spinal column or an even lower part of the motor system, rather than the brain, and that it is only with great effort that these motions may be brought under conscious command. Whatever the biological mechanisms that control these particular gestures, I would argue that the student still has a stance on her gestures and that this stance is operative both while the student is unable to control the gesture and while she has mastered the technique.

My earlier discussions of the dialectic of productive practice and perceptual constitution and of Merleau-Ponty's notion of chiasm are relevant here. In everyday gross motor behavior—say, moving the arm up and down the guitar neck—the guitarist controls her motions, literally producing the behavior; at the same time, she constitutes that gesture in visual and proprioceptive sense perception. Now imagine that our student is still learning the fingering exercise, but that her hand was numbed by an anesthetic and her eyes were blindfolded. Again, she plays the descending interval and her fingers jump far away from the fretboard. In this situation, she is completely unaware of the length of her fingers' gestures, and, considered as an isolated event, we could rightly say that she had no stance upon it. However, this is *not* the situation described initially. In the exercise, she is under no anesthesia; she feels her fingers fly off the neck and experiences the fact that the fine contours of the gesture are outside of her control. Though she can't control the fine-grained elements of the motion, she still has a stance upon it—frustration, surprise, annoyance, and, perhaps, determination. Here, the fact of this chiasmatic interplay of perception and action transforms the mere physical motion of a hunk of flesh and bone into a practice with a stance. Her stance here (one of surprise and frustration) is not merely on the perception of the gesture but also on the action itself—even though she cannot as yet control it. Indeed, the stance quality on the action itself is precisely that: the shock-of-failed-control. Again, this is a stance in the formal sense developed in chapter 1: the affective, valual, or stylistic quality with which a person engages an entity in her experience. Here, the student constitutes her out-of-control manual gestures in her experience. She is aware of her hand, and that awareness is not formed in a disinterested manner; rather, she attends to her hand with rich detail, with frustration and determination.

This example may seem to be a very specific and particular one, but we can use it to open the discussion onto broader dimensions of stance. So far, I have primarily discussed stances on actions in the small time-scale of immediately situated events. It is true that one's experiences and one's stances on them are always constituted in the actuality of specific events and situations. However, such lived phenomena may be so intimately tied to past experiences—and to the anticipation of future ones—that any discussion of stance must account for the issue of long time-scales in lived experience.

Consider our young guitarist a few years ago, when she first tried to teach herself to play. Though she had never picked up a guitar before, in her first months working at the instrument, she situated her actions within a lifetime of learning motor skills. On the first day that she touches the guitar, she plucks a few notes awkwardly; the results are far from musical, but she has a foot in the door, so to speak, and can at least make sounds. Her older sister shows her how to finger the G and C chords, and at first she is incapable of fretting them at all. Having the experiences of motor skills typical for our species, though, she knows that while these gestures are completely impossible now, focused attention and repetition will eventually transform the impossible into the possible-but-awkward-and-unreliable and, hopefully, into the smooth-and-effortless. Fast-forward to the first practice sessions with the new finger exercises that her teacher showed her. She is completely unable to control the gesture that the exercise requires of her, and her stance on the action alone is the shock-of-failed-control. But this description is not sufficient. Even though she has absolutely no control whatsoever of the fine contours of the gesture during the first minute of her first practice session, there is something more to her stance—a "protention" that *this* act is part of a long-scale series of acts that will eventually result in her being able to play with her teacher's technique. *Protention* is a term from Husserl's phenomenology that refers to possible future events experienced continuously with the present moment.[11] I have already discussed some of Husserl's ideas on time consciousness in the previous chapter, and to examine the question of stance on long time-scales, it will be necessary to return to this topic again.

Time is a notoriously difficult element of lived experience to discuss, and the notion of protention can be easily misunderstood. Protentions are not, as the phraseology may seem to suggest, a supernatural divination of the future. There is, of course, never any guarantee that a protended occurrence will indeed take place. Thinking of protention as an experience of the future that makes no claim to clairvoyant vision, we may be tempted to equate protention with anticipation. But protention is no fantasy or conjecture actively posited in imagination, as when a child tries to guess if it is a coin or a candy that one has hidden in one's hand. Protention is distinct from the everyday notion of anticipation in that protentions do not take the form of reflexive thought in words or images cordoned off in a realm of mere fantasy or speculation. To the contrary, my experience of the recent past, events in what Husserl called the "now-point," and the protended future exist simultaneously with one another, and taken together they form what Husserl called the "living present."[12] Playing an ascending major scale in C on the guitar, for example, I play a C and at the same time I protend the sound of the D and E in the near future, the gesture of making those notes, and even the continued persistence of my body and the guitar neck. Of course, even the latter, most fundamental protentions may not be fulfilled; the temperature may suddenly drop 200 degrees and the guitar may shatter, or a sudden, unexpected sword blow may chop off one of my arms. However, I must protend the upcoming moments and retain the past moments; otherwise, we could not have the temporal space, so to speak, in which to have experience, and neither would we be able to make any kind of sense or meaning. The understanding of even the simplest temporally extended entity, like a sentence, would be impossible without the protentions and retentions that constitute the living present. To understand the sentence "Jane hands John the pen," for example, I must simultaneously retain "Jane" while I experience "hands" in the now-point and protend the fact of direct and indirect objects as yet unspecified. When the sentence has been heard or read, I retain it, not as a series of isolated moments, but as a temporal unity extruded across and receding as a unit within the living present. If I did not retain and protend, I could not experience the sentence as having any meaning, since neither "Jane," "hands," "John," "the," nor "pen" as isolated fragments (nor all five words as a simultaneous atemporal unity) have the meaning of "Jane hands John the pen." All noetic processes, their valual qualities with them, emerge in and move through the living present.

Returning to the issue of stances and long temporal scales, the key point is that individual stance qualities are not merely continuous across the living present of a single event. On the contrary, in many cases the valual quality of stance may connect experiences across events, and that connection may be fundamental to those experiences. Consider again our teenage guitarist. During the third day of her classical guitar exercises, she focuses attention and tries with only slight success to bring her finger movements under control. The stance quality of surprise has almost completely faded, although still present is frustration each time an otherwise responsive finger leaps away from the neck. However, there is something more here. Valual and affective stance qualities associated with temporal events on long time-scales are more subtle than the primary-color affects of happiness or sadness, the emotional equivalents of Romper Room Red and Playskool Blue. Phenomena such as breaking free from a long-standing frustration, digging in for the long haul, muddling through, being defeated after a good battle, or being determined to win at all costs exemplify some of the types of experiences I wish to focus on at this juncture. We are all familiar with such states, and the kind of experience I want to discuss here takes place when such states are not merely thematized as distinct phenomena, but emerge for the person as stance qualities — as the affective dimension of a situated act of constituting experience. Such stance qualities are a crucial part of our lives, and they gain their weight and power because they link our past and present with our understandings of what we experience our future might become. The full stance quality of the guitarist working and largely failing her exercise is one of digging-in-for-the-long-haul, and the Husserlian temporal terminology can help us see precisely how such qualities emerge in experience.

Digging-in-for-the-long-haul is not merely a simple affect, a quality that cannot be broken down into simpler parts. Neither is it an intention in the mundane sense of the term, a plan formed in mental words to pursue a course of action. While the stance quality of digging-in-for-the-long-haul may be accompanied by an explicit thought ("I will keep working at this till I get it!"), such a reflexive plan is different from the stance itself. As a lived stance quality, digging-in-for-the-long-haul is a stance of committed determination on present action, tied to and informed by a backgrounded awareness of protentions of future actions, and of one's own future determined stances upon them. Of course, the existence of protentions never guarantees their actualization: one may perform an exercise, and in so doing have protentions of many future hours at the instrument, only to lose interest in music, master the exercise quickly, or die suddenly the next day, never having had the opportunity to actualize one's protention. However, if the stance quality that one experiences is indeed digging-in-for-the-long-haul proper, rather than a short-term determination, then it will be a quality of a long-scale protention, regardless of the real-world actualization of that protention in future practices. In a parallel fashion, other stance qualities emerge from retention. Two weeks into her fingering exercise routine, our guitarist grasps the neck with a new and complex valual quality. Her immediate stance has been more or less the same throughout this period, but with two weeks of hard practicing and small gains made each day, the affective valence of her engagement with her present act is tied to and informed by the affective valence of her past acts, thus constituting a complex stance quality we may call satisfaction-of-making-steady-progress. The examples so far have largely been positive, optimistic ones, but not all such stance qualities are so pleasant. We have all seen individuals who are beaten down in life. This isn't merely a single emotion that wells up at a given time, though it may emerge in that manner. To the contrary, such feelings often become present as stance qualities—the way a mop is held or a cardboard sign ("Will work for food") is grasped, with the weight of past mistreatments weighing like an anchor and the protention of an identical future shutting out any gesture of pleasure or hope.

It is worth emphasizing here that stance on long temporal scales is indeed a type of stance in the formal sense that I defined in chapter 1. In the present situation, I am not only aware of the objects immediately before me. I may also have a backgrounded awareness of retentions of the long-scale past and protentions of the long-scale future. I do not merely experience these retentions and protentions, I have a relationship to them: I focus on the moment and hold my fears at bay; I grit my teeth and take my medicine, settle in comfortably, or dig in for the long haul. In this way, the backgrounded past or future is an element of experience, and stance on long-scale retentions and protentions is the affective, stylistic, or valual quality with which I engage those elements of experience.

As always in the reading of stance, there is no guarantee that one's interpretation of another's stance in long time-scales is veridical—that is, that the retentions into which stance qualities are invested are retentions of the real historical past or that protentions into which stance qualities are invested are protentions of a future that will be actualized. The interpretive issues here are vastly complex. For example, consider the great actor whose rich imagination of past humiliations gives her performance of begging on the street the ring of truth, when in fact the protended future of hopeless begging is that of the fictitious character, not the thespian in her actuality. In a very different example, a delusional office worker may interpret every insignificant pleasantry as a winking affirmation that she is destined for great things. Seeing herself as a rising star and actively compensating for what she sees as her public reputation, her presentation at the departmental meeting is one of self-assured calm informed by a long history of perceived winks and nudges. Here, her co-workers see her as self-effacing and fail to realize that this modesty is informed, not by a lived past of uncertain interchanges and low expectations, but by the weight of a thousand perceived exhortations of the "you go girl" variety and the lived protention of a high-status position.

Because acts of constituting experience on long time-scales are an element of our experience, it is not uncommon to have a meta-stance upon them. Return to the guitarist from the earlier example. It is now ten years later and she is in the second semester of a master's program in music. She has long ago assimilated the basic hand postures discussed above and a host of other fundamental guitar techniques; further, she has a good knowledge and an intuitive grasp of her own processes of learning. After a semester at the conservatory, she has learned well a few difficult pieces, but in the last few weeks she has come to realize the depth of the repertoire that she has to master. On one particular occasion, she sits down to work on a long, complex composition that is a standard part of the guitar literature, and with a smooth facility she settles into the usual process of reading through the score to find the technically difficult or interpretively complex passages. After mapping out the main sections she will need to address, she begins to work on the first tough passage, which requires the difficult juggling of two independent lines. Her acts of reading through the score, isolating specific gestures, repeatedly articulating them, lightly monitoring various hand and body postures, and listening intently throughout are all enacted with a stance that we could call settling-in-for-the-long-haul. Her movement between the steps in the practicing process has become smooth, almost automatic, even as the parts she is rehearsing are rough and difficult; in addition, the present acts of smooth focus are synthesized with a protention of the years that will be required to master the basic repertoire and the retention of her past achievements in the practice room.

Toward the beginning of the practice session—just as the process of isolating, reading, repeating, listening, and monitoring takes hold—she grasps this protentional-retentional structure of cozy practice rooms, musical accomplishment, and aesthetic pleasure with a meta-stance of warm embrace. As the session continues, that meta-stance fades into the far background of experience, but the valence of that meta-stance colors every element of her session. Speaking loosely, one could say that she was throwing herself into her music making. Such an act of throwing oneself into a course of conduct is the constitution of a meta-stance. Her long-scale noetic acts connect present practices with a long time-scale past and future and do so with a specific affective valence; further, her reflexive consciousness embraces all of that in an assertively affirmative grasp of her stance on herself. This reflexive awareness is focal at the beginning of the practice routine and then rests in the defining background of her experience as the session progresses.

Of course, meta-stances on the long scale need not operate in this fashion. Consider an alternative scenario in which the student has become dispirited by the challenge of mastering such a large repertoire and the time involved in practicing. Activities outside of music (community work and politics) have begun to interest her, and she has started to resent the great number of hours that she has to spend at her instrument. As before, she sits down to practice, and while the series of isolating, reading, repeating, listening, and monitoring acts takes hold, she grasps the smooth process and the protentional-retentional structure to which it is connected in an act of reflexive consciousness. Here, however, her engagement with this long-scale noetic act has a very different valual quality. Becoming focally aware of the very facility of her learning process and its embedding in a lived project that stretches both backward and forward to encompass a large stretch of time, she grasps the situation with dismay, even a mild revulsion. Like a cook plucking a rotten bag of salad from her refrigerator, our guitarist holds her practice skills at a mental distance. In an act of reflexive self-consciousness, she freights the past years in the rehearsal room (here perceived as cramped and dank) and the potential future in music (here seen as lonely, isolating, and self-absorbed) with disgust. She quickly relaxes her arms and back, which have just tensed, and is successful in backgrounding this reflexive awareness, but nevertheless it lurks at the edge of her experience. Rather than affirming her acts past and future, she rejects them and divides herself against herself. Her meta-stance creates a complex and dissonant set of valences in the overall gestalt of her experience. A sensitive teacher listening to a tape of the practice session might recognize a note of reluctance in her playing, even as she commends the student on the efficiency of her practice routine.

With this discussion of long-scale acts of forming experience, the types of stances that accompany them, and the distinctive ways in which interpretive and reflexive processes play out there, we can begin to get a glimpse of the ways in which individual situations fit into the larger context of a person's life.

We start at the opposite pole: the example that began this section of the guitarist unable to control her fingers. Ordinarily, when we consider gross movements of our bodies, we unite the motion of a limb with the reflexive monitoring of that limb in vision and proprioception; further, one's stance on the action and one's stance on the perception are often one and the same thing. In the guitar exercises example, though, these two elements are separated. The musician certainly has a stance on the data that her eyes and proprioceptive senses deliver, but the production of motor behaviors is out of her control. In fact, one might be tempted to say that in such a case, the guitarist's hands were part of her body but not part of her person or subjectivity, and she only rightly had a stance on the perceptual, but not the motor, phenomena. Such a perspective is inaccurate. The guitarist's proprioceptive and visual perception of her present action combine with her lived awareness that such a gesture might someday come under her control, thus transforming the experience, giving her a stance on both the perception and the motor function together, and bringing her fingers back into the ambit of her person. Here the protention of future acts turns the lack of control into a phenomenal presence, an experienced absence that I referred to earlier as the shock-of-failed-control.

The connections across experiences on long scales of time form one dimension in which the person is potentially constituted. It is this sense of oneself on long time-scales that allows one to partially recontextualize and thus bring differing meanings to the immediate situation. As the example suggests, this sense of one's self need not take the form of a series of ideas explicitly formulated in words, a mental biography or manifesto. While one may actively stop and think, "I have spent sixty hours a week in this cozy [or cramped] practice room, and I have ten more years ahead of me in this paradise [or prison]," more often than not such words are an interpretation of long-scale protentions and retentions lurking in the background of one's experience of the immediate situation. Such mental words need not be formed in the center of experience (or at all) for the past to inform the present. Rather, the complex gestalt of the valual qualities of the retained elements of the past and the protended potential of a particular future or set of futures, combined with the valual qualities of the immediate situation and the overall stance with which all of this is laid out in lived consciousness, sets the larger valual environment for our experience at any moment.[13] The dialectics of retrospection and iteration illustrated earlier with examples of stance on small time-scales are parallel to the interplay of the immediate situation and experiences on large time-scales, although this latter set of dialectics is vastly more complex. This constant negotiation and renegotiation of past and future in the present enables people to have what in everyday language we loosely describe as *lives,* rather than either a long series of moments strung together or a single unified essence that just happens to be invested in a temporal world.

Just as stance in the production or reception of expressive culture is the pivot on which aesthetic effects turn, so is stance on large time-scales the pivot on which the meaning of lives turns. If one's connection of the situated present to specific elements of the lived past and the potential future is one of the ways in which one's life is constituted, then it is the stance with which such connections are made that frames, tints, and shades those connections. Of course, people connect the immediate situation not only with their own, directly lived pasts. As Alfred Schutz's monumental *Phenomenology of the Social World* ([1932] 1967) so richly illustrates, we have a lived awareness of people and peoples in times and places distant from the present situation, an awareness that is no less lived and significant for being highly mediated and subject to error. For example, the guitarist in our earlier illustration may not only locate her immediate practicing situation within the personal history of hours spent in the practice room, but also within her personal experience of sexism in the classrooms, lounges, and rehearsal halls of a patriarchal music school and also within her more mediated experiences of the long-scale history of women's exclusion and marginalization from the Western conservatory tradition that have entered her consciousness through books, articles, Web sites, magazines, and lectures. This positioning of the immediate lived situation within history and society makes explicit the connections between stance and social dynamics beyond the immediate situation and moves us closer to the politics that I have pointed toward throughout. The next chapter addresses these issues directly.

Before embarking on that discussion, I would like to emphasize that attention to these issues has a direct relevance for fieldwork on expressive culture. In witnessing a concert, a play, or a ritual, the ethnographer sees only the bodies of the people before her; she doesn't see experienced pasts or protended futures. Nevertheless, she can more fully see these bodies as three-dimensional people by recognizing that even the most mundane action of the present situation is experienced against the backgrounded awareness of a life and that stance on the long scale binds the situation and the life together. A singer may experience this gig as a key performance that will lead to a new career, for example, or only as one of a series of jobs necessary to raise some extra money; a listener may be dramatically and reflexively aware that this story is the last one that she will hear her grandmother narrate, or her listening acts may be accompanied by the feeling that these tales have become routine. Whether such connections construe the event as important or mundane, the immediate situation is always located in the context of the person's life, and we enrich our work by being sensitive to those linkages. In interviews and feedback interviews, and also in participant observation and interpretation, we can look to see the ways in which this event or this kind of event is tied to the large scale of the participants' lives.

Though the topic of lives involves the particulars of individual people, it is also directly related to partially shared experiences of collectivities and larger social contexts, an issue that I will take up in greater detail in the next chapter. On a basic level, the past experiences and future expectations that people have in their lives—that singing in this genre can lead to a full-time career in my country, that people from my ethnicity or gender aren't allowed to become famous singers—are shaped by the social world in which they are situated and its relations of power. Further, individual performances of expressive culture are tied to a lifetime of events beyond expressive culture. The act of grasping the guitar neck with heavy metal rage or righteous, pacifistic fervor may be shaped by the retention of a thousand days working in a dead-end service-sector job, or, in a different context, the protention of a thousand nights spent fighting in a Southeast Asian jungle. In varied and complex ways, long-scale protentions and retentions are the concretely lived background against which individual events occur, and stance on those long-scale experiences makes a person own and inhabit that life in all of its contextual richness. A sensitivity to the dynamics of situations, stances, and lives can make our interpretations of expressive culture richer and open up the analysis of individual events to larger contexts.

At the end of the previous chapter, I suggested that the fundamental fact that experience must be *sustained* across an event illustrates the underlying substratum of agency by which all social life is constituted. That is, I suggested that for an event to take place, the participants must actively sustain their experience through a course of time, and this makes the situated, partial agency of everyday practice the material out of which interaction is worked. The partial linkage of present acts to the person's lived past and future and to a larger social world infinitely broadens this stratum, and it does so along two dimensions. First, it connects lived experience with history and social life, giving a substratum of partial agency to the full sweep of social time and social space; at the same time, it adds a valual dimension to history and social life, undergirding them with the richness of lived meaning. In other words, that substratum of partial agency is the material from which history and social life are made, and stance is the valual grain of that material. Expressive culture is one of many domains of this substratum, one of the places where this material is worked. Among other things, it is the space where this material impinges back on itself—a place of social reflexivity where enstanced agents engage with and reflect on their own agency, a knot in the grain of social life whose whorls are formed of the stances of the everyday displaying themselves to themselves. But just as a knot may produce a rupture in the surface of a plank of wood or become a feature around which the grain flows, so is expressive culture's place in social life complex and varied. The relationship of expressive culture to the rest of the social world has often been represented in one-sided ways—the linchpin of revolutionary change, a ventilator of social tensions, a tool for inculcating normative beliefs, a sprig of parsley on the plate of more fundamental political realities, or a humanizing safe haven for creativity and pleasure in a world of tedium and domination. In the next chapter, I will try to gain perspective on these one-sided visions of expressive culture by showing how the notion of stance fits into a practice-based approach to social life.

CHAPTER FOUR

The Social Life of Stance and the Politics of Expressive Culture

We encounter an incredible variety of things in our lives: physical objects, texts, rules, moods, our own bodies, other people. The diversity is vast and it can seem overwhelming. The foundational insight of Husserl's phenomenology is that no matter how varied are the things that we encounter, we can find a common structure in all of our experiences. That structure is intentionality, a subject engaging an object, not merely passively registering that object but actively constituting it in experience. Stance is the quality with which those engagements take place. While the forms of stance are as diverse as the things that we engage—stance on a musical composition or stance on the practice of reception, stance on the rules or moves of a game, stance on another person, stance on one's own life in its long time-scale— all of these types of stance are fundamentally united by that intentional structure. Whether we consider a writer handling characters in a sensitive or callous manner, a music fan listening to a CD with an open or closed mind, a stand-up comic addressing an audience gently or in a combative fashion, or a graduate student in music viewing a lifetime in the practice room as an appealing future or a jail sentence, we see the common fact of a person grappling with the things of her world and bringing them into her experience. The quality of that grappling plays a key role in the overall meaning of things for her.

Throughout this discussion, I have understood the constitution of experience as a kind of *social practice*, in the sense of that term elaborated in the classical formulations of practice theory—a kind of process that is both actively achieved by the person and profoundly informed by situated and large-scale social contexts (see, e.g., Giddens [1976] 1993, 1979, 1984; Bourdieu 1977).[1] The social dimensions of such constitutive practices have run through every element of my discussion. From an audience member who listens uncomfortably to works from a tradition that she cannot call her own, to the jazz musicians who grapple competitively with each other on the stand, to the guitar student who struggles to come to terms with a future shaped by the power relations of the Western conservatory—all of the types of stance that I have discussed emerge within and are shaped by a larger social world. The relationships between stance and that larger world are complex, and to introduce a systematic examination of this topic, I want to use ideas from practice theory to re-read one of the basic concepts in contemporary scholarship—context.

From Alan Dundes ([1964] 1980) and Dan Ben-Amos ([1971] 2000) to Alan Merriam (1964) and John Blacking ([1967] 1995), *context* was one of the fundamental keywords in the folklore and ethnomusicology of the 1960s and 1970s. Scholars placed texts "in context" and sought to understand the relationship between what seemed to be disparate kinds of objects of study: texts (such as pieces of music, material artifacts, or narratives) and contexts (cultures, histories, and societies). In the very best work of the period, scholars drew connections between the meanings of texts and the lives of the people who make them. Too often, though, the texts of expressive culture were seen to be "in context" in the same way that a cow is in a corral or a car in a garage—as a well-bounded thing enclosed by a container. But texts and contexts are not two different types of study objects, two different orders of reality; they are made of the same "stuff"—social practices. Clearly, we cannot deny that texts often have an objectlike quality and at least a partial autonomy from any given person who produces or receives them. No creative act of reception can find a B-major 7 chord in Bob Dylan's original recording of "All Along the Watchtower," nor can a reader of the Grimms' version of "Cinderella" claim to find a scene in which Jack steals an iPod. Yet, for expressive culture to have any significance at all, it must be brought into lived experience, and that process deposits a layer of practice in the text that is fundamental to its meaning. The first chapter of this study used the composition class and recital example to lay bare that practice stratum of expressive culture, and here I want to suggest how ideas from practice theory can show how context is based in practice.

"Man makes history," runs the common paraphrase of Marx's famous quote, "but not in conditions of his own choosing,"[2] and in differing ways Anthony Giddens and Pierre Bourdieu forwarded that orientation by showing how such "conditions" were a residue of past practices sedimented in the present and taking the form of social structure. Rather than reducing society to a collection of individuals or denying the very real ability of power relations to shape and inform a person's action, Giddens and

Bourdieu illustrated how the interplay of past and present practices constituted the very social forces that would constrain and enable future practices. Seen in the light of phenomenology and practice theory, expressive culture is not one order of reality that exists in the context of another order of reality, such as society and history; rather, these things are merely differing domains of practice. This perspective is part of a broader current in the scholarship of the last thirty years. While older forms of analysis had labored to connect objectlike expressive texts such as songs, material artifacts, or folk narratives with objectlike political phenomena such as society and history, more contemporary approaches in a range of fields emphasize their common grounding in practice. Here, the scholarly focus is on the politics of social acts such as factory work or housework, campaigning or voting, and teaching or learning, and on the expressive practices of producing or receiving material culture, music, or verbal art. Performance-oriented research has furthered this trend by revealing the embedding of expressive practices within political ones (such as the use of verbal art, dance, or music in politics; see, e.g., Parmentier 1993, Gilman 2009, Askew 2002) and also the political significance of seemingly innocent expressive practices (such as the ways in which fundamental ideas about gender are negotiated in the dance performances of the Greek culture that Cowan [1990] discusses). This theory of stance seeks to continue the advance of practice- and performance-oriented traditions of scholarship by exploring the most fundamental connection between text and practice—the fact that texts of expressive culture emerge for audiences and performers only in practices of constituting experience. By examining the layers of meaning that emerge from such practices and attending to stance, we can reconnect text and context at its constitutive level and dissolve the remainder of textualism in performance studies.

The political significance of this practice foundation is substantial. In everyday life, practices are separated into differing domains. It is obvious that a person would encounter serious obstacles if she tried to pay her property taxes in the break room at a local fast-food restaurant or get tested for strep throat at a museum of colonial American decorative arts. However, the *meanings* of practice often flow across the boundaries between domains. The anxieties, the desires, or the frustrations felt on the factory floor, in the living room, or in the public square may express themselves in the ways a microphone is grasped, the characters in a narrative are handled, or, to borrow again from Merleau-Ponty, the way a viewer's eye "palpates" the contours of a painting. Of course, this traffic among domains of practice is nothing if not complex. As the traditions of social history flowing from Michel Foucault's work illustrate, the formation of differing domains of practice and their boundaries—what counts as medical or sexual or legal practices—are historically emergent and tied to patterns of domination and resistance. And as performance studies scholars within and beyond folkloristics have shown, both the boundary between expressive and instrumental practice (see, e.g., Bauman and Briggs 1990, Del Negro 2004) and the meaning and prestige of individual media and genres of expressive culture (see, e.g., Auslander 1999) are constantly being negotiated. The previous chapters have suggested the implications of stance for the social and political dynamics of expressive culture, and what remains is to make those dynamics explicit here.

The Social Life of Stance

While people have some level of control over the affective, stylistic, and valual qualities with which they constitute their experiences, that control is not absolute and neither is it exercised in a vacuum. On the contrary, a person's constitution of stance is profoundly influenced by the situated and larger social contexts in which she finds herself. The most basic dynamics of this relationship are relatively straightforward, and a closer examination of the social life of stance and its political contexts will reveal greater subtlety and complexity.

Stance and Culture

Traditional visions of culture provide what can be seen as a first-order approximation for understanding the shaping of stance by its social world. In older forms of anthropology and folklore studies, for example, cultures are understood as sets of beliefs and practices that relate to one another in a systematic fashion. Here, each society is seen to have its own culture, which imbues any given act with meaning; attention to cultural context is, therefore, fundamental for understanding any individual practice. Conceptualized in this way, the stances that a person takes in producing or receiving expressive forms, or in any other domain of practice, would be influenced by the culture in which that person lives. Ignoring historical change, treating group boundaries as natural barriers rather than as negotiated processes, and ignoring the politics of representation, this kind of approach has a range of problems and comes from a past moment in the history of the humanities and the humanistic social sciences. Despite its difficulties, this approach does have the virtue of highlighting the social nature of human activity, and it can be used to capture some of the grossest dynamics of stance.

Claims in this older tradition can be made to take the form "Culture X favors stance Y in context Z." For example, Italian culture, it could be argued, favors a stance of *disinvoltura* (poise, ease of manners) during the ritualized evening promenade known as the *passeggiata*. As Giovanna P. Del Negro's work illustrates (2004), the passeggiata is made up of a wide range of expressive practices, including walking, observing the walks of others, and engaging in polite conversation. Disinvoltura is the ruling aesthetic of the passeggiata, and it can be understood as a kind of stance—an affective and stylistic quality with which acts of strolling, observing others, and conversing are engaged. Neither an aerobic workout nor a lazy saunter, the proper passeggiata walk, Del Negro observes, should be performed in a graceful, smooth, and effortless fashion. The observation of others should be equally *disinvolto*; betraying neither an anxious scrutiny nor a bored detachment, one should gracefully acknowledge the gaze of others and effortlessly attend to the spectacle of strollers on display. Because the passeggiata is an interactive event with many participants playing the role of both performer and audience, and because it is an event in which people from all segments of the society participate, the generalization "Italian culture favors a stance of disinvoltura in the passeggiata" is an effective first approximation of the social organization of stance there.

While many examples such as this one can be found in the academic literature, more contemporary approaches to the underlying phenomena understand society, as Del Hymes once expressed it, as an "organization of diversity" (1974:433)—an array of social positions organized systematically, each with its own differentiated sets of beliefs and practices. Add to this the observation that behaviors are influenced by the situation in which they occur, and we come to a more fine-grained, second order of approximation.

Del Negro notes, for example, that older women in small-town Italy have greater license to transgress the canons of disinvoltura and gaze in an open, disapproving, and even aggressive manner at the strolling of others. In so doing, they perform the act of passeggiata viewing with a kind of vigilant, even judgmental stance. Turning from societies to "scenes" or "social worlds" (flexible social formations that exist within or across societies and that have their own particular sets of beliefs and practices, see, e.g., Cohen 1999), one can likewise see that stance is shaped by culture and understand culture as an organization of difference. In the world of competitive figure skating, the skaters are expected to enact their jumps, spins, and footwork with an effortless quality, and for many skaters the expression of a uniquely personal approach is valued. In contrast, judges are expected to achieve their practice (gazing, analyzing, and evaluating) with an eagle-eyed attention to

detail: whether a judge's scrutiny is smooth or labored is of little consequence. Not merely differentiated by positions in a social system, stances
also vary by situation. The professional skater who moves with a completely
effortless stance in performance may be labored in rehearsal. Taking an
afternoon to work with youngsters just starting their careers, that same professional may go so far as to take on the demeanor of a drill sergeant, actively
dramatizing the hard work and effort involved in certain exercises. Alternatively, while the most common onstage stance of the extreme metal guitarist
is one of intensely aggressive, even straining energy, in rehearsal she may
focus on having a relaxed hand posture. While teaching a lesson, such a musician may have to remind her student that the electronics of the guitar do
the work of amplifying the sound, and she may display this by playing lines
with an overtly smooth and effortless style. In all of this, the kind of stance
that one takes is influenced by one's culture, social role, and social situation.

To achieve an even higher order of approximation, we must shift from
traditional constructions of culture to practice-oriented ones. From this
perspective, we may observe that any individual, stanced performance is
not merely an example or an instance of an existing cultural model or cultural norm for a person at a given social position in a given situation within
a given culture. Applying the practice theory ideas discussed earlier to the
notion of culture, we can observe that a cultural model or norm is a context
of past practices to which the person's present, at least potentially agentive
practice responds. Of course, such agency is never purely free, unconstrained action. Some models or norms of practice may be so deeply sedimented that the individual is unaware of other ways of doing things. In
other situations, the person may be sharply aware of other ways of acting,
but particular practices and their stances are heavily or even brutally en-
forced by techniques of power. Despite the fact of constraint, in many situations actors have 'at the very least the potential to reject cultural models
and enact a non-normative stance.[3] In most situations there is more than
one norm—a norm and a counternorm, or a set of competing norms, to
which the actor's enstanced practice responds—and in all situations, a
norm must be interpreted for the actor to make sense of it.

For example, comparing the later episodes of the 1950s American television show *The Goldbergs* with the bawdy routines of Jewish American
women stand-up comics from the same period, Del Negro (2009) illustrates how differing performers situated themselves in the context of the
gender and ethnic cultural norms of the day—an ocean of past practice cir-
culating through currents of everyday behavior, popular and academic
writing, and varied genres of expressive culture. Both Gertrude Berg, the
actress who played the mother on *The Goldbergs*, and night club comedians

such as Belle Barth delivered Yiddish-inflected homespun wisdom in their performances. The delivery of their lines, however, could not have been more different. Even if we set aside the stand-up's use of ribald material in her routines and focus only on her performative stance, it is clear that Barth's stance transgressed norms of middle-class female respectability. Loud, unconstrained, and aggressive, the stance of Barth violated the dominant American norms of proper white, bourgeois womanhood that Berg sought to reproduce, exemplify, and co-opt for her assimilating, upwardly mobile Jewish audience of the period. Del Negro shows how Barth and her cohort combined the normative, mouthy styles of contemporary male Jewish comics with the counter-normative red-hot momma style of women vaudevillians past to forge their unique styles. By contrast, Berg, in her later work, combined June Cleaver respectability with a mild, sanitized Jewish identity. In all of this, we see agents drawing on practices from the ocean of surrounding social life and reproducing, reinterpreting, and remaking the stances of others—all the while creating a context for the stanced performances of those in the future. It is worth noting that the circulation of these practices in the media was not unconstrained. Berg had a long run in television, while Barth and her cohort primarily worked in nightclubs and released records on small independent labels—media that the entertainment business censored in a limited manner or not at all.

The larger point to see here is the ways in which the cultural shaping of stance can be read through the lens of practice—to see that a rich dialectic of agency and the constraining and enabling context of the practices of others shapes the stance of performance. Further, attention to the agentive side of practice highlights a fact that is significant for all performers: practice is never a fait accompli, a deal that is done as soon as the intention is formed. On the contrary, stance must be enacted, brought into being, and made real by the person.[4] Many forms of stance require rehearsal and training (either formal or informal) to be enacted effectively, but even with such a background, stances may be enacted well or poorly. The highly trained performer may have a bad day and fail to enact a practice with her desired stance, while even the novice may get lucky and pull off a difficult performance. It is the anxiety about the reality of enactment that makes skating fans hold their breath when the champ performs the final jump in the last performance of a high-profile competition, even, or especially, if it is a simple one.

So far in this chapter, I have intentionally avoided the most micro-level analyses of lived experience. More of the richness and complexity of the situation comes into view, however, when we realize that all of the dynamics outlined in the previous two chapters (facet stance, meta-stance, total stance, the maintenance of stance in iteration and retrospection, the situation of stance within large time-scales, etc.) are subject to a dialectic of culture and agency. In the social world of the Western conservatory, a stance of smooth facility with the composition is almost universally valued for performers, while counter-normative values exist for the meta-stance upon that facility: some musicians, conductors, critics, and listeners prize a performer who actively embraces her technical abilities, while others prefer a meta-stance that does not so assertively highlight the performer's facility. These values were precisely reversed in the American hardcore punk scenes of the 1980s. Despite the genre's reputation for an anarchic, "anything goes" aesthetic, a range of stances on the composition were valued there. While bands like Rites of Spring and Black Flag actively embraced a raw, clumsy stance, others like Shudder to Think or Fugazi displayed polished technical abilities in performance. What was far more uniform, however, was the meta-stance on performative facility. Virtually no technically adept bands approached facility with a meta-stance of celebration and embrace. Indeed, it was the meta-stance that held these skills at bay and cordoned off the more technically adept punk bands from equally polished metal acts. The shaping of a specific form of stance by social context is not an unusual occurrence. All of the large-scale social dynamics discussed in this chapter apply to even the most fine-grained structures of lived experience discussed in the previous chapters. All are practices and emerge from a dialectic of culture and agency. It is this variegated field—which is neither a site of unconstrained individual actors nor a marionette performance in which culture pulls the person's strings—that is the space within which the social life of stance plays out.

Cultures of Stance. Text-prominent and Stance-prominent Cultures

The examples I have focused on in the last few paragraphs emphasize social scenes where stance is merely one element of practice among many that are shaped by culture. Before I turn to specifically political issues in the analysis of stance, it is worthwhile to pause and examine a category of social formations that invert the relationship between stance and culture. In these social formations, stance is not merely one phenomenon among many that are shaped by culture; on the contrary, here a specific stance is the guiding theme around which the social formation itself coalesces. Such social formations could be referred to as *cultures of stance,* and the notion can be understood as a phenomenological reinterpretation of the idea of subculture elaborated by Dick Hebdige in his classic 1979 text of the same name.

Using the semiotics of Julia Kristeva and Roland Barthes to reinterpret the then dominant subculture theory in sociology, Hebdige understood a subculture as a small group whose members share a common style and which is situated within a larger society. Where some subcultures could be differentiated from one another by their class affiliation or ideology, Hebdige argued, a higher-order distinction could be made by attending to the ways in which subcultures handle the semiotics of style. In this view, all subcultures draw on the set of signs found in their parent culture, but they differ in the "signifying practices" with which those signs do their work. Some, like the teddy boys or the skinheads, simply recombine the signs of their parent culture to express new, but fixed meanings. Other subcultures, such as the punks, handle the signs in an ironic fashion. Achieving a more radical rejection of the parent culture than would be possible merely by saying "no," the punks drew attention to the process of signification itself, drained any individual sign of its meaning, and put the larger symbolic system of the parent culture in question.

One of the great triumphs of Hebdige's approach (and that of Birmingham School cultural studies in general) was its focus on the issue of style and its search for meaning across diverse media and genres of expressive culture—primarily music and dress, but also everyday practices such as speech and forms of interaction. But his reliance on Tel Quel semiotics meant that the issue of the handling of signs became divorced from their emergence and weight in lived experience. As a result, the discussion focuses on isolated items (particular forms of clothing such as "drainpipe" pants or ripped T-shirts), not on the way that those items are concretely grasped. I would argue that here, "signifying practice" (1979:117–27) is not the practice of practice theory—concrete action that is both achieved by the person and influenced by situated and large-scale social context. On the contrary, "practice" here is merely a question of how a given sign is set in a text—as an entity that bears a meaning directly or as one that highlights the fact of its being a sign and means only absence, revolt, or refusal. This type of focus on signs fails to account for the forms of meaning that emerge from the structure of lived experience (whether a sign is grasped glancingly in the background or highlighted in the center of attention; whether a sign emerges in memory or anticipation). Also lost are the forms of meaning that depend on their placement in the chain of production and reception (rehearsal or performance, listening to a record at home or to a live band at a club) and the role of embodied action in meaning (whether the musician or audience member is "on" during this particular evening or is having a bad night).[5] In other words, this kind of approach obscures the full reality of practice as concrete action that is always both social and agentive. Taking the stance-oriented approach that I have described in the previous chapters, we can begin to recover the fullness of practice and gain access to a range of meanings that would other otherwise be lost to interpretation.

One of the critiques leveled against the notion of subculture is that it implies a greater uniformity within a given group than actually exists. Much to his credit, Hebdige recognized that there may be internal variation within subcultures (121), thus opening a door to the looser notion of popular culture "scenes" now dominant in popular music studies. The idea of stance cultures fits nicely with this new orientation. Because stances emerge in social practice, they are the result of actors and actions, are variable across situations, and are subject to historical change; as a result, stance cultures have precisely the kind of flexibility characteristic of scenes. Like any canonical work, *Subculture* has been widely discussed in the years since its publication, and my goal here is not simply to find flaws with this foundational study. By reinterpreting its older approach to style through the lens of phenomenology and practice theory, I hope to suggest a different perspective on a long-standing concern of popular music studies scholars and show the relevance of this new interpretation for contemporary work on the relationship of expressive forms to their social base.

One further insight in Hebdige's work bears reinterpretation in the light of phenomenology. Toward the end of *Subculture*, Hebdige notes that the ironic handling of signs that disrupts the communication of meaning can lose its quality of shock and negation over time. With images of everyday objects clipped from magazines and newspapers and then rearranged on a page, the surrealist technique of collage, explains Hebdige, was once a highly disruptive device. Over time, though, collage became commonplace and lost its power to disrupt. What remains unclear in Hebdige's analysis is why signs have this historical quality; why—if meaning is a product of the setting of signs in a text—*signifiance* must always give way to signification; why, to repeat the line from André Masson that Hebdige quotes, "this meeting of an umbrella and a sewing machine on the operating table [the disruptive effect of collage] happened only once" (Masson in Hebdige, 130). Such dynamics, I would suggest, are fundamentally grounded in the kinds of dynamics of practice that attention to stance reveals.

Distinguishing between two differing types of social formations that may emerge around genres of expressive culture—text-prominent ones and stance-prominent ones—can help to make this kind of issue more tractable. Any culture or scene in which participants tend to focus on decontextualized texts and background their practices of production or reception can be understood as text-prominent. Such social worlds include those in which performers are expected to follow the text closely and enact the author's intentions or those in which the audience of expressive culture treats texts as isolated objects for appreciation or analysis. Here, stance is still present in experience, but it appears as an ineffable quality, that element of meaning that escapes analysis precisely because it is bracketed at the outset of explicit exegesis. Such social worlds contrast with stance-prominent ones—places in which performance is foregrounded and prominence is given to the singer over the song, so to speak. All forms of expressive culture involve both texts and stances, so the distinction between these types of scenes depends on where participants place the emphasis, on how text or stance is situated in the foreground/background structure of experience, not an exclusive focus on one or the other. The dynamics of stance differ sharply in these two types of scenes.

Consider, for example, the music of the now canonical mid-1970s British punks. On a basic level, aggression, energy, and a seeming absence of technical ability (the much vaunted "three chords and an attitude") were the stance qualities valued in music performance. As I discussed earlier, stance qualities are qualities of action, and their expression in media is a complex affair. In punk, a rushing-but-unified time-feel in the ensemble, certain kinds of rough or lo-fi vocal or instrumental timbres, the use of aggressive pick attack by the guitarists, and a set of verbal and linguistic devices were among the signs that initially expressed this stance. Highly prizing the affective qualities that these signs embodied, punk musicians and their audiences moved them to the center of their attention. No longer an element of the background, these now focal elements became the point of the event. In the language developed in the previous chapters, the shift from fringe to focus transformed them from expressions of stance into *quasi-texts*.

The consequences of this transformation are obvious: as quasi-texts, a rushing-but-unified time-feel, rough timbres, and so forth can no longer be interpreted by punk audiences as a reflection of an aggressive, energetic, or amateurish stance; often, they are instead interpreted as stylizations of past performances and objectlike features of the genre. To keep in the stylistic game, performers over time must find fresh signs to embody the stance or take up a meta-stance on those features, one that embraces and forwards them. These dynamics are made more complex by the fact that the expressions of stance are often not strictly arbitrary signs. In the context of the parent music culture's ideas about ensemble coordination, a rushing, almost uncoordinated time-feel, for example, can easily be interpreted as the product of a group of musicians who have an excess of energy, aren't penned in by a machinelike sense of ensemble coordination, and don't have the training to keep an absolutely steady tempo. In the context of mid-1970s rock music, the punk time-feel did express these qualities.

To embody an aggressive stance, punk bands in the later 1970s played at faster tempi or performed their amateurishness by allowing performance to occasionally lapse into a completely uncoordinated state. The issue of rough vocal timbres and lo-fi guitar distortion is more complex. Raspy singing and distorted guitar sounds were commonplace in the polished corporate rock of the day, and in order to maintain a punk stance, singers had to find more nasal or piercing timbres and avoid richer or smoother forms of guitar distortion.

This discussion illustrates some of the interpretive dynamics found when performers and audiences foreground stance over text, and it also helps explain why the semiotic shock that concerned Masson and Hebdige (and which played out in the punk musical style) happens only once. Understanding signifying practice in the narrow sense that Hebdige inherited from then contemporary French semiotics, meaning is rooted in the arrangement of signs. Informed by practice theory, a stance-oriented approach grounds meaning in situated acts of engaging signs; signs are still important, but their meaning depends in part on the way that performers and audiences take them up, people whose acts in the immediate situation are informed by past situations. In the early phase of the punk history, the distinctive musical features of punk performance are read as indications of stance; highly prized, they are shuffled to the foreground of attention. Over time, though, the weight of past experiences influences the way that people familiar with this music form present interpretations. Musical features that had been taken as evidence of stance become so familiar that they are taken as quasi-texts—preestablished features of the genre rather than traces of the performer's immediate actions. Prizing stance, particularly an immediate and rebellious one, the present performance is heard as less effective. Musicians must therefore find new ways to display their stance of rebellious immediacy, and it is in this way that meanings like the shock effect are lost.[6] Speaking more broadly, we can say that in stance-prominent cultures, an ever-expanding interplay of text, quasi-text, stance, and meta-stance often becomes the order of the day. The opposite dynamic takes place in text-prominent scenes or in any situation where text is habitually the focus. Here, text is thematized and stance operates as a kind of open secret of meaning—a set of features that, one might say, are hidden in plain sight in the background of lived experience, informing the foregrounded text and coloring the overall meaning of the event.

The distinction between text-prominent and stance-prominent social formations also speaks to some of the complexities associated with the notion of genre. When texts are created in text-prominent social worlds, the notion of genre may be complex, but practices of production are geared to an awareness of texts as products, and questions of genre analysis are at least tractable. In fact, genre analysis in these contexts means interpreting the sets of intertextual links, those that connect this text to other texts and highlight their distinctively genre-based features. In situations in which stance is made prominent, however, genre analysis can be more confusing. It is here that we find people placing texts with no formal relationship to one another in the same generic cubbyhole or making broad, cross-generic connections: seeing any form of lament as a blues, or, as we observed earlier, representing a restaurant as offering "post-punk cuisine." Here, a complex set of stance interpretations, however accurate or inaccurate they may be, allows the flashy generic connections. Tenor Nathan Granner has stated that "Mozart was the world's first well-known punker, the first rock 'n' roll punk band," and "I would liken Mozart to the Clash. He just wanted to write his music and play it. He didn't care about norms. His first concert was canceled because people didn't like what he was doing" (quoted in Horsley 2006). Here, Granner makes a pair of broad stance interpretations (punk music as rebellious; Mozart as rebellious) that allow the generic connection. While claims like these are often used in marketing and advertizing, stance-oriented genre designations can also emerge from deeply held ideological commitments, such as those of activists who see a common generic link in the music of resistance from singers of widely disparate ethnic groups and historical periods.

The preceding discussion has moved from those social formations in which stance is an element of practice shaped by a culture to those in which stance is the focus of a culture—from stance in culture to cultures of stance. Here, it is worth emphasizing a point that I alluded to in the preceding chapters: in any given culture or scene, there may be explicit ideologies of stance—formal or informal discourses about whether the dynamics of stance or any of its elements (facet stances, meta-stances, etc.) should be foregrounded or backgrounded and what stance qualities are to be valued. Where ideologies of stance are discussed explicitly, the interpreter of culture usually has little trouble in starting to understand the politics of this expressive feature. Where stance is backgrounded, placed outside the bounds of discourse, or explicitly framed as unrelated to power, more interpretive work is necessary to make clear the relationships among expressive culture and the broader forms of power in the social life of its adherents. The specifically political dynamics of stance—the role of stance in the politics of the production and reception of expressive culture, the linkages of these practices and their meanings to politics in other domains—is a complex topic that requires careful attention.

In the preface, I briefly sketched why the interpretation of stance might be useful for scholars interested in the relevance of expressive culture for issues of politics and power. Stance is a fundamental element in the meaning of expressive culture; therefore, stance is relevant to politics inasmuch as meaning in expressive culture in general is relevant to politics. Here, I want to suggest that the political significance of stance plays out in two main ways: a dynamic in which stance is simply one factor among many in the expressive forms of a given social world and a dynamic in which stance is the focus of that social world. I will explore each of these in turn.

Stance as an Element of Meaning

When stance emerges as one element in the overall mix of meanings in an expressive form, its political significance can operate in a range of ways. For example, on a basic level, the macho texts of many all-male pop metal bands in the 1980s were performed with macho stances and enacted a particular vision of masculinity. Stance, however, can also comment on and complicate the meanings that are presented in a text, as when vocalist David Lee Roth's performative stance either betrayed a comic irony about his drooling rake image (in his 1980s cover of the standard "Just a Gigolo") or nuanced that image with unexpected moments that involve a more tender stance (as in his performance of "Dance the Night Away" during his days with the group Van Halen). Simple or complex, these last few descriptions are, of course, scholarly interpretations of meaning in a particular situation. What is significant, either in this case of the politics of gender or more generally in the politics of any expressive form, is not one scholar's reading of the meaning of the texts in question, but the ways in which those meanings play out in the lived experiences of their audiences, the influence of those meanings on people's reproduction of or resistance to power relations in practices already existing in a society, and the patterns of domination and subordination to which those meanings are tied. The audience's stance in the practice of reception is crucial here and operates in several layers. Considering the Roth example, audiences may simply fail to interpret his ironic or tender moments. Alternatively, they may place his tender or humorous stance in the near background of the experience of listening to these songs and see those stances as facets of what Phil Auslander would refer to as Roth's "musical persona"—the social identity that the musician attempts to construct in performance (2006).[7] Here, the nuancing of his machismo may perversely allow audiences to tolerate and accept the traditional vision of men's sexuality that is the focal meaning. Alternatively, the irony and tenderness may clash against the more straightforwardly macho antics, the dissonance of text and stance popping suddenly into the center of attention and causing listeners to notice, and perhaps question, dominant visions of gender.

Which meanings are constituted by whom, how often, and with what consequences are complex questions that are as interpretive as they are empirical. As I have argued elsewhere (1999), when viewed from the perspective of practice, the politics of meaning in expressive culture turns on questions of *consequences*: how do the meanings of X piece or genre play out in the lived experiences of its adherents, and what are the consequences of those meanings for practices outside the domain of expressive culture? The issue of consequences is precisely the one to consider here, but in the context of the criticism of heavy metal music, the word *consequences* raises unfortunate associations: parents worrying that the images of chaos and violence in heavy metal will turn their children into sociopaths, delinquents, or Satanists. Expressive culture is, of course, not a magic force of corruption or hegemony that controls weak minds and programs them to act in certain ways; while expressive culture does bear meanings, its works and genres must also be interpreted, and they always operate within situated contexts, the everyday life of mundane practices and their politics, discourses of representation, and large-scale social forces. This complex interpretive reality offers substantial challenges to researchers. It requires the scholar to have sophisticated interpretive apparatuses for understanding the rich experiences of meaning that varying audiences may have; it also requires equally sophisticated historical and ethnographic methods to understand how those meanings are situated in the audiences' larger social lives and how they reproduce, inflect, or resist the politics that is found there. As one factor in the production and reception of meaning, stance is thus fundamental to the politics of culture.

Stance-on-power

There is a second way in which the phenomenon of stance in expressive culture may play out in the politics of a social world—stance as a posture in a social field. Considered formally, this is not so much a separate interpretive dynamic as much as it is a subcategory of the first.

Earlier, I suggested that in many expressive genres stance is not merely one element among many; it is the focus or even the raison d'être of the expressive form. This situation is not limited to those sharply demarcated social worlds that coalesce around genres of expressive culture, such as traditionally conceived music subcultures. On the contrary, many expressive genres that circulate broadly within or across societies are ones in which performative stance is highly prominent. In the work of stand-up comics such as Totie Fields or Brad Garrett, for example, the text of their routines is not the focus of attention. After the performance, one may recall a line or two, but the text of their routines is neither particularly witty nor original. To the contrary, such comics evoke laughter because of their so-called funny bones. Here, the comic's performative stance on the delivery of the lines of the routine, the characters portrayed in the comic narratives, the performer's ensemble of bodily gestures, and her/his interaction with the audience construct a sense of who that comic (or stage persona) is, and the unfolding of that stance across the span of the performance is what evokes the laughter. In such a situation, the prepared lines primarily serve as a medium in which stance can be worked, like the clay or marble that an artist molds or chips to form her sculpture. Likewise, in music the singer's stance on her body, the composition, the other musicians, the audience, and so forth may be the focus of attention. In forms of communication that are framed as having more explicitly instrumental purposes, such as the political debate or the academic lecture, it may be hard to background the text completely, but what moves an audience to vote in a certain way or care about a body of material is often the debater's or lecturer's performative stance. Further, it is easy to see how the stances found in expressive culture could be intended or interpreted as models for ways of being in other social situations.

To make clear the inherently political dimensions of this idea, I want to return again to Samuel Todes's work on embodiment. By extending his profound insights into the role of the relationship between the body and its physical environment in the constitution of the person, we can gain new ideas about the fundamental connections among practice, the person, and power. Specifically, I will show how enacting a stance operates both as action and as the posture from which action springs, and I draw on Todes's perspectives to suggest a broad vision of the subject as an agent that operates in and through a world of forces.

In *Body and World* ([1990] 2001) Todes seeks to critique the idealist tradition in philosophy exemplified by Immanuel Kant, which claims that all understanding of the world happens through concepts, and to show that pre-conceptual, embodied forms of understanding are the fundamental form of knowing upon which conceptual knowledge rests. Building on the work of Maurice Merleau-Ponty, Todes offers a rich phenomenology of what he calls "practical perception." Most relevant here is his discussion of the vertical field of gravity in which bodily practice takes place, our reaction to that field in balance, and our poised bodily engagement with objects.

Todes begins his discussion by observing that our pre-conceptual bodily activity happens in a field of gravity. Gravity, he argues, is not merely a contingent set of forces that we deal with in a piecemeal fashion. "The influence of the vertical field on its contents [people and objects]," Todes writes, "is not *a* particular influence *on* its contents *to* which they react in any way—either by conformity or resistance. It is a *field* of influence *in* which its contents first have and can exert their *own* various kinds of influence on each other" (124–25).[8] In other words, being bodies, we aren't contingently in some kind of neutral space, but inherently exist within an oriented field of force and power. Balance is our fundamental grappling with that field, and it is inherently embodied and pre-conceptual. As embodied subjects, "[o]ur initial [and ongoing] problem is to balance ourselves upright in this field of influence. Our problem is neither to conform (accede) *to* this influence, nor to offer resistance *to* it . . . [but] to orient ourselves effectively rather than ineffectively *in* this field of influence; to align ourselves in this field in such a way that it dependably enables us to do what we need to do in it" (125). In this context, "[b]alance is neither purely active, like moving, nor purely passive, like being moved. It is both active and passive, and one only through the other. We balance ourselves only by actively orienting ourselves so as to be held in balance by the pull of the earth drawing down through us from the heavens above" (125). Here, balance is not something that an absolutely free subject happens to do, being contingently in a physical world that happens to have a certain particular force. Rather, balance is the action of a subject that is inherently embodied and inherently in a world, a world defined by a field of power and to which action is inherently oriented.

Built up upon balance is a phenomenon that Todes calls "poise," the pre-reflexive grappling with objects in the horizontal space of the world. As physical bodies, we are not merely oriented toward the vertical field of gravity in space; we are oriented toward a perceptual engagement with other physical objects, which can reveal themselves through bodily exploration. Rather than being a pure subject that is in a body and happens to discover a world, we are, Todes argues, first physical bodies in a world of physical objects, and our existence is oriented toward dealing with them. "[N]ot merely a matter of internal bodily coordination, but also of skill in handling things (and persons) about us" (66), poise exists prior to and is a necessary precondition of the concept of "objects" and any conceptual knowledge or exercise of will in dealing with those objects. Todes's point is that both skeptical arguments, which question the existence of the world, and idealist perspectives, which treat space and time as conceptual categories that the mind imposes on the world, are wrong because they ignore the fundamental grounding of embodied subjectivity that is revealed in balance and poise.

Todes develops a critique of Kant by comparing the results of his (Todes's) phenomenology of perception with those from a phenomenology of imagination that he develops in one of the book's later chapters. If practical perception is the operation of an embodied subject in a real physical world that is other to her, then imagination, Todes argues, is a body subject retreated into a space of her own creation. Here, there is still a subject and a world, but the "world" is "the subject's *own* imaginative capacity" (154). Todes's larger goal is to critique Kant's categories as "imaginative idealizations of perceptual [i.e., embodied] categories" (202); that is, Todes sees embodied engagement as ontologically fundamental and Kant's idealism as a powerful analysis of the subject that ultimately fails because it reduces perception to imagination.

Whether one sides with existential phenomenology or transcendental idealism in questions about embodiment, Todes's phenomenology is a profound exploration of perception and imagination. (It should be clear by now, I hope, that my example of the composition class discussed in chapter 1 was inspired by Todes's approach to the imagination.) Abstracting the issue of embodiment from Todes's phenomenology, one finds a vision of the person as inherently situated in a world. In this vision, the relationship of subject and world is not an impediment to the subject's agency, but its condition. In this abstracted reading of Todes, subjects are subjects through their action, which depends first and foremost on their grappling in a world of forces (balance) and with objects (poise). To my reading, this vision at least partially characterizes the nature of the social subject as well. To be a social subject is to act in a social world of forces. In this context, balance and poise are to the field of gravity and to objects what the social dimensions of stance are to social structure and immediate, concrete others.[9] Like balance and poise, stance is both a kind of action and the posture from which all other actions spring. Also like balance and poise, stance can be brought under reflexive control but is no less agentive when it exists in its primary form, as the pre-reflexive, taken-for-granted valual dimension of action.[10]

When seen in this light, one particular form of stance comes to the fore—not affect, style, or value writ large, but a specific form of stance that cuts across them and can be referred to as *stance-on-power*. Anthony Giddens (who, like Todes, was influenced by Merleau-Ponty) argues that power is a fundamental feature of all action and that it has a twofold nature—power as the ability to do or achieve things (what Giddens calls power as the "transformative capacity of human action," [1976] 1993:117) and power as domination (the power to shape the action of others, "power 'over' others," [1976] 1993:118).[11] Understood in this way, society is a field of power, and stance-on-power is one's orientation to that field.[12] Stance-on-power is one's relationship to one's action as it takes place in a field of power relations. The point is critical. The stance qualities of stance-on-power are not "domination" and "subordination," but the affective and stylistic relationships to one's own actions within a particular situation and at a particular social position in a world of sedimented structures of domination and subordination. It is worth emphasizing here that stance-on-power is indeed a type of stance in the formal sense that I defined in chapter 1. Stance in general is the quality with which a person engages an object and brings it into experience. In the previous chapter, we saw how one's own actions can be the focus of one's attention and one can have a stance upon them. Placed in that context, we can say that we have a stance-on-power when we regard our actions in a particular way, not viewing them alone but rather placing them in the context of a field of power relations. Stance-on-power is the quality with which we constitute that complex of our actions and our perception of those relations.

Describing such stances is inherently complex. Since such stances are the person's stance on her action in a larger social world, they stem from and make up her interpretation of that social world; thus, all descriptions of stances-on-power are second-order interpretations, interpretations of interpretations. The act of reading such stances is made even more complex by the fact that all action takes place within multidimensional contexts of power, including those of particular small-scale groups (families, cohorts, communities, institutions) and also those wider environments of domination tied to race/ethnicity, class, gender, or sexual orientation.

Despite this complexity, stance-on-power is not an obscure phenomenon. Examples of it can be found in the tenor of both everyday and extraordinary actions and are as familiar to our experience of life and intimate to our understanding of ourselves as our hands, our tools, or our most cherished sentiments. In an office or store, for example, actions as mundane as writing an e-mail message, brainstorming ideas in a meeting, stocking shelves, or chatting in the break room are achieved with a stance toward one's location in an environment of power—a cozy (or frustrated or insecure) embrace of a niche in the system, an obsequious (or begrudging or automatic) deference to authority, a bellicose (or saccharine or uncaring) pressing of advantage. In informal, non-institutional, or less obviously hierarchical situations, power may not take the obvious forms of domination and subordination, but action is still power in the sense of doing, and stance-on-power is no less in effect. In a committee of equal partners deciding the direction of their venture, a family camping trip, or a musical performance, acts of debating, setting up camp, or taking a solo are all achieved with a stance-on-power—an approach to carrying out one's own action and coordinating it with the actions of others that may be assertive, flexible, openhanded, self-deprecating, or submissive. In explicitly political contexts, stance-on-power resonates with the political character of the action that one is undertaking to produce complex, hybrid qualities. Urging an ally to make a particular move, denouncing an opponent in a public forum, or acquiescing to a demand in a conflict are all achieved with a stance-on-power that spins and shapes the meaning of the act and is crucial to its rhetoric. To say that all action involves a stance-on-power is not to retreat to a Hobbesian view of life and reduce all interaction to domination or subordination, or all actors to masters or slaves. Renunciation of privilege, resistance to injustice, and openhandedness are all possible stances in a field of power, and at least a percentage of social life involves stances of bland, unreflective reproduction or minor postures of resistance and accommodation. Further, insisting on the ubiquity of stance-on-power does not confuse the quality of an action with the reproduction of or resistance to power relations. Whether the guards in a prison put down a revolt begrudgingly, in a neutral fashion, or with sadistic zeal, the only thing that matters for *this* moment's reproduction of power is whether or not they retain control of the prisoners. But this is not to say that stance-on-power is insignificant for issues of domination and subordination. Without an overall commitment to resistance, actors cannot achieve social change, and stance-on-power is part of the mix of meanings in everyday behavior and the affective life therein upon which organized domination and resistance rest. The overtly begrudging or sadistic stance of the prison guards in yesterday's revolt may itself inspire future acts of submission or resistance among prisoners. My point here is to identify stance-on-power as a fundamental, ongoing feature of social action.

The relevance of stance-on-power for the politics of expressive culture is substantial. As a kind of social practice, the production or reception of expressive culture involves a stance-on-power. Of equal importance, however, is the fact that in many genres of expressive culture, performers seek to display and foreground—"dramatically realize" in Goffman's terminology (1959:30)—their stance-on-power. Consider Ray Romano and Tim Allen, the comic everymen of 1990s popular culture. In their stand-up routines and their televised situation comedies, Romano and Allen dramatize a stance-on-power to which we might refer as a cozy, lighthearted embrace of their social world. Whether they are positioning themselves in the narrative world of the first-person stand-up routine or the dramaturgical world of a sit-com plot, Ray and Tim (both the characters and the performers, the line is intentionally blurred) find themselves responding to the day-to-day problems of family life and work, gender and class, with a posture that is alternatively clever, whiny, or long-suffering. Underlying it all, though, is a comic, lighthearted, and ultimately cozy acceptance of their niche in a white, middle-class suburban social space. There is no explicit ideological agenda here, and the vision of the social world portrayed by these performances involves anything but a recognition of the politics of suburbia. Nevertheless, this interpretation of the white, American middle-class suburban family is, of course, a deeply political interpretation. Indeed, it takes no great work of social insight to see that the worlds of *Everybody Loves Raymond* or *Home Improvement* involve specific representations of gender, class, and race/ethnicity. Rather, my point here is that the main characters' stance-on-power, the posture of their actions in response to this social world, is the focus of the performance. Ray Romano and Tim Allen were not trying to persuade their audiences of a political perspective. To the contrary, they sought to make their audiences laugh, and they did so by pointing out the minor frustrations experienced by a character in a social niche and celebrating that character's response to them. Indeed, these nettled but ultimately happy characters were largely defined through the work of displaying their stance-on-power in their fictive worlds.

Some of the complexity in the interpretation of stance-on-power stems from the differing ways in which social worlds, and the stances upon them, are invoked. In realist narrative genres like situation comedy, the expressive form explicitly depicts a social world, locates the actions of the performers within it, and dramatizes a fictive stance-on-power. Contrast this with non-narrative and non-realist genres of expressive culture. In certain works of abstract expressionist painting, like those of Jackson Pollock for example, the image created is most commonly interpreted as an expression of behavior. While the canvas certainly can be seen as nothing more than a visual texture or as a structure of colors and shapes, such work is often produced and received in the context of the romantic notion of the artist as a creative genius—an individual who has intense emotions, resists conformity, and must constantly break the confining bounds of tradition. In this context, the drips of color in Pollock's action paintings are often interpreted as evidence of his stance while painting—fiery, unique, and unconstrained. Such qualities are a stance-on-power inasmuch as they are interpreted as existing in the context of a perceived world of traditional art and a broader society that seeks to confine the individual's creativity and emotions. Comparing the sit-com example with the abstract expressionism example, we see two cases in which stance on a social world of power is dramatized, and the differences stem from the ways in which the social world is evoked. In *Everybody Loves Raymond,* the performance directly evokes a fictive contemporary Long Island, and Romano's acting dramatizes the stance of his fictional character (Ray Barone) on that social world and its relationships. In the Pollock example, the painting itself does not explicitly depict its context. There are no images of conforming traditional artists, narrow-minded art critics—or, more broadly, constraining bourgeois society—in Pollock's paintings. Rather, the drips from Pollock's brushes are seen as a trace of his stance in the act of painting, which, given common assumptions about art and artists in mid-twentieth-century America, many audiences placed in the context of a perceived world of mainstream conformists and creative, non-conforming artists.

Of course, the interpretive situation in both the Romano and Pollock examples is more complex than this quick snapshot. Romano not only dramatizes Barone's stance on the fictive Long Island, he also enacts and dramatizes his stance on the real world of the other actors in the scene and the live studio audience, and part of the success of the show is the way in which his stance in the real world of those interactions echoes Barone's fictional stance. Indeed, the character and the actor share a first name, and it is well known that Romano's character emerged from the first-person narratives of his stand-up routines. Following the conventions of mainstream American television and movies, many U.S. audiences are expected to partially conflate the real and the fictional Rays, seeing Barone's stance in the fictive world as tied to Romano's stance in the real world. As always, the audience's stance interpretations may be inaccurate. Romano may seem to be affably effortless in his interactions with the cast, but off the set he may be coercive or manipulative; likewise, Pollock's drippings and splashings may have been enacted with a cool and calculating desire to make money, not a fiery effort to break the confines of the conventional world in unconstrained emotional expression and stylistic exploration. My point here is to suggest the differing ways in which social worlds are evoked in two differing genres of expressive culture and the way in which stance-on-power underlies them both.

A further example will deepen our sense of these dynamics. In the performances of explicitly political singer-songwriters, a very specific macropolitical world is referenced, and the singer's stance-on-power can be read in that context. In terms of the music culture of 1960s American folk revival and U.S. popular music in general, vocalist Joan Baez had a wide vibrato, a full timbre, precise diction, marked use of dynamics (especially dramatic forte passages), and limited use of ornamentation. In first-person narrative songs, these features could dramatize the stances of the character in the social world depicted by the song or the stance of the singer in the social world of the performance, or both. While her quivering vibrato and powerful forte passages may have been meant to evoke the affective stance of the character in whose voice the events of the narrative are described, her precise diction, controlled ornaments, and full timbre are indicative of her performative stance on the song and her interaction with the audience. For example, the character who is the first-person narrator in "House of the Rising Sun" would not have used the dialect that Baez employed in her performances of this song. Further, in the character's everyday interactions, the question of whether or not to use an occasional glissando or a brilliant timbre in the upper register would not be relevant. To the contrary, these features constitute Baez's relationship with her own voice, the ensemble, and the piece—her polished skill at delivering a line, her emotional but understated engagement with the melody, her command of her vocal apparatus. In non-narrative, first-person lyric songs, such as "Blowin' in the Wind," the text depicts a social world that is clearly intended as the large-scale society in which the performance event is situated, and the narrative voice shifts from that of a character to that of Baez's stage persona itself. Here, all of the elements of performance are meant to directly reflect her stance on 1960s America. Whatever differing objects they deal with and however they straddle differing social worlds, Baez's facet stances nevertheless add up to a larger stance-on-power, one that might plausibly be characterized as emotionally intense but controlled and dignified; placed in the context of her stage behavior and the society that her lyrics evoke, her performances dramatize a stance-on-power of earnest resistance to domination, knowing experience, brave and understated commitment. Differing audiences may, of course, interpret any of those features in differing ways. Further, even if one agrees with these descriptions of Baez's stance, one may place differing valences upon it—self-important, bourgeois, inspiring, or even soothing. The point, however, is that despite the interpretive flexibility of the particulars of this case, stance-on-power is a key component of the meaning here, and my goal in this discussion is to suggest some of its structures in lived experience.

One of the crucial objects that stance-on-power may address is its place in the social world of production, either the immediate context of performance or larger institutions. Stage fright, for example, is a stance-on-power—a fearful posture toward one's acts in front of an audience. Its opposite is charisma or stage presence, a confident or authoritative stance on one's own behavior as a performer and on one's relationship to one's audience. Performances that take as their theme the media industries (such as the films *The Player* and *Hollywoodland*; songs like the Kinks's "Working at the Factory," the Barenaked Ladies's "Box Set," or any tune that urges the listener to "Turn the radio up!") evoke the larger world of their own production, and here the stances of the performers inevitably operate as explicit stances-on-power in that world. Such social worlds can be evoked more elliptically, as when performers or audiences in low-prestige or marginalized media or genres produce or interpret their expressive forms in implicit juxtaposition to the perceived dominance of high-prestige or mainstream media.

The examples so far have focused on performative stance, but the audience's stances also involve a stance-on-power. For audience members, all stances-on-the-other involve stances-on-power by constituting a relationship to the action of the immediate social situation of the performance; the stance qualities discussed above, such as listening with an open mind or being a tough audience, are thus types of stance-on-power. Postures such as "Go ahead and entertain me, I dare you," "I better get my money's worth," "I am honored to be in the presence of such a genius," or "A dummy like me will never understand this; I don't know anything about art," all reflect differing perceived power relations between audience and performer, and differing stances upon them. Such stances may be kept private, or they may be dramatized in audience responses of laughter, applause, or the throwing of rotten fruit. Made public, stances may even be made into framed performances of their own, such as the judging of competitive performances exemplified most notoriously by Simon Cowell, the vitriolic judge on the *American Idol* television song contest.

Reception is situated in large-scale as well as small-scale contexts, and stance-on-power may engage these broader worlds directly. Perhaps the most commonly discussed example of audience stance in popular music studies is the self-consciously transgressive one of teenagers listening to the music of racial or class others—be it the songs of Chuck Berry or Chuck D, Johnny Cash or John Lydon. The warm embrace or bored rejection or ambivalent reception by an audience member of the expressive culture marked as belonging to one's own or another's ethnicity, region, gender, or sexual orientation are differing stances-on-power, and all of the interpretive and performative dynamics explored above apply here as well. Further, in such situations, the formation of a stance in the practice of reception may not merely be one element in the mix that shapes the meaning of the performance for an audience member; it may be the very point of attending the event. For example, an audience member may attend a concert of music from her ethnic group in order to have the opportunity to enact her ethnicity. Here, focusing on the appropriate musical dimensions, catching the cultural references, and grasping the music with affection, the audience member's stance is not merely a stance on the music, but on the music as actively situated in a larger world of ethnic politics, and such practices of reception are understood by that person as constituting behavior within that world. Of course, it is not only in performances of ethnicity that audience stance is a stance-on-power. All of the situated orientations of the audience to the power relations of the performance event mentioned above may be inflected through larger social forces: "*Your ethnic group* is supposed to be funny; make me laugh, clown," "*My ethnic group* is always getting ripped off; this show better be good," "*Those big city performers* came all the way out to the sticks to perform for us; I am lucky to see them," or "*A working man* like me will never understand this high-brow stuff." These examples just scratch the surface, but they give a sense of the range of ways in which reception can be a form of stance on the power relations of the performance or of its larger social world.

The Expressive-political Nexus

In performance, stance-on-power may be more or less explicitly connected to a representation of a social world, an ideology, or a call to action, and exploring the relationship among these four elements is the first step in making explicit the kinds of significance that expressive culture can have for the politics of social life. I will use the term *expressive-political nexus* to refer to the configuration of these four elements in any work of expressive culture. Though it may be clear from the preceding discussion, it is worth emphasizing that the elements of the nexus are always interpretations of a social world. As a result, they are not unambiguously expressed in media but must be interpreted by performers and audiences.

Some forms of expressive culture directly connect stances-on-power with representations of the social world, political ideologies, or calls to action. Joan Baez's performances do more than dramatize a stance of passionate but dignified resistance; they situate that stance in a world of injustices grounded in race/ethnicity, class, and gender. They explicitly reference a social justice ideology and call for people to enact a broadly resistant stance in political behavior. Hatecore—a small subgenre of heavy metal music that explicitly espouses white supremacist views—offers a configuration of elements similar to those of Baez's music. Both involve resistant performative stances, as well as explicit interpretations of the social world, ideologies, and calls to action. The affective valence of their resistant stances and their readings of the social world are opposed, of course, with hatecore bands offering a macho and bellicose stance and interpretations of society that, perversely, see white men as the victims of racism and sexism.

In both of these examples, the connections among the performer's stance-on-power, representation of the social world, ideology, and calls to action are tightly forged, but a wide variety of other kinds of relationships among them are possible. In earlier work (1999), I noted that death metal musicians may enjoy the aggressive, resistant sounds of punk music, but they often object to what they see as the heavy-handed interpretations of social life and propagandistic calls to action common in the music. For them, death metal is certainly about performances that dramatize an aggressive and resistant stance-on-power, but their music takes a different stance on the audience than that of the punks. Where the punks patronized their audiences by telling them what to do, the metalheads said, we respect our audience by telling them to make their own decisions. In the terminology I have been developing here, we could say that their stance-on-the-other respects their audience's autonomy, and their ideology only says "take our stance-on-power and do what you will with it." In much expressive culture, these relationships are made even more loose and ambiguous. Translating Hebdige's ideas into my language, one might say that punk music sought a way of dramatizing a stance of generalized resistance that was not, and indeed could not be, connected to any ideology—even, paradoxically, its own.

Betraying a related but distinct dynamic, a common technique in popular music making is to write songs that explicitly dramatize an appealing stance, but which are less specific or even actively ambiguous in their reading of their social world or their ideological implications. This is exemplified in "You Gotta Be," the 1994 single from Afro-British pop singer Des'ree. The verses of the song urge the listener to trust her instincts and retain her dignity in the face of a difficult world, while the hooky and often-repeated chorus exhorts the listener to be resilient by offering a litany of desirable qualities. The first two lines explain that "you gotta be bad, you gotta be bold," and the "you gotta be" formula continues with "wiser," "hard," "tough," "stronger," "cool," "calm," and so forth. A flowing dance groove underlies the track, and a smooth Fender Rhodes–like synthesizer part lays out the harmonic rhythm, which by turns resolves to the major tonal center or its relative minor. The song's second-person address speaks directly to the listener, and the precise intonation, rich timbre, even dynamics, and sparing use of blues ornaments make clear that Des'ree is enacting the stance that she is advocating for others—one of intense but controlled dignity. The social world evoked by the song is vague; beyond brief references to the potential cruelty of lovers and to economic scarcity, society is depicted mostly in an implicit fashion—loosely, as the place where one constantly faces obstacles. No explicit reference is made to racism or sexism.

However, the vocal track would make the racial and gender identity of the singer clear to most listeners in the United States or the singer's native United Kingdom, and it would be easy to read the challenges of the world depicted by the song in those terms. "You Gotta Be" exemplifies a configuration of stance, evocation of a social world, and ideology that are far from those of Joan Baez. Des'ree's song offers a clear stance, which, I suspect, is the primary focus of interest for most listeners and, perhaps, the performer as well. While this stance (a dignified resilience in the face of social pressures) is certainly a stance-on-power in the sense I described above, it is only loosely connected to a racial and gender identity and evokes only the most ambiguously drawn social world. Respect for elders and love of learning are briefly mentioned in the song's second verse, but, presenting only the vaguest ideological sentiments, the song issues no calls to collective action. Offering stance-on-power as the focus of enjoyment but with the fewest possible political specifics, such an approach, when performed with skill, can often find a large audience.

Still other kinds of connections among the elements of the expressive-political nexus are possible, and an examination of these issues shows the diversity of ways in which the links among them can be forged. The rawest form of stance-on-power is decontextualized affect—texts that sound happy or sad. Strictly abstract music, dance, or imagery are all examples here. The reference to some kind of social context can begin to make those affects relevant for a social world, however abstract.[13] These connections can be further specified by identifying particular dimensions of identity in a social world—race/ethnicity, gender, or region, for example. Ideology can be fleshed out to greater or lesser degrees, as can calls to action. It is worth emphasizing that even in the absence of text in language or other explicitly political signs (such as a melodic quote from a national anthem or the image of a flag), a stance-on-power can, for knowledgeable audiences, be connected to an ideology or a call to action. For example, the musician's stance-on-the-other always functions as a stance on the social relations of the performance event and possibly on broader social relations as well. "Giant Steps," a piece of instrumental jazz by John Coltrane, is well known in the genre as an extremely challenging work; when played by the members of an ensemble whose stances on one another are markedly supportive (or, alternatively, markedly aggressive), an informed audience may hear the musicians' stances-on-each-other as giving an ideological inflection to the role of this piece in the repertoire—a repudiation or embrace, respectively, of the competitive tradition within jazz.[14] Titles and other media extrinsic to a work give an ideological spin to otherwise abstract affects. For example, the serious, lamenting, almost menacing tone of the instrumental version of

Charles Mingus's "Fables of Faubus" are, for knowledgeable audiences, given an ideological weight by the title's reference to Orval E. Faubus, the notorious governor of Arkansas who defied the U.S. Supreme Court's order to integrate the Little Rock public schools. The reputation of the performers (in the media or the local community) can certainly situate affect with regard to position in a social world, ideology, or call to action. Indeed, where the social identity of the performers and the cultural connotations of the work or genre that they perform are apparent, some kind of ideological valence, however loose, often emerges in performance, even in the absence of explicitly ideological messages.

However the stance-on-power is connected to other elements of the expressive-political nexus, it is clear that in many situations stance-on-power is the element of performance to which people are attached. It would seem that the purpose of comedy is to evoke laughter. But many Ray Romano fans may enjoy a rerun of *Everybody Loves Raymond*, even if they do not once crack a smile. What they enjoy in this context, I think, is Romano's stance-on-power—his frustrated, whiny, clever, but ultimately cozy embrace of a social niche. For progressives or radicals dissatisfied with the world that Romano so happily embraces, his stance-on-power is precisely what makes the show annoying. Likewise, a recording of a Joan Baez performance from the 1960s may explicitly urge opposition to the U.S. war in Vietnam, and while the specific ideological issue at hand is no longer in play, the song may inspire affection or opprobrium in contemporary audiences because of the stance-on-power that it dramatizes.

The intense emotional attachments that audiences and performers have to stances-on-power make this topic an important one, and stance-on-power is a key part of the politics of expressive culture. Because expressive culture is a domain of social action, it entails power in both senses of the word that I elaborated earlier—power in the sense of the ability to act and power in the sense of domination. As a stretch of social behavior, for example, the performance is a space where power is enacted, where audiences and performers negotiate and coordinate their behavior together in the context of sedimented past practices. That soloists should or should not lead the direction of the rhythm section, that a woman can or cannot play first violin, that a comic does or does not command authority over her audience, that a Latina did or did not get top billing, that a famed pianist or a no-name graduate student has come to play in our little burg—all of these instances illustrate how the performance event is shot through with power. As a dimension of action and frequently the pivot of meaning, stance-on-power plays a key role in the social dynamics of power and performance. Further, many forms of expressive culture are tied to large-scale processes of production and reception, and the dimensions of power in situated practice here are obvious. Actively patronizing or boycotting an artist or a production company; using Big Money to elbow aggressively into a local media market; tenaciously building up a local music scene so that people in the community will not be dependent on national touring acts for entertainment; busily downloading music before the technology or laws have changed; obsequiously or subtly or resentfully jockeying for position in a music community, company, or industry—large-scale structures are constituted by and from the context of situated practices, and all of these involve a stance-on-power.

Power and Expressive Culture: Relations of Consequence

While the power relations of large-scale structures of production and reception are important, many in the humanities and humanistic social sciences care about the relevance of expressive practice for other domains of social life—structures of domination that play out in the workplace, the home, the hospital, the public square, and the legislature; that is, *power* in the broad sense of the term. I observed earlier that issues of the political significance of expressive culture turn on the question of consequences, the question of the relevance of the lived meanings of expressive culture for practices in other domains of social life. The notion of stance-on-power and the relationships among the elements of the expressive-political nexus highlight a particular set of dynamics in the consequentiality of expressive culture. This final section examines this topic.

The Political Dynamics of Activist, Ideological, and Stance-oriented Expressive Culture

I begin at a first order of approximation. To choose an obvious starting point, observe that the stances-on-power dramatized in explicitly ideological and activist expressive culture can be picked up and enacted by audiences in other domains of practice. The music of liberation movements offers the tightest connections among the elements of the expressive-political nexus, and it is no doubt the case that on some occasions the dramatized stance of pro-active social engagement and of resistance to power inspires people to become involved in political struggles and take up those stances in the political practices of the battlefield, the street, the courtroom, or the legislature. This is clearly a limiting case, and equally common are all manner of slippages among dramatized stance, interpretation of the social world, ideology, and action. Depending on the level of abstraction at which one reads both songs and society, one may see little or no slippage when a thirty-year-old recording by Joan Baez inspires resistant political behavior and a resistant political stance among those who oppose the Iraq war. Greater slippage can be found in the case of the use of civil rights songs by the opponents of abortion; here, the active and resistant stance dramatized by the music still inspires political action with a similar affective and social valence, but this stance is oriented toward a different struggle (reproductive rights) and to many the "resistance" sides with, not against, domination. Even more slippage can be found in nostalgic readings of protest music. In some contemporary situations, what was intended as the dramatization of a dignified courage is read as a soothing evocation of the past or a ridiculous display of naïveté and can inspire contented apathy or even regressive political sentiments.

Other dynamics of social influence and social slippage occur with expressive culture that depicts a clear stance-on-power but is more ambiguous about its representation of the social world, ideology, or calls to action. While they may differ in their affective valences, the fine points of their ideologies, and the subject positions from which they hail, the universal negation of classical Hebdigian punk music, the darkly aggressive individualism of 1990s death metal, and the affirmative, resilient individualism of singers like Des'ree all offer a pro-active stance-on-power (resistance), an abstract vision of the social world, and no direct call to action. Such expressive forms are intended to inspire a stance of individual fortitude in the face of situations unforeseen. Social theorist Michel de Certeau ([1974] 1984) referred to uncoordinated everyday acts of opposition as "tactics" (as opposed to the systemic maneuvering done by people in power), and there is no question that individualist expressive forms may have inspired countless isolated postures of feisty opposition and acts of tactical negation. The larger implications of such acts for structures of domination, however, can be read in many ways. It is true that the decentralized acts of individuals may bring down oppressive governmental regimes in quiet revolutions, and in everyday life acts of opposition predicated on the notion that "the personal is the political" may resist everyday acts of domination. However, stances-on-power abstracted from explicit interpretations of social context or ideology may also inspire people to participate in practices that are not in their own interest or that serve radically differing ends. For example, while the resilient stance-on-power dramatized by Des'ree's music may inspire a woman to leave an abusive husband, it may also inspire that woman's boss to crack her whip and make her department meet quarterly earning projections. If political activists often worry that the minor gains they have won may be nothing more than fleeting accommodations to power, the gains of the individualist must be even more ephemeral. Indeed, the fate of stances-on-power unmoored from interpretations of social context, ideology, or activism is *by definition* up for grabs. Paradoxical political figures like the "rebel conservative" or the victim of "reverse racism" stem from attaching resistant stances (feisty opposition, the desire for redress) to interpretations of the social world that confuse domination with oppression. And just as stridently ideological and activist expressive culture may inspire apathy or reactionary behavior among an audience (as among those metalheads who are turned off by the perceived preachiness of hardcore punk music), loosely stance-prominent expressive culture may inspire a resilient stance that leads to doctrinaire activism among some audiences. The examples of the stance-prominent, loosely ideological, and activist expressive forms I have emphasized have all been assertively individualist, but other social postures (e.g., a go-with-the-flow quietism, an embrace of in-group identity) may be represented here as well.

Still other dynamics of influence and consequence occur when a vision of the social world is specified and an ideology made prominent, but calls to action are left vague. Consider didactic realist narratives. The film *North Country,* for example, portrays a working-class woman who confronts the misogyny of a Minnesota mining company and the complicity of the small-town residents who depend on that company for their livelihood. The narrative dramatizes the main character's determined efforts to unite the women who work for the company in a class-action lawsuit that ultimately yields a redress of grievances. Here, the protagonist's stance-on-power is the focus of the drama, the interpretation of the social world is explicit, the ideology clear, and explicit calls to action absent. It is important to see that the relationships among the elements of the expressive-political nexus can be analyzed independently of the stances, social visions, or ideologies they portray. Consider the nostalgic situation comedy *Happy Days;* a popular American television show about the 1950s, it aired in the 1970s and depicted the conspicuously wholesome life of a cheery, midwestern teenage boy and his family. Like *Everybody Loves Raymond* and *Home Improvement,* the stance-on-power of the protagonist is a cozy embrace of a niche; the social world is interpreted as a convivial place where gender roles are fixed and unproblematic, and class is invisible. For most audiences, I would suspect, the highly stylized dramas and the omnipresent period markers raise the prominence of the show's ideological position, which could be summed up as "all's right with the world." Unsurprisingly, the show offers no calls to action. In mainstream American media, few narratives could be as different as *North Country* and *Happy Days.* However, the structural relationships among the parts of the expressive-political nexus are the same in these examples: the stance is prominent and dramatized, the vision of the social world and ideology are clear, and calls to action are absent.

Situated between those kinds of expressive culture in which the elements of the nexus are explicitly drawn and tightly forged (Joan Baez, hatecore) and those with loose connections among the elements and more ambiguous ideologies (Hebdigian punk, death metal, or stance-prominent pop songs such as "You Gotta Be"), explicitly ideological, non-activist expressive forms like *North Country* and *Happy Days* also have their own characteristic types of influence on other domains of social life and distinct varieties of meaning slippage. Just as pop music audiences often misunderstand lyrics and focus on the mood or groove of a song, viewers of explicitly ideological expressive forms may focus on the stance-on-power, disengage it from the ideology, and carry it forward into other aspects of their life. This form of slippage converts ideological expressions to stance-prominent ones, and all of the types of slippage I list above with regard to expressive forms like "You Gotta Be" would apply. Inversely, other audiences may convert ideological works into activist works. In terms of the practices of production and reception, this could be done simply—for example, by showing *North Country* at a women's center and, after the film is over, passing out leaflets about a local labor action. Again, all of the dynamics of influence and slippage found in activist expression like that of Joan Baez would apply. But ideological expression often is intended to operate in a different fashion—to raise consciousness, heighten awareness, instill a perspective, educate, or inform. While the makers of *North Country* may have hoped that their film would encourage women to speak up at work, pursue grievances, or file lawsuits, their most immediate focus, I suspect, was on drawing attention to the problem of sexual harassment and the value of collective action. Likewise, while the producers of *Happy Days* may have imagined that their show might lead to greater civic participation in the United States, one would suspect that they saw the main political effect of the show as instilling a positive image of 1950s America and Americans in general. The difficult-to-theorize social miasma that such forms of expressive culture are believed to impact is referred to by a vast array of fuzzy nouns—attitudes, beliefs, opinions, perspectives, worldviews, assumptions, disposition, and sensibilities. There is no doubt that expressive culture can impact the ways in which people interpret and act in the social world, but the issues of slippage here are notoriously complex. Producers of ideological expressive forms may quite rightly have a host of concerns about this topic: that their work will be too vague to be interpreted as they intend or too didactic to appeal to people and change their minds; that they will end up only preaching to the choir or enflaming the opposition; or that even if they communicate their ideas and inspire their audience, their message will be forgotten once a person leaves the theater or turns off the TV set. I do not wish to suggest that the fostering of dispositions is insignificant. Seeing a thousand television shows in which men play dominant roles, in which people of color are marginalized, or in which gay, lesbian, bisexual, and transgender people are absent or stigmatized cannot help but have an impact on the assumptions that a person brings to social interaction in other spheres of social life. I do want to say, though, that it is only through such impacts that expressive culture can carry its political weight.

Stance in the Politics of Everyday Life

The last point brings us to a key issue—the complexity and multifacetedness of stance in both the experiences of persons and the broader social life of political practice. Considering this carefully will refine our understanding of the relationship between power and expressive culture. Both scholarly and popular interpreters of the politics of culture make arguments premised on the idea that the stances dramatized in expressive forms may be the model for behavior in social life. Such arguments can be crude and ill-founded (as in the claims of cultural conservatives that heavy metal music makes children suicidal or rebellious), or they can be more subtle and richly developed. That expressive culture must always be interpreted to have its effects and that such interpretations are always made in the context of a concrete world of social relations are well known. What I want to emphasize here is a fundamental quality of both persons and social movements: their reliance on a diversity of stances. While the mindlessly conformist cult follower and the lone-wolf cowboy may exemplify limiting cases of people with a narrow repertoire of stances-on-the-other in social interaction, most people have a broader range of ways of behaving in everyday life—domineering in some contexts and submissive in others, by turns expressive and dour, extroverted and shy, confident and insecure. The question of the impact of stance-on-power for a political system rarely turns on creating a new stance from whole cloth, but rather on situating existing stances relative to structures of power relations sedimented in practice and on fostering or diminishing stances in the overall ensemble of social postures a person may adopt. It is for this reason that stances-on-power fully disengaged from representations of society and ideology are particularly ambiguous in their politics. Speaking broadly, if in the most conservative vision of the United States, men, for example, are encouraged to be submissive to their presumably male bosses and domineering with their presumably female spouses, then it is unclear how to read the political meaning of expressive forms that celebrate an aggressive stance. The politics of such stances depends on the contexts in which they are employed.

The situation with regard to stances within social movements is equally complex. By definition, liberatory social movements, in the long view, require a resistance to power, and oppressive movements require submission to it. However, in the practice of situated social interaction, a range of stances emerge in any kind of social world. Among all but the most rigorously voluntarist collectives, a certain amount of deference to others (if not to authority) is required; likewise, every society short of the strictest totalitarian hierarchy involves situations where people are expected to work together more or less as equals. Where issues of power are complex, ideological and activist expressive forms must carefully calibrate their fostering of stances with their vision of the social world, and the more subtle the calibration, the more vexed the interpretive questions for the audience. Committed to a continuity of means and ends (of situated practices and macro-social patterns), some brands of anarchism and pacifism may completely reject obedient or aggressive stances, respectively, and seek to narrow the stances-on-power that they promote, within both the movement and society at large. It is certainly the case that social justice can never spring from a cultish obedience to authority or a delight in physical violence for its own sake. However, it is also true that anti-authoritarian small group collectives may—in their love of strictly voluntarist, self-willed action—fail to achieve consensus and through inactivity play into the authoritarian power; likewise, pacifism may, at least in certain situations, function as an accommodation to power or a form of apathy. As with individual persons and mundane practices, the world of social movements involves an ensemble of stances inflected by social situation and ideology.

Taking an even broader view, hegemony—the ongoing negotiation of power relations by differing segments of society—can be seen as a massively complex ensemble of ensembles of stances enacted in practice. Considered alone, the hegemony of capitalism in a society, for example, depends on the mix of stances among its participants: how many of the political and economic elite take a bellicose stance of pushing their advantage, how many seek to offer concessions within the system, and how many identify downward and renounce their privilege; among the managerial and working classes, how many identify with the elites and seek upward mobility, how many seek only concessions and accommodations within the system, and how many seek systematic change; among the underclass, how many focus solely on survival, how many resort to self-interested criminality or clannish gangsterism, and how many are willing to engage in revolutionary struggle. *Examined in the context of the preceding discussion, though, the situation is far more complex.* Such broadly dispositional attitudes toward power (identifying upward or downward, seeking power, accommodation, or systematic change) require a range of concretely enacted stances in real-world practice. To achieve a broadly resistant dispositional attitude to power, for example, one must accommodate the bad jokes of one's compatriots, obediently show up to the rally at the city center on time, and struggle with one's opponents; in other words, one must foster the proper stance in the proper context toward the proper sets of others. Finally, any such dispositions must play out in practice and be achieved. This is not only a question of walking the walk (rather than just talking the talk), but also a question of walking the walk *effectively*—of maintaining the solidarity of the group by competently suppressing annoyance at a compatriot or really showing up at the rally on time, of struggling with one's adversary in an efficacious manner.

The previous paragraph was framed in broadly Gramscian, class-oriented terms, but the point applies to the relationship between stance and power generally. Stance-on-power plays a crucial role in social life; it never does so alone, though, but always as arrayed in complex ensembles of the person, society, and practice. *This* is the larger social life that the stances-on-power of expressive culture must influence if they are to matter for politics. It is *this world* of complex ensembles of stances enacted in concrete, situated practices that the dynamics of influence and slippage that I have outlined in the previous section must engage. For those interested in the politics of expressive culture, this is the field of phenomena to be explored. Activist, ideological, or with stance unmoored from social life, expressive culture shapes society only through the situated interpretations of audiences and then, later, through its impacts on their actions. Or, to put the horse where it should be—before the cart—social agents are situated in a world of power, and the meanings they find in and bring to expressive culture are one element in the mix that shapes their reproduction or transformation of that power.

Putting Power and Expressive Culture in Perspective

Throughout this discussion, my goal has been to chart the varying ways in which stance may play into social life in general and into power relations in particular. I sought to map the terrain in which particular expressive forms play out, sensitize scholars to the range of phenomena that they might encounter in the world, point out the pitfalls of confusing local situations with universal conditions, and critique simplistic claims on this topic that overplay the progressive or regressive potential of art.

In laying out the differing relationships between the meaning of expressive culture and practice in other domains of social life, I have tried to give equal emphasis to situations in which expressive culture influences other forms of practice and those in which the influence fizzles out or slips in some unforeseen direction. In seeking to debunk simplistic and overbroad claims about the efficacy of expressive culture, I may have seemed to place special emphasis on examples of slippage and unmoored expressive culture from other domains of practice. To ward off the impression that I am skeptical about the social significance of expressive culture, I would underscore that expressive culture can and does have an impact on the rest of society. Indeed, that role can be profound. But however great or minor its role, expressive culture has an impact on social life only in and through practice. Neither the prominence of one element in the expressive-political nexus (stance-on-power, representation of the social world, ideology, call to action) nor any specific configuration of elements can guarantee impact or guard against slippage. *No theory can identify forms of expressive culture that are inherently democratic or life-affirming, because power—or more precisely, domination—cannot be reduced to any other social phenomenon.* This idea is well known, but its significance is often forgotten. The irreducibility of power stems from the most fundamental nature of practice and agency, and examining this concept will put into perspective the relationships among expressive culture, stance, and power.

In any situation, domination refers to relationships between practices—relationships of control and of inequity, of who can do what, of who can have what, of who gets to say "Jump!" and who has to say "How high?" In other words, domination in any place and time is made up of the relationships between the things that people do, and no social phenomenon other than those doings can correct inequities and end domination there. To argue otherwise would be to suggest that the agency of the people involved in those actions is merely an effect of some external force. An endless array of social phenomena have been posited as capable of undermining domination—democratic institutions, the raising of consciousness, education, social critique, liberatory ideologies, a spirit of dissent, good intentions, and, of course, various forms of expressive culture. Domination is reducible to none of these things. As constituted in practice, any of these things may *influence* the set of practices that make a relation of power, but only a change in the practices themselves can be said to end a state of domination.

Institutions, for example, do not exist apart from the practices that constitute them, and the existence on paper of "democratic institutions" in a particular time and place does not mean the end of domination there. Only institutional practices that constitute equitable social relations can be said to undo domination. In the U.S. civil rights struggle, it isn't the 1968 Fair Housing Act *on paper* that could end inequality of housing for African Americans and other people of color; on the contrary, only the enactment of non-discriminatory housing practices by real estate agents, bankers, sellers, and buyers (and, in addition, the activities of the police and federal agents to enforce the law and require those who discriminate to comply) could be said to do that; given the real-world persistence of structural racism in housing and the failures of enforcement of the act (Lipsitz 1998: 25–33), it is clear that racist domination of the U.S. housing market still persists.[15] Whether ending domination in any particular case will require revolutionary destruction of existing institutions or their reconstruction from within, it is never the reified institutions themselves that bring about social justice, but the constitution of just relations between people's practices that make things just.

Likewise, liberatory ideas cannot undo domination or can only undo it in a very narrow domain. Anti-racist consciousness-raising, feminist education, LGBT social critiques, anti-capitalist ideologies—and, of course, resistant forms of expressive culture—may have an impact on ideas or feelings. Inasmuch as domination affects how people think about the social world and make value judgments, ideological practice may undo these forms of domination. But practices of maintaining feelings of fear, hate, or disdain for people from particular groups (others' or one's own) are only the tip of the iceberg of dominating practice. The bulk of that frigid mass is inequitable relations in practices of work in the home, the farm, or the factory; of acquiring and maintaining housing and food; sexual practices; practices of child rearing, medicine, and elder care—the whole of social life. Acts of consciousness-raising, education, and social critique are all extrinsic to, or are only a small part of, these practices. As a result they resist domination only inasmuch as they may influence how the practices of domination, subordination, and resistance in these other domains are carried out.

Theory can never find a necessary connection between a configuration of the elements of the expressive-political nexus and a type of impact on the social world. While an analysis of many case studies may someday suggest that certain types of expressive culture may be more consequential or more prone to slippage in certain kinds of social formations and contexts, such an analysis could never do anything more than identify tendencies. For it to do otherwise would require that expressive culture really did control society, that the agency outside of performance events was shaped or controlled by the agency within it. Searching for such broader generalizations about such connections—however contingent and tentative they may be—is a worthwhile project for those who study the politics of culture. In developing the notion of stance, identifying the elements of the expressive-political nexus, exploring the relationships between expressive practice and the practices in other social domains, and suggesting the limits of theory, I hope to have mapped the broadest outlines of the space in which some of these dynamics may play out and to have pointed toward new topics for research. The fact that theory has limitations does not invalidate theoretical work—just as the boundaries of the case study do not invalidate that form of inquiry. Grounded on the most basic structures of experience and dialectics of practice, our broadest theoretical ideas can suggest the outlines of the possible, and theoretically informed analyses of sets of empirical situations can reveal tendencies and patterns that help us make sense of the world, however limited such general insights might be.

The interpretation of stance does not only serve those interested in the politics of culture. Illuminating specific meaning making processes, I hope in this book to have shed light on the ways in which expressive culture moves us, or more accurately, the ways in which, by engaging expressive culture, we move ourselves as we move toward it and toward others. Beyond these broad theoretical projects in politics and aesthetics, I hope that the ideas about stance that I have offered here can also serve the needs of the ethnographer or historian primarily interested in the interpretation of individual cultures. In the field, the archive, and the library, our research can come to understand the effects that expressive culture concretely has for particular people in particular situations. Expressive culture is important because people find powerful meanings in it and because those meanings may have an impact on other parts of their lives. Stance often plays a key role in those meanings, and understanding the interpretive processes that it involves can help scholars to more richly come to grips with the forms of expressive culture we find in the world, get closer to the experiences of the people we study, and explore the connections between their expressive practices and the rest of their social lives.

As I have tried to show in this chapter, only inasmuch as experiences of expressive culture might foster or resist domination in other domains of social life can it be said to matter for questions of power. This final section has sought to map the differing ways in which it might. While expressive culture can be a crucial influence on practice in other domains, it is just that—an influence, one factor among many that shape the social life of power. Every genre of expressive culture has its florid celebrants, those who see it as the key to liberation, and at least since Plato expressed his distrust of music, every genre has had its bellicose detractors as well. Likewise have higher-order categories of expression (folklore, popular culture, high art) been celebrated or damned. Neither angel nor demon, expressive culture is simply a part of social life, and we do no service by making it into something it is not. Only by grounding the study of expressive culture in lived practice and experience can we do it justice. Given the reality of its richness and its unadorned potential for shaping our lives, what field of inquiry could be more deserving of our attentions?

Notes

Preface: What Phenomenology Can Do for the Study of
Expressive Culture (pp. vii–xix)

1. The term *expressive culture* is used by scholars in a wide range of disciplines to refer to any type of social behavior with an aesthetic dimension. This includes genres traditionally studied in the humanities such as music, dance, theater, and painting, but also everyday forms of aesthetic practice like storytelling, jokes, dress, graffiti, and ritual.

2. The word *valual* is the adjectival form of value. In everyday life, we experience things not only as having factual properties (size, shape, weight, etc.), but also as having qualities that involve their value for us. For example, we may experience an object on a store shelf as desirable or repellent, useful or useless, exciting or soothing, comfortably familiar or disturbingly strange. It is the broad domain of experienced features such as these that I wish to indicate by the expression "valual qualities."

Chapter 1: Locating Stance (pp. 1–26)

1. On the notion of expressive culture, see note 1 in the preface.

2. Closely related to one another, ethnographic, contextualist, and performance-centered approaches have become central to folklore studies and inform much of the contemporary discipline. Some classic examples include Abrahams (1964), Seitel (1969), Ben-Amos ([1971] 2000), Gossen ([1972] 2000), Kirshenblatt-Gimblett (1975), Bauman (1977), and Stone (1982).

3. See Berger (1999:3–4) on textual empiricism.

4. Like the ethnographic, contextualist, and performance perspectives discussed above, reception-oriented approaches have played a key role in studies of music, folklore, and popular culture. Radway (1984), Walser (1993), Weinstein (2000), Cavicchi (1998), Cowan (1990), and Bacon-Smith (1992) represent some of the broad range of scholarship that involves attention to reception.

5. Here and throughout, I intend the term *reception* in a broad sense to include all of the ways in which a person engages a work, from the immediate activities of sense making by which words and gestures have their mundane meanings for us to the most formal exegesis, as well as all forms of affective, sensual, or bodily responses to works of expressive culture.

6. Since the 1980s, a number of scholars in ethnomusicology (e.g., Stone 1982, 1988; Feld [1984] 1994; Titon 1988, 2008; Rice 1994, 2008; Friedson 1996; Berger

1997, 1999; Berger and Del Negro 2004; Porcello 1998; Wolf 2006) have used ideas from phenomenology. Firmly grounded in a nuanced reading of Alfred Schutz's Husserlian scholarship, Ruth Stone's *Let the Inside Be Sweet* (1982) forged the path for phenomenological ethnomusicology, and the sophisticated theoretical framework established in that book laid out the key themes in this line of scholarship—the music event as a situated, cultural interaction in which participants actively make meaning. Stone furthered this perspective in *Dried Millet Breaking* (1988) and explored the role of time consciousness in music events. A number of other scholars have also done important work in ethnomusicology's phenomenological tradition. Developing related ideas, Steven Feld's "Communication, Music, and Speech about Music" ([1984] 1994), for example, used a communication approach to critique Charles Seeger's work on the relationship between speech and music and explored the "interpretive moves" and framing processes by which music is made meaningful. Rich ethnographies by Jeff Todd Titon and Timothy Rice follow another strand in the phenomenological tradition, hermeneutics, to depict musical interpretation as an open-ended process. Paul Ricoeur's work informs the "interpretative dialogues" that Titon uses in *Powerhouse for God* (1988) to thoughtfully explore the processes by which members of an Appalachian Baptist church interpret music and verbal art and make them integral to their lives. Rice's *May It Fill Your Soul* (1994) draws more heavily on Hans-Georg Gadamer for its sensitive portrayal of music making in Bulgaria and its broader reflections on musical understanding. Titon and Rice discuss the relevance of hermeneutics for ethnomusicological fieldwork in their chapters in *Shadows in the Field* (Barz and Cooley 2008), the well-known, edited volume on research methods in the discipline, first published in 1997. Martin Heidegger is the inspiration for *Dancing Prophets* (1996), Steven Friedson's important study of the role of music in Tumbuka healing rituals. In this book, I seek to build on these works and advance the orientation toward experience that they champion. For a review of some other phenomenological approaches to music, see Berger (1999).

It is worth noting that Titon uses the term *stance* in a 1985 article on fieldwork that draws on phenomenological ideas. There, he defines stance as the social position that a research participant assigns to a fieldworker when the fieldworker enters her music culture (18); this sense of the word *stance* is different from the one I am developing in this project.

7. Phenomenological orientations have been used in anthropology by a range of scholars, including William F. Hanks (e.g., [1987] 2000, [1989] 2000a, [1989] 2000b, [1989] 2000c, 1990, 1996), Thomas J. Csordas (1993), Michael Jackson (1989), C. Jason Throop (2003), Throop and Keith M. Murphy (2002), and Charles D. Laughlin and Throop (2006). Hanks's work combines ideas from phenomenologists Roman Ingarden, Alfred Schutz, and Maurice Merleau-Ponty with approaches from a wide range of thinkers who work on language and social life. Most significant here is Hanks's important book *Language and Communicative Practices* (1996), which builds on Pierre Bourdieu's practice theory to reconcile what he calls "formalist" and "relationalist" approaches to language. Here, Hanks extends Ingarden's ideas to show how the active work of an interpreting subject is needed to make texts in language meaningful, while Merleau-Ponty is employed to illustrate how linguistic meaning depends on an embodied subject situated in the physical and social world. Hanks's massive *Referential Practice* (1990) employs a similar synthesis to yield new insights into the phenomenon of referential meaning in language. Time is a key concern in both of these works, and here and elsewhere Hanks takes up ideas from phenomenology, or a generally phenomenological outlook, to explore how linguistic resources are used to bring together differing temporal orders in performance ([1989] 2000b, [1989] 2000a). Csordas (1993) uses

phenomenological ideas about embodiment to rethink the concept of culture and develop a notion of "somatic modes of attention," by which he means culturally specific modes of focusing on one's own body or that of another. Csordas richly compares Merleau-Ponty's notion of perception with Bourdieu's ideas about practice to depict embodiment and textuality as competing views of culture, the ultimate priority of which is "indeterminate," and he argues that this indeterminacy is a central issue for ethnography. Drawing on Husserl and Schutz, C. Jason Throop (2003) has shown how ideas from phenomenology can provide a firmer grounding for the notion of experience than is found in contemporary anthropological theories and also how a phenomenological attention to the temporal dimension of experience can help ethnographers gain richer insights into the lives of their research participants. Throop further develops these ideas in his collaborative publications. Throop and Murphy (2002) argue that ideas in Bourdieu's work have their origin in the writings of Husserl and Schutz and that those thinkers more effectively theorize agency, while Laughlin and Throop (2006) offer a complex theory of cultural neurophenomenology to connect the fields of anthropology and psychology.

While studies of language and affect, such as those of Niko Besnier (1990) and Judith Irvine (1990), and works in the anthropology of emotions, like those of Catherine Lutz and Geoffrey White (1986) or Lutz (1988), do not cite thinkers from the phenomenological tradition or explicitly employ its intellectual tools, such research resonates with many of the concerns of this book. Besnier's review of the language and affect literature (1990), for example, illustrates how thoroughly language is saturated with emotion. Drawing on ideas from Peircian semiotics, he shows the diverse ways in which affect is indexed by language and profoundly shaped by culture. In a powerful piece of analysis, Irvine (1990) argues that the linguistic registers of a society do not merely link sets of linguistic features together with social groups and situations; they also have affective dimensions that connect them to the society's broader ideological currents and social structures. Since all talk takes place in a register, Irvine suggests, the expression of affect in language is deeply informed by larger social forces. The piece's theoretical insights are grounded in a case study of Wolof verbal interaction, and Irvine notes that she has "not much treated questions about what emotions Wolof speakers 'really feel'" (155); however, she goes on to observe, quite rightly, that the shaping of affective expression by language cannot help but inform people's affective experience. Likewise, Lutz's well-known ethnography of everyday life on a Micronesian atoll (1988) illustrates how emotion saturates all of social life and language, ties us to the world, is fundamentally shaped by culture, and is negotiated in situated and large-scale social contexts. Seeking to overturn Western assumptions that depict emotion as biologically universal or strictly internal and subjective, Lutz shows how emotions and talk about them can never be viewed as referencing universal affective states; rather, they index a culture's larger assumptions about the nature of the person, which is in turn shaped by the ideologies and power relations of the society in question.

I see my project as complementing that of these various anthropologists. While this study does not seek, as Lutz does, to reveal the ethnopsychological implications of individual affective terms, I recognize that experience is fundamentally social, not radically individual, and emphasize that all of social life is shot through with affect. Taking expressive culture as my topic, I put structures of lived experience at the center of my analysis and examine the culturally specific ways in which musical sound, narrative, and other expressive forms are situated relative to them.

8. Scholars in linguistics and related fields also use the word *stance,* but they and I mean differing things by this term. Reviewing some of the literature on stance in the disciplines of language research, Mary Bucholtz and Kira Hall (2005) explain that there, the expression refers to "the display of evaluative, affective, and epistemic orientations

in discourse" (11). As I explain more fully later in this chapter, I use the term *stance* to refer to the affective, stylistic, or valual qualities with which a person constitutes her experience. Thus, while stance in my sense can be depicted in language, it is not the linguistic display of an orientation but a particular form of that orientation as constituted in a specific structure of lived experience. In the course of developing his own theory of stance in language, Paul Kockelman (2004) reviews a wide range of scholarly literatures that use this term, including linguistics and philosophy. Writing in the *Journal of Linguistic Anthropology*, Kockelman defines stance as "the semiotic means by which we indicate our orientation to states of affairs, usually framed in terms of evaluation (e.g., moral obligation or epistemic possibility) or intentionality (e.g., desire or memory, fear or doubt)" (127). The article understands such orientations to be a crosslinguistic feature of interaction and social life, which is encoded differently in the grammatical and lexical structures of differing languages. A careful comparison of English and Q'eqchi'-Maya is used to show two of the many ways in which language might represent these orientations. Again, the focus is on the ways orientations are expressed in language, rather than structures of lived experience, although, like Irvine (1990:155; see my discussion of her in note 7 above), he rightly asserts that structures embedded in language often shape the perspectives of their speakers (138).

It is worth noting that Kockelman and I both employ the term *intentionality*, but our uses are quite distinct. Kockelman is a linguistic anthropologist whose philosophical references are, to my reading, all outside the phenomenological tradition. He doesn't discuss structures of experience in the phenomenological sense, and, to my reading, it is clear that intentionality here does not refer to Husserl's idea of the necessary link between consciousness and its object. For example, in a passage in his review of the philosophical literature on stance (129), he mentions the "intentional stance of mankind," which, after Daniel Dennett, he says refers to "the tendencies of humans as a species to interpret behavior in terms of putative mental states." The differences between our perspectives is most clear in his closing paragraph, in which he writes that his analysis of stance is based "in terms of crosslinguistic categories, whose properties . . . are characterized by social and semiotic features (e.g., participant roles and morphosyntax) rather than psychological or metaphysical ones (e.g., evaluation or subjectivity)" (144).

9. In the Western music conservatory, the term *interpretation* refers to the performer's manner of playing a piece. In much Western art music, the pitch and duration of the notes of a composition are specified precisely by a score, and the interpretation refers to the performer's ways of playing other sonic elements, such as dynamics (loudness and softness), tempo (the speed with which the music is played), and timbre (the tone color used, see note 12 below). A related but distinct sense of the word *interpretation* can be found in contemporary humanities scholarship. Drawing on continental European philosophy, humanists employ the term *interpretative framework* to refer to a set of ideas used to make sense of a text or social interaction; likewise, the word *interpretation* is broadly used to refer to the process of meaning making. Throughout this example, I have tried to use these terms in such a way that the context clarifies which sense I intend.

10. Throughout this example, I have tried to use the kind of language that composers, performers, and audiences in this tradition would when talking about music. A crescendo is a technique in which the performer makes the music increasingly loud during a specific passage. To accent a note is to place a greater emphasis on it. One can use rhythm to accent notes by, for example, pausing slightly before or after the note is played. The term *cadence* refers to the end of a passage or section in a piece of music, and a cadential chord is the chord (group of notes played at the same time) occurring at a cadence. Throughout this section, understanding the fine details of music terminology is not strictly necessary for following the larger argument.

11. The term *dynamic* refers to the loudness or softness of music sound. When using a dynamic accent, the performer emphasizes an individual note by playing it louder.

12. The term *timbre* is usually glossed as tone color. Consider the situation of a person listening to two notes, the first played on a guitar and the second played on a piano. Both notes have the same pitch (say, a C) and the same level of loudness or softness (say, moderately loud) and are played for the same amount of time (say, one second). Despite these similarities, a person who listened to these two notes would still hear a difference between them. That difference is defined as timbre. A single instrument can often play with many differing timbres, and the range of timbres that the ear can discern is large. *Bright, dark, clear,* and *raspy* are a few of the many English language words used to describe timbre.

13. One scholar who explores this issue is Roman Ingarden ([1933] 1989). For him, the musical work is not a subjective and mental thing, but neither is it ideal or real. Rather, he argued that it must be considered as an "intentional object," which has inherent features that can be apprehended by a performer or listener. In addition to its "tone formations," Ingarden suggests, the musical work's inherent features include "emotional qualities" and "aesthetic value qualities," and these are completely distinct from the composer's intentions or any meaning projected onto the work by a performer or listener. At the same time, though, Ingarden argues that compositions necessarily contain "places of indeterminacy" that must be filled out in individual performances, and that the musical work includes both those elements specified by the score and the full range of potential performances that the score's indeterminacy leaves open. Hanks draws on Ingarden's ideas on the literary work, particularly his ideas about indeterminacy ([1989] 2000c; 1996). Ingarden's notion of intentional objects is derived from the idea of intentionality developed by Husserl, with whom he studied. While Husserl's notion of intentionality is critical for my project, my interpretations differ in many ways from those of Ingarden. I give far less autonomy to the musical work than he does, and my reading of Husserl is inflected through later phenomenologists of the body, such as Merleau-Ponty and Todes.

14. In this context, the term *voice* refers to an independent part, not a singing voice. Thus, a composition with four voices would have four separate musical lines. Such lines could be sung by four singers, played by four separate instruments, or played on one instrument (such as a piano), if that instrument is capable of producing them. The limitations on the composition described in this sentence would be common ones for an assignment in a beginning music theory class. It is not necessary to understand the nuances of the music terminology used here (diatonic harmony, parallel perfect motion, pivot chords, key changes) to get the main point of this argument.

15. In her rich phenomenology of narrative, Katharine Galloway Young (1987) makes a similar observation, noting that "Taleworlds [the places depicted in stories], whether fictive or real, are brought into being, sustained, and banished by the attention of tellers and hearers" (197). Discussing the ontological status of musical works, Ingarden develops a related but distinct perspective when he argues that "musical compositions are nothing mental and nothing 'subjective' . . . but are objectivities of an altogether special kind and mode of being, although it is of course entirely true that they would not even exist without the composer who created them and without the listeners who apprehend them cognitively and aesthetically" ([1933] 1989:22).

16. In differing ways, Ingarden's discussion of the ontological status of musical works ([1933] 1989), Hanks's Ingardenian analysis of the status of texts ([1989] 2000c; 1996:122–28), and Young's exploration of the ontological status of narrated events and speech events (1987) all give a limited autonomy to the object of attention and all recognize the role of the subject in constituting meaning.

17. Indeed, a long-standing dilemma of modern Western philosophy centers around what seems to be the impossibility of immediate experiences of oneself. For a fuller discussion, see Berger (2004).

18. See Berger (1999:149–73).

19. The term *affect* broadly refers to the lived experience of emotion, as opposed to its narrowly physiological dimensions. The term *valual* is the adjective form of the word *value*. For a further discussion, see note 2 in the preface.

20. While Husserl's thought changed across the span of his career, this notion of epoché is fundamental to all but his earliest work and is richly developed in his major statements such as *Ideas* ([1913] 1962) and *Cartesian Mediations* ([1931] 1960). Throughout this book, I have drawn on useful works of secondary literature, including Kohák (1978), Hammond, Howarth, and Keat (1991), Schmidt (1985), Ihde (1986), Kockelmans (1994), and Natanson (1973).

21. By asserting that the epoché is never to be removed, phenomenology does not deny the existence of phenomena like mirages or suggest that any given momentary experience is a complete and accurate understanding of the physical world. Rather, phenomenology offers the notion of the epoché as a way to reconnect the subject with the world, which idealist philosophy had sharply separated, and explore the linkages between them.

22. This reading is derived from Sartre's brief essay "Intentionality: A Fundamental Idea of Husserl's Philosophy" ([1939] 1970) and the discussion of Sartre's ideas in Hammond, Howarth, and Keat (1991).

23. These ideas are richly explored by Todes's work on embodiment ([1990] 2001). See my discussion of Todes in chapter 4.

24. A number of philosophers have argued that the for-a-subject qualities of noema are not fundamentally constructed in after-the-fact thinking acts deduced from sensations. In everyday life, at least a sizable percentage of our actions are carried out without preexisting planning in words and concepts. While one does, on occasion, have to stop and actively think about how to use objects from the world around one, that thinking, such philosophers argue, emerges against a background of objects already for-a-subject and actions already in progress. For a further discussion of the priority of action over reflection, see Dreyfus (1991, 1992).

25. The notion of the mutually constitutive nature of the person and the world is a view central to existential phenomenology, and some in that branch of the tradition claim that it is in Husserl's transcendental phenomenology as well (see, e.g., the discussion of the relationship between Merleau-Ponty and Husserl in Schmidt 1985). In this view, neither person nor world is possible without the other. This isn't to say that if all people died tomorrow in a nuclear holocaust, the rocks and gases of all planets and suns would wink out of existence. However, were there never to have been subjects, there never would have been rocks as rocks in the mundane sense of the word.

26. Drawing on the work of Merleau-Ponty, Csordas (1993) also emphasizes the ways in which the constitution of experience is shaped by culture. His work understands the practices of Catholic Charismatic healers and spirit mediums in Puerto Rico as examples of "somatic modes of attention," culturally specific ways of "attending 'with' and attending 'to' the body" (138).

Chapter 2: Structures of Stance in Lived Experience
(pp. 27–53)

1. I alluded to this idea earlier when I suggested that the analysis of stance would lead us to find the dimensions of interpretation in production and the productive elements in reception.

2. Irvine (1990) and Hanks (1996) both address related issues in their analysis of language and practice. Discussing the affective dimensions of linguistic registers, Irvine shows how "fluency" in prosody, phonology, morphology, and syntax all index affect, and how the interpretation of that indexical relationship is shaped by ideological forces. Hanks suggests that persons engaged in communicative practices must concern themselves with the "feasibility" of particular acts, and that the fluidity, tempo, and timing of speech in social interaction cannot help but index a wide range of meanings (231).

3. In chapter 4, I will return to this topic and explore an additional type of stance quality: stance-on-power.

4. While Hymes's formulation of *style* in "Ways of Speaking" (1974) nicely captures the everyday sense of this word and the common scholarly approaches to the topic, his profound discussion of the concept there far transcends mundane usages. Seeking to identify elements of language that had been overlooked in linguistics or treated as of secondary importance, Hymes takes style as a fundamental component of language. He explores how linguistic features can serve either "referential" or "stylistic" functions (1974:436). Further, he shows how styles may be tied to groups, situations, persons, or genres (440); color speech across contexts or serve to define a genre or context (441); and shape language change (449). Perhaps most significantly for our purposes, Hymes distinguishes genre from performance ("genres . . . are not in themselves the 'doing' of a genre," p. 443). Developing this idea, he emphasizes how speakers may have differing ways of engaging with a genre or work and sees types of "performances as [having] relationship[s] to genres, such that one can say of a performance that its materials (genres) were reported, described, run through, illustrated, quoted, enacted" (443). Discussing work with a related orientation, Hymes cites Stanley Newman's research on style in the Yokuts language in order to emphasize that, in knowing a language, speakers do not merely have and enact a grammar, but have a style that shapes the way that they employ the strictly structural forms imposed by that grammar (447–49).

To be clear, Hymes does not employ phenomenological methods, analyze structures of experience, or discuss the Husserlian "act character" of intentionality. In "Ways of Speaking," a style is understood as a dimension of a given language and the property of a speech community, agency in language is not explicitly theorized, and the "cognitive orientations" (449) inculcated by linguistically specific styles are said to partially shape thought (450). Stance and style are thus distinct concepts. However nuanced by differences within a community, genre, or function, style in Hymes's sense is a structural feature of a language and a community, where stance is the valual quality of intentionality—the valence we attach to our fundamentally agentive engagement with our objects of attention in the constitution of our experience. Style, as an element of language and an expressive resource, is thus a thing that a person may have a stance upon. One might be able to argue that Hymes's model transfers the structural qualities ascribed to grammar to a new domain of analysis (style), and, as an explanation for the expressive force of language, the notion of style is, I believe, susceptible to the reductio ad absurdum problems I discussed in chapter 1. But social and cultural theory operates as much in the theorist's handling of his/her subject matter as it does in that writer's formal definition of terms. To my reading of "Ways of Speaking," a sense of agency in linguistic practice is very much preserved in Hymes's treatment of the notions of language, style, and speech. I would like to think of this theory of stance as an attempt to use phenomenological approaches to forward the impulse that animates Hymes's work.

5. Using the intellectual tools of linguistic anthropology, one might understand the typical prosody, contour, and timbre of the pedantic proverb telling that I discussed here as an example of elements of a *linguistic register* in Judith Irvine's sense

of the term (1990)—a conventional set of linguistic features associated with a typical social situation, shot through with affect, and tied to larger social ideologies. As conventionalized expressive resources, the various registers existing in a particular language and community can be seen as operating as sedimented quasi-stances.

6. Grounded in the analysis of language, not structures of experience, Kockelman also develops a notion of meta-stance (2004:143–44), and his ideas differ from mine. See my larger discussion of Kockelman's work in chapter 1, note 8.

7. Precision and ambiguity are the axes around which many aesthetic ideologies revolve, and while it is beyond the scope of this study to explore this topic, an analysis of such phenomena in these terms could prove useful in a range of contexts.

8. See below for a further discussion of stance and time consciousness.

9. Exploring this example further, we can specify four dimensions of thinking and four corresponding ways in which we have stances upon it. First, there is the temporal dimension of thought and the pacing of ideas within our experience. Each thought comes quickly or slowly, and one holds a stance upon this pacing. A math student may, for example, find herself working to coax out each slowly emerging line in a mathematical proof or frantically resisting the torrent of ideas that flow forth. These two alternatives involve a quality of effort or work, but when thoughts emerge at a desirable tempo, we have a more relaxed relationship to their passing, not unlike that of a sailor who allows a rope to glide through her grasp as she pays out line, lightly controlling its speed and registering its movement. Such quasi-passivity is still invested with valual qualities, as when a writer enters "the zone," the sentences flow effortlessly through her mind, and she grasps the train of thoughts lightly and with pleasure. A second dimension in which stance is defined is with regard to the intensity with which thoughts emerge. For example, having occasionally had problems with insomnia, I know that I am more likely to get to sleep if my nagging thoughts emerge not only more slowly, but also with less intensity. A loose and detached affective stance toward nagging thoughts helps make them emerge less vividly in experience. Third—and closely related to the topic of intensity—is the location of thought in the foreground/background structure of lived experience. As I discussed previously, experience is rarely composed of only a single phenomenon. Images, bodily sensations, thoughts, feelings, and myriad other types of phenomena are present in awareness, and they are usually structured into a vivid and detailed focus and a less intense and dimmer fringe, which trails off into the horizon. Grasping one phenomenon intensely, we shuffle other phenomena into the background of attention, and these processes of arranging and organizing attention—and the affective quality of this organization—are basic to stance. One final dimension is the meaning content of the thoughts themselves, and the complexity of stance on the meaning content of experience is as complex as meaning itself. One's stance on the meaning content of a train of thought in words, musical sounds, or images refers to the valual quality of one's engagement with those meanings. Which meanings in the train are emphasized? Which are given less stress? What is the affective weight with which those meanings are experienced? And what is the style or manner of those constitutive and interpretive processes? In thinking that Jeff lied to me, for example, do I highlight the fact that it is *Jeff* who lied to me (because, perhaps, I had thought him a paragon of truthfulness) or that I was the victim of a *lie* (rather than a slight or some other social wrongdoing)? The fact that we always have a stance on our thoughts adds a layer of interpretive richness to even our most mundane thinking.

10. As Paul Provenza and Penn Jillette's 2005 film *The Aristocrats* shows, there was not complete consensus on these questions; some in the audience shouted "too soon," but the majority of the crowd of comedians and entertainers roared with laughter at the comic's material.

11. In phenomenology and phenomenologically informed research into expressive culture, much attention has been paid to the role that time plays in meaning making. See, for example, Ingarden ([1933] 1989), Ihde (1976), Young (1987), Hanks ([1989] 2000b, [1989] 2000a, 1996), and Throop (2003), as well as my own work on this subject (1999, Berger and Del Negro 2004).

12. My use of the term *iterative* is derived from its everyday meaning in mathematics and the sciences. There, an iterative system is one in which what happens at one stage in a process shapes what happens during the next stage of the process, which in turn shapes what happens at the following stage, and so forth. The concept is a relatively straightforward one, and it should not be confused with *iterability*, a complex notion advanced by Jacques Derrida and later carried forward by Judith Butler and others. Very loosely speaking, iterability there refers to the capacity of signs to be repeated. This capacity is seen as a fundamental quality of signs, and scholars in the deconstructive tradition have argued that it has broad implications for the philosophy of language and the nature of gender.

13. Folklorist Katharine Galloway Young explores related dynamics in a chapter of her rich phenomenology of narrative, *Taleworlds and Storyrealms* (1987:69–99). Examining the storytelling sessions of an English community, Young looks at the ways in which meanings unfold as a series of narratives are presented. Drawing on work in folklore studies, phenomenology, sociolinguistics, and Erving Goffman's interpretive sociology, Young shows the complex ways in which a teller's choice of narrative can reinterpret the significance of previous narratives in the session and form a context of meaning for subsequent narratives. Ingarden touches on similar dynamics in music, noting how the succeeding movements of a sonata, or any large-scale musical work, may color our aesthetic and emotional apprehension of the ones that follow ([1933] 1989).

14. The preceding examples of this section are ones that emphasize formal structures on the scale of entire works and narrative closure. Of course, not all social groups place a premium on coherence among phenomena in the long scale, and the differing aesthetics of such groups highlights the role of culture in the constitution of experience. For example, attending to nineteenth-century symphonic music, a knowledgeable listener will keep the long-scale fullness of the tonal narrative in her living present. For devotees of rock groups in the jam band tradition of the Grateful Dead or Phish, the accretion of experience in what Henri Bergson (1913) would call the growing durée of the living present is no less fundamental to experience, but the pursuit of coherence and unity drops away. The transitions from one timbral, harmonic, or rhythmic texture to the next are crucial, but often the listener seeks no return to an initial state of completion or larger narrative flow. New moments are not grasped as completions of form, but past passages are retained in the present moment to allow the awareness of contrasts across sections. Other music genres operate in a different fashion. As Anne Danielsen's rich work on James Brown and Parliament has shown (2006), devotees of funk music focus attention on short time-scales, exclude from experience the awareness of large-scale musical form, and drop into a temporally thin but emotionally powerful moment (see also my own remarks [2004] on electronic dance music). Whatever aesthetic of the living present is preferred, the temporal shape of experience that a person constitutes will depend on that person's active and culturally informed engagement with her objects of attention.

15. This vision of time as a series of expanding moments is informed by Ruth Stone's important work in *Dried Millet Breaking* (1988). A rich study of the Woi epic of the Kpelle people of Liberia, Stone's ethnography shows how Kpelle experience the performance event as a series of moments—temporal units that can be "expanded" or "deflated"—and how musical and social processes serve as the means by which such units are constructed and managed.

Chapter 3: Stance and Others, Stance and Lives (pp. 54–96)

1. My understanding of Merleau-Ponty throughout this passage is informed by Reynolds (2001). For a discussion of the notion of the chiasm in both Husserl and Merleau-Ponty, see Schmidt (1985).

2. On the role of tactile feedback in writing, see Goldberg (1987).

3. See Hahn (2006) for a discussion of the ways in which culture shapes judgments about the extremity of sensual experience and an examination of the larger significance of extremity for ethnography.

4. A range of authors have discussed the role of non-arbitrary signs in the aesthetics of expressive culture. For example, building on Keil's notion of participatory discrepancies, Steven Feld argues that iconic and metaphoric relationships among musical practices, musical form, a group's relationship to nature, and its styles of social interaction are the root of music's affective power ([1988] 1994). For a rich discussion of non-arbitrary signs in the aesthetics of verbal art and a review of the contemporary literature from linguistic anthropology on this topic, see Webster (2008).

5. Taking language as his center of gravity, Hanks has developed related points about the central role of practice in meaning making (1996). The formal structures of language alone cannot explain meaning in linguistic interaction, he argues; rather, they are only one element of "communicative practices." Drawing on Bourdieu's practice theory, he argues that practice isn't merely the application of a linguistic code to a situation but is itself a ground for shared meaning, and he shows how understanding between people depends on a range of practice-based features, including orientation to the other as an embodied subject in time and space, the "feasibility" of particular kinds of action (231), and the cultural norms of practice that Bourdieu has called "habitus."

6. In Western music theory, tempo is to be sharply distinguished from rhythmic density. For example, a musician may feel the basic pulse of a piece as fifty beats per second, tap her foot to those pulses, and play a melody that starts with a series of eighth notes (two notes per beat). As she continues to tap her foot with the same basic pulses, the melody may then shift to a series of sixteenth notes (four notes per beat). In such a case, the tempo hasn't changed because the rate of the underlying beats has remained constant. What has happened is that the rhythmic density of the melody has increased.

7. Drawing on Bourdieu, Hanks also explores the role of tempo and timing in the meaning of social interaction and the culturally specific ways in which units of time are construed (1996:231, 271–72).

8. A number of other scholars have made related observations and discussed similar ideas. For example, richly exploring the "mystery of ornamentation" in Bulgarian bagpipe music, Timothy Rice (1994:76–85) notes that to a novice player from outside the culture, the ornaments that pipers use to decorate Bulgarian melodies are bewilderingly complex and varied. Rice's ethnography traces the path by which he learned to play the bagpipes and assimilate the local style of ornamentation. Following his teacher's instructions and immersing himself in performance, Rice solves the mystery by conceptualizing the melody note and its ornaments by way of a single set of hand gestures, rather than thinking of each melody note and ornament as requiring its own gesture (82–83).

In a sophisticated analysis of improvisation in music and verbal art, R. Keith Sawyer approaches related issues (1996). Building on the work of Harold S. Powers, Sawyer suggests that "[s]ome improvisational forms (e.g., Javanese gamelan, Rotinese parallel oratory, Slavic epic poetry) are constructed by the performer out of pre-existing units" (1996:285). The size of these units is one dimension along which traditions of improvisation may vary, and Sawyer observes that the size and relative fixity of ready-mades are related to what he calls the "density of decision points" in a genre—the number of moments in a piece at which the performer can introduce new ideas. In both of these works, we see differing ways in which expressive forms are organized into units in lived experience and the significance of this kind of organization for performance.

9. Skepticism about the ability of audiences to read the stances of others may cause some readers to doubt the importance of stance in general in the interpretation of expressive culture. To address this concern, we need only gesture to the wide range of situations in which producers actively seek to display or even fake their stances—musicians who tremble with emotion, camera operators whose shaky grasp on their cameras conveys energy and excitement, professional wrestlers whose skin bulges performatively with flexed muscles and taut tendons. If their audiences didn't seek to read stance, at least in certain cultures and contexts, producers of expressive culture wouldn't have to fabricate them.

10. For a discussion of "seeing as" that centers in other terms, see Kohák (1978).

11. The literature in phenomenology on the temporal dimension of experience begins with Husserl's *Phenomenology of Internal Time-Consciousness* ([1929] 1964), and this discussion is grounded in that work. For a rich exploration of these ideas, see Ihde (1976). For an application of these ideas to music, see Schutz (1976). Though Henri Bergson was not part of the phenomenological tradition, his *Time and Free Will* (1913) elaborates related ideas on temporal experience. I have discussed time consciousness in music throughout my work (1997, 1999, 2004). In this section, the discussion of intention in the everyday sense of that word is grounded in Schutz's *Phenomenology of the Social World* ([1932] 1967).

12. Events from the recent past that persist in the living present are called *retentions*. See my discussion of time consciousness in the previous chapter.

13. The precise ways in which past experiences are freighted with valences and situated in the complex gestalt of the living present are undoubtedly one of the components that make up mood. However, exploring this important topic is beyond the scope of this project.

Chapter 4: The Social Life of Stance and the Politics of Expressive Culture (pp. 97–135)

1. The classical formulations of practice theory are an important foundation for this study, and what I derive from them is a very specific set of ideas about the nature of practice and its relationship to social structure: that practice is always both agentive and shaped by situated and large-scale social contexts; that agency and structure are, in Giddens's terms, a "duality"; and that present practice is both constrained and enabled by the context of past practices and the anticipation of future ones. Viewed through a practice theory lens, social structure is composed of nothing but practice, but this does not return us to radical individualism or deny the existence of domination or larger social forces; rather, it more effectively explains the reproduction of structure and the mechanisms of domination by grounding them in the concrete world of socially situated agents. In past work (Berger 1999; Berger and Del Negro 2004), I have explained how perception in particular and the constitution of experience in general should be understood as kinds of social practice, and that perspective permeates this work as well.

A variety of scholars have explored the relationship between Pierre Bourdieu's ideas and phenomenology. Bourdieu discussed this issue explicitly (e.g., 1977), and Hanks (1996:240; [1987] 2000) and Csordas (1993) have both examined the relationship between his work and that of Merleau-Ponty. An important article by

C. Jason Throop and Keith M. Murphy (2002) reviews some of Bourdieu's writings on the relationship between Bourdieu and phenomenology, argues that many of his ideas have historical precedents in the work of Husserl and Schutz, and suggests that his debt to these earlier scholars was not sufficiently acknowledged. Throop and Murphy go on to suggest that Bourdieu's vision of practice is overly deterministic and argue for the advantages of a phenomenological perspective. A brief reply to Throop and Murphy can be found in Bourdieu (2002).

It is worth noting that the notion of stance is quite different from Bourdieu's concept of *habitus*. For Bourdieu, habitus is a disposition to engage in certain kinds of practices. It is internalized from past practice, shapes future practice, and is deeply informed by social structure. While less rigid and reified than a rule and while it enables contextually sensitive improvisation, habitus is not conscious intent, and it is largely taken for granted. All of this is quite different from stance, which is not a disposition in any sense of the word. While the stance a person takes is certainly informed by situated and larger social forces, it isn't the tendency to act in a certain way but rather the affective, stylistic, or valual quality of a person's constitution of experience.

2. A common translation of the original quote reads, "Men make their own history, but they do not make it just as they please; they do not make it under circumstances chosen by themselves, but under circumstances directly found, given, and transmitted from the past" (Marx [1852] 1972:594).

3. This is not in any way to say that culture is opposed to agency or that it only limits behavior. A wide range of scholars have shown that, to use the most common construction of this idea, culture both constrains and enables practice. It is certainly true that in any given situation, the power relations of a culture may impose norms that limit an individual's action; however, culture is the unavoidable context and the condition of practice, and therefore facilitates as well as limits what people may do.

4. For Schutz and Luckmann, this fact—that practices in the world are not accomplished merely by forming a plan or a wish, but must be actively and concretely achieved—is the hallmark of experiences of reality, as opposed to experiences of dreams or of fantasies (1973). Their analysis of these differing "provinces of meaning" turns on this distinction.

5. When Hebdige turns to the "relationship between experience, expression, and signification" (1979:120), "experience," it seems to me, does not refer to the concretely lived world of objects grasped and actions taken—to the contents of consciousness—but only to a much looser notion of one's experience of holding a generalized position in society (as a youth or a working-class person). As a result, Hebdige can talk about the semiotics of the punk subculture as breaking "not only with the parent culture[,] but with its own *location in experience*" (121; emphasis in the original).

6. Of course, not all stance-prominent scenes prize shock. When an ideology of nostalgia and fidelity to tradition is strong in a stance-prominent scene, audience members may hold events from the recent past at bay and set the present performance in the context only of ones from an originary age. In such a situation, performers are supposed to conserve the tradition, so hearing a feature of performance as a quasi-text doesn't freight that feature with negative valences. Rather, it is read as evidence that the performer knows the genre and is carrying it forward into the present. For example, in those bluegrass scenes that are musically conservative, stance is important, but listeners do not need to hear some new way in which this musician displays her engagement with the music. Rather, listeners place the features of the present performance in the context of those of musical heroes like Bill Monroe or Ralph Stanley, hearing the musician's stance as evidence that she gets involved the same way that Monroe or Stanley does, and an ever deeper engagement

with the original recordings and traditional performances leads listeners to an ever more sensitive engagement with stance.

7. Seeking a performance studies approach to music research, Auslander builds on the work of Erving Goffman and urges scholars to conceptualize music events as situations in which the musician performs a social identity for an audience (2006). Auslander emphasizes that audience reception is the arbiter of a musician's successful performance of identity, and he also explores the ways in which some musicians construct complex identities by performing in more than one musical genre.

8. One might well argue that gravity is indeed contingent on the planet on which one happens to be acting, and that this contingency invalidates the ontological claims that Todes draws from his analysis of balance in a vertical field. While I am not aware of any place in which Todes addresses this issue, reading his further discussion of poise, I have developed the view that this criticism would not be valid. While bodies floating in space may not deal with a field of power drawing them in a direction that is by definition down, the need to maintain an oriented poise in relationship to a field of other objects becomes *more* urgent in this context, not less so, and the significance of embodiment more apparent.

9. The ideas about the social subject that I have presented here as an abstraction from Todes's body phenomenology diverge, I think, from that author's own views on the topic. I express uncertainty here, because his thoughts about the social subject were never fully elaborated. They are briefly sketched out in the "Anticipatory Postscript," which, according to an editor's note in *Body and World*, was written "in 1990 for the Garland Press edition of Todes's dissertation, published under the title *The Human Body as Material Subject of the World*" (Todes [1990] 2001:277). (*Body and World*, the text that I have consulted here, is the most recent edition of that work, and his "Anticipatory Postscript" is included there as an appendix. Todes's dissertation was completed in 1963.) The postscript outlines the argument of an in-preparation book entitled *The Human Body as Personal Subject of Society*. Sadly, Todes died in 1994 before completing the project.

In the postscript, Todes suggests that the human subject and its capacity for action emerge in stages, each of which is grounded on the last—a body subject engaged with an actual physical world, a thinking subject that transforms the freedom of the originary bodily subjectivity to produce ideas, and a social subject that transforms the freedom of the subject again and realizes thoughts by acting in a social world. Adults can move among these forms of subjectivity, Todes suggests, but all are grounded on the bodily subject. Todes's ideas are not fully elaborated, but he suggests that the body subject is developmentally prior to the social subject and to society (287–88). Given this, I suspect that he would resist my impulse here to theorize a more abstract vision of the subject as an agent operating in a field of forces.

10. Discussing Todes's ideas in an endnote in his introduction to *Body and World*, Dreyfus explains that the word *poise*, "which usually [in everyday usage] describes a static stance [in the mundane sense of the word, not in my specialized usage], is a rather misleading term [for what Todes wishes to describe]. . . . The reader must always keep in mind that, for Todes, poise is a characteristic of skillful *activity*" (293; emphasis in the original). This dual sense of poise—as both a necessary feature of activity and as the process that allows the world to appear and activity to proceed—is parallel to the dual nature of stance I have discussed here.

It is worth noting that the "Anticipatory Postscript" discusses three "stances" of understanding ("standing-up," "standing-back," and "standing-for," p. 289) that characterize Todes's three forms of subjectivity. In chapter 4 of *Body and World*, Todes uses the term *stance* to refer to the bodily posture one must maintain to deal with an object in the world (120), and he distinguishes between "effective stance" (the posture one must adopt to skillfully deal with an object) and "actual stance" (any given instance of such a stance, which may be effective or ineffective). His use of the word *stance* in these contexts is unrelated to the sense of that term that I develop in this project.

11. Giddens intended his theory of structuration to unite disparate branches of the literature on power, which he argues are largely grounded in either one or the other meaning of this term. While he sees the transformative capacity to act as the more "general" sense of the word and domination as a more "restricted" or "relational" sense ([1976] 1993:117), this construction is not intended, I think, to downplay the significance of domination in social life, at least in his work through the mid-1980s. For example, in *The Constitution of Society* he states that "'Domination' and 'power' . . . have to be recognized as inherent in social association (or, I would say, in human action as such)" (1984:31–32). As practice is at the root of his social theory, and as power in both senses of the word is basic to practice, Giddens clearly depicts power as a fundamental part of social life.

12. Without carrying the metaphor too far, I think it can be noted that both the physical and the social fields are constituted by the ensemble of objects within them. Subjects are susceptible to those fields because it is the subjects' very being that generates them. There are important differences between social and physical fields, though. To my rudimentary understanding of physics, it is only the mass of present objects in space that generates the gravitational field around them. The social field, to the contrary, is not only shaped by the interactions among present subjects, but also by the actions of subjects distant in time.

13. Approaching related ideas from a semiotic perspective, Jan Hemming (2003) has discussed the ways in which differing kinds of signs combine in musical works to give political valence to the affective content of music. The notion of scalars and vectors from mathematics and the physical sciences serve as the central metaphor in his discussion. In math and the sciences, a scalar is any thing that can be accounted for by a single number, while a vector is a scalar oriented in a direction. (The speed "five miles per hour," e.g., is a scalar, while "five miles per hour heading northeast" is a vector.) Building on the semiotics of Ferdinand de Saussure, Hemming argued that while some elements of music sound may signify their meanings in an arbitrary fashion, others do not, and the two work together in complex ways. The non-arbitrary signs in music, he argues, function as a scalar quantity of musical meaning and signify affect. In this context, lyrics or other ideological signs may serve as vectors and "point" those scalars in one political "direction" or another.

14. The argument of Steven Feld's "Aesthetics as Iconicity of Style (uptown title); or (downtown title) 'Lift-up-over Sounding': Getting into the Kaluli Groove" ([1988] 1994) suggests a related set of dynamics. Building on Charles Keil's notion of participatory discrepancies and broad trends in ethnomusicology linking music and society, Feld argues that the musicians' style of interactions in an ensemble can serve as a metaphor for the predominant style of social interaction in their culture, and that when such iconic relationships are constituted, they give music great affective power. Here, musical texture and rhythmic coordination ("groove" in Keil's sense) carry an ideological weight, even in the absence of texts in language. See also Keil and Feld's dialog about this article in their collection *Music Grooves* (1994:151–80).

15. As George Lipsitz shows (1998:28–29), the 1968 Fair Housing Act was designed to make it difficult to punish discriminatory real estate agents and bankers. But even if it had been written in such a way that its enforcement would have been easy, it is only actual non-discriminatory real estate transactions and actual, on-the-ground enforcement of the Act that would lead to a fair American housing market. Further, the fact that the law was written with lax enforcement in mind illustrates

that it is not standards and rules on paper that can constitute equitable social relations, but rather fair standards enacted in fair social practices. This logic applies to institutions as well. Had the law been written to facilitate enforcement but the institutional structure thus described not been enacted, the power relations in housing would still have remained. None of this is to reduce structure to individual action or to downplay the importance of institutions in social life, but to emphasize that power relations are relations of social practices and that institutions are constituted of practice.

Works Cited

Abrahams, Roger D. 1964. *Deep down in the jungle. . . : Negro narrative folklore from the streets of Philadelphia.* Hatboro, PA: Folklore Associates.

Access Atlanta. 2004. Best bets by cuisine. http://www.accessatlanta.com/restaurants /content/restaurants/diningguide/spring04DGlista.html (accessed July 28, 2004).

Askew, Kelly M. 2002. *Performing the nation: Swahili music and cultural politics in Tanzania.* Chicago: University of Chicago Press.

Auslander, Philip. 1999. *Liveness: Performance in a mediatized culture.* London: Routledge.

———. 2006. Musical personae. *TDR: The Drama Review* 50(1):100–119.

Bacon-Smith, Camille. 1992. *Enterprising women: Television fandom and the creation of popular myth.* Philadelphia: University of Pennsylvania Press.

Barz, Gregory F., and Timothy J. Cooley, eds. 2008. *Shadows in the field: New perspectives for fieldwork in ethnomusicology.* 2nd ed. Oxford: Oxford University Press.

Bauman, Richard. 1977. *Verbal art as performance.* Rowley, MA: Newbury House Publishers.

———. 1986. *Story, performance, and event: Contextual studies of oral narrative.* Cambridge: Cambridge University Press.

Bauman, Richard, and Charles L. Briggs. 1990. Poetics and performance as critical perspectives on language and social life. *Annual Review of Anthropology* 19:59–88.

Ben-Amos, Dan. [1971] 2000. Toward a definition of folklore in context. In *Toward new perspectives in folklore,* edited by Américo Paredes and Richard Bauman, 3–19. Bloomington, IN: Trickster Press.

Berger, Harris M. 1997. The practice of perception: Multi-functionality and time in the musical experiences of heavy metal drummers in Akron, Ohio. *Ethnomusicology* 41(3):464–88.

———. 1999. *Metal, rock, and jazz: Perception and the phenomenology of musical experience.* Music/Culture series. Middletown, CT: Wesleyan University Press.

———. 2004. Horizons of melody and the problem of the self. In *Identity and everyday life: Essays in the study of music, folklore, and popular culture,* 43–88. Music/Culture series. Middletown, CT: Wesleyan University Press.

Berger, Harris M., and Giovanna P. Del Negro. 2004. *Identity and everyday life: Essays in the study of music, folklore, and popular culture.* Music/Culture series. Middletown, CT: Wesleyan University Press.

Berger, Harris M., and Cornelia Fales. 2005. "Heaviness" in the perception of heavy metal guitar timbres: The match of perceptual and acoustic features over time. In *Wired for sound: Engineering and technologies in sonic cultures,* edited by Paul D. Greene and Thomas Porcello, 181–97. Music/Culture series. Middletown, CT: Wesleyan University Press.

Bergson, Henri. 1913. *Time and free will.* Trans. R. L. Pogson. New York: Macmillan.

Berliner, Paul F. 1993. *Thinking in jazz: The infinite art of improvisation.* Chicago: University of Chicago Press.

Besnier, Niko. 1990. Language and affect. *Annual Review of Anthropology* 19:419–51.

Blacking, John. [1967] 1995. *Venda children's songs: A study in ethnomusicological analysis.* Chicago: University of Chicago Press.

Bourdieu, Pierre. 1977. *Outline of a theory of practice.* Trans. Richard Nice. Cambridge: Cambridge University Press.

———. 2002. Response to Throop and Murphy. *Anthropological Theory* 2(2):209.

Bucholtz, Mary, and Kira Hall. 2005. Identity and interaction: A sociocultural linguistic approach. *Discourse Studies* 7(4–5):585–614.

Cavicchi, Daniel. 1998. *Tramps like us: Music and meaning among Springsteen fans.* Oxford: Oxford University Press.

Cohen, Sara. 1999. Scenes. In *Key terms in popular music and culture,* edited by Bruce Horner and Thomas Swiss, 239–50. Malden, MA: Blackwell Publishers.

Cowan, Jane K. 1990. *Dance and the body politic in northern Greece.* Princeton: Princeton University Press.

Cowdery, James R., Dane L. Harwood, James Kippen, Michelle Kisliuk, David Locke, Eddie S. Meadows, Leonard B. Meyer, Ingrid Monson, John Shepherd, Christopher Small, and Christopher Waterman. 1995. Rejoinders. *Ethnomusicology* 39(1):73–96.

Csikszentmihalyi, Mihaly. [1975] 2000. *Beyond boredom and anxiety: Experiencing flow in work and play.* Twenty-fifth anniversary edition. San Francisco: Jossey-Bass Publishers.

Csordas, Thomas J. 1993. Somatic modes of attention. *Cultural Anthropology* 8(2):135–56.

Danielsen, Anne. 2006. *Presence and pleasure: The funk grooves of James Brown and Parliament.* Music/Culture series. Middletown, CT: Wesleyan University Press.

de Certeau, Michel. [1974] 1984. *The practice of everyday life.* Vol. 1. Trans. Steven Rendall. Berkeley: University of California Press.

Del Negro, Giovanna P. 2004. *The passeggiata and popular culture in an Italian town: Folklore and the performance of modernity.* Montreal: McGill-Queens University Press.

———. 2009. From the nightclub to the living room: Gender, ethnicity, and upward mobility in the 1950s party records of three Jewish women comics. In *Jews at home,* edited by Simon J. Bronner. Jewish Cultural Studies, Vol. 2. Oxford, UK: Littman Library of Jewish Civilization.

Dreyfus, Hubert L. 1991. *Being-in-the-world: A commentary on Heidegger's "Being and Time, Division 1."* Cambridge, MA: Massachusetts Institute of Technology Press.

———. 1992. *What computers still can't do: A critique of artificial reason.* Cambridge, MA: Massachusetts Institute of Technology Press.

Dundes, Alan. [1964] 1980. Texture, text, context. In *Interpreting folklore,* 20–32. Bloomington: Indiana University Press.

Feld, Steven. [1984] 1994. Communication, music, and speech about music. In *Music grooves,* 77–95. Chicago: University of Chicago Press.

———. [1988] 1994. Aesthetics as iconicity of style (uptown title); or (downtown title) "Lift-up-over Sounding": Getting into the Kaluli groove. In *Music grooves,* 109–50. Chicago: University of Chicago Press.

Fine, Elizabeth C. 1984. *The folklore text: From performance to print.* Bloomington: Indiana University Press.

Friedson, Steven. 1996. *Dancing prophets: Musical experiences in Tumbuka healing.* Chicago: University of Chicago Press.

Giddens, Anthony. [1976] 1993. *New rules of sociological method: A positive critique of interpretive sociologies.* 2nd ed. Stanford: Stanford University Press.

——. 1979. *Central problems in social theory: Action, structure, and contradiction in social analysis.* Berkeley: University of California Press.

——. 1984. *The constitution of society: Outline of the theory of structuration.* Berkeley: University of California Press.

Gilman, Lisa. 2009. Genre, agency, and meaning in the analysis of complex performances: The case of a Malawian political rally. *Journal of American Folklore* 122(485).

Goffman, Erving. 1959. *The presentation of self in everyday life.* New York: Doubleday Press.

Goldberg, Natalie. 1987. *Writing down the bones: Freeing the writer within.* Boston: Shambhala Publications.

Gossen, Gary. [1972] 2000. Chamula genres of verbal behavior. In *Toward new perspectives in folklore,* edited by Américo Paredes and Richard Bauman, 188–218. Bloomington, IN: Trickster Press.

Hahn, Tomie. 2006. "It's the RUSH": Sites of the sensually extreme. *TDR: The Drama Review* 50(2):87–96.

Hammond, Michael, Jane Howarth, and Russell Keat. 1991. *Understanding phenomenology.* Oxford, UK: Basil Blackwell.

Hanks, William F. [1987] 2000. Discourse genres in a theory of practice. In *Intertexts: Writings on language, utterance, and context,* 133–64. Lanham, MD: Rowman & Littlefield.

——. [1989] 2000a. Copresence and alterity in Maya ritual practice. In *Intertexts: Writings on language, utterance, and context,* 221–48. Lanham, MD: Rowman & Littlefield.

——. [1989] 2000b. The five gourds of memory. In *Intertexts: Writings on language, utterance, and context,* 197–217. Lanham, MD: Rowman & Littlefield.

——. [1989] 2000c. Texts and textuality. In *Intertexts: Writings on language, utterance, and context,* 165–96. Lanham, MD: Rowman & Littlefield.

——. 1990. *Referential practice: Language and lived space among the Maya.* Chicago: University of Chicago Press.

——. 1996. *Language and communicative practices.* Boulder: Westview Press.

Hebdige, Dick. 1979. *Subculture: The meaning of style.* London: Methuen.

Hemming, Jan. 2003. The case of new fascist rock music in Germany: An attempt to distinguish scalar and vectorial sign components. Paper presented at the biennial conference of the International Association for the Study of Popular Music, July 3–7, 2003, McGill University, Montreal, Quebec, Canada.

Horsley, Paul. 2006. Mozart was a punk, so Schubert was a goth: Musicians travel the country to prove classical is anything but dull. *Kansas City Star.* http://www.kansascity.com/mld/kansascity/entertainment/music/15520469.htm (accessed September 27, 2006).

Husserl, Edmund. [1913] 1962. *Ideas: General introduction to pure phenomenology.* Trans. W. R. Boyce Gibson. New York: Collier Books.

——. [1929] 1964. *The phenomenology of internal time-consciousness.* Trans. James S. Churchill, ed. Martin Heidegger. Bloomington: Indiana University Press.

——. [1931] 1960. *Cartesian meditations: An introduction to phenomenology.* Trans. Dorion Cairns. The Hague: Martinus Nijhoff.

Hymes, Dell. 1974. Ways of speaking. In *Explorations in the ethnography of speaking*, edited by Richard Bauman and Joel Sherzer, 433–52. London: Cambridge University Press.

Ihde, Don. 1976. *Listening and voice: A phenomenology of sound*. Athens: Ohio University Press.

———. 1986. *Experimental phenomenology: An introduction*. Albany: State University of New York Press.

Ingarden, Roman. [1933] 1989. The musical work. In *The ontology of the work of art*, trans. Raymond Meyer with John T. Goldthwait, 3–133. Athens: Ohio University Press.

Irvine, Judith. 1990. Registering affect: Heteroglossia in the linguistic expression of emotion. In *Language and the politics of emotion*, edited by Catherine Lutz and Lila Abu-Lughod, 126–61. Cambridge: Cambridge University Press.

Jackson, Michael. 1989. *Paths toward a clearing: Radical empiricism and ethnographic inquiry*. Bloomington: Indiana University Press.

James, William. [1890] 1981. *The principles of psychology*. Cambridge, MA: Harvard University Press.

———. [1904] 1967a. Does "consciousness" exist? In *Essays in radical empiricism and A pluralistic universe*, 1–38. Gloucester, MA: Peter Smith.

———. [1904] 1967b. A world of pure experience. In *Essays in radical empiricism and A pluralistic universe*, 39–91. Gloucester, MA: Peter Smith.

———. [1909, 1912] 1967. *Essays in radical empiricism* and *A pluralistic universe*. Gloucester, MA: Peter Smith.

Keil, Charles. [1966] 1994. Motion and feeling through music. In *Music grooves*, 53–76. Chicago: University of Chicago Press.

———. [1987] 1994. Participatory discrepancies and the power of music. In *Music grooves*, 96–108. Chicago: University of Chicago Press.

———. 1995. The theory of participatory discrepancies: A progress report. *Ethnomusicology* 39(1):1–20.

Keil, Charles, and Steven Feld. 1994. *Music grooves*. Chicago: University of Chicago Press.

Kirshenblatt-Gimblett, Barbara. 1975. A parable in context: A social interactional analysis of storytelling performance. In *Folklore: Performance and communication*, edited by Dan Ben-Amos and Kenneth Goldstein, 105–30. The Hague: Mouton.

Kockelman, Paul. 2004. Stance and subjectivity. *Journal of Linguistic Anthropology* 14(2):127–50.

Kockelmans, Joseph J. 1994. *Edmund Husserl's phenomenology*. West Lafayette, IN: Purdue University Press.

Kohák, Erazim V. 1978. *Idea and experience: Edmund Husserl's project of phenomenology in "Ideas I."* Chicago: University of Chicago Press.

Laughlin, Charles D., and C. Jason Throop. 2006. Cultural neurophenomenology: Integrating experience, culture, and reality through Fisher information. *Culture & Psychology* 12(3):305–37.

Lipsitz, George. 1998. *The possessive investment in whiteness: How white people profit from identity politics*. Philadelphia: Temple University Press.

Lutz, Catherine. 1988. *Unnatural emotions: Everyday sentiments on a Micronesian atoll & their challenge to Western theory*. Chicago: University of Chicago Press.

Lutz, Catherine, and Geoffrey White. 1986. The Anthropology of emotions. *Annual Review of Anthropology* 15:405–36.

Marx, Karl. [1852] 1972. The eighteenth brumaire of Louis Bonaparte. In *The Marx-Engels reader*, edited by Robert C. Tucker, 594–617. New York: W. W. Norton and Company.

Merleau-Ponty, Maurice. [1945] 1981. *Phenomenology of perception.* Trans. Colin Smith. London: Routledge.

———. [1964] 1968. *The visible and the invisible.* Trans. Alphonso Lingis, ed. Claude Lefort. Evanston: Northwestern University Press.

Merriam, Alan P. 1964. *The anthropology of music.* Evanston: Northwestern University Press.

Monson, Ingrid. 1996. *Saying something: Jazz improvisation and interaction.* Chicago: University of Chicago Press.

Natanson, Maurice. 1973. *Edmund Husserl: Philosopher of infinite tasks.* Evanston: Northwestern University Press.

Nettl, Bruno. 1964. *Theory and method in ethnomusicology.* Glencoe, IL: The Free Press.

———. 1974. Thoughts on improvisation: A comparative approach. *Musical Quarterly* 60(1):1–19.

Parmentier, Richard J. 1993. The political function of reported speech: A Belauan example. In *Reflexive language,* edited by John A. Lucy, 261–86. Cambridge: Cambridge University Press.

Porcello, Thomas. 1998. "Tails out": Social phenomenology and the ethnographic representation of technology in music-making. *Ethnomusicology* 42(3):485–510.

Provenza, Paul, and Penn Jillette, 2005. *The aristocrats.* Thinkfilm and Lions Gate Entertainment. DVD.

Radway, Janice A. 1984. *Reading the romance: Women, patriarchy, and popular culture.* Chapel Hill: University of North Carolina Press.

Reynolds, Jack. 2001. Maurice Merleau-Ponty (1908–1961). In *The Internet Encyclopedia of Philosophy.* http://www.iep.utm.edu/m/merleau.htm (accessed January 15, 2007).

Rice, Timothy. 1994. *May it fill your soul: Experiencing Bulgarian music.* Chicago: University of Chicago Press.

———. 2008. Toward a mediation of field methods and field experience in ethnomusicology. In *Shadows in the field: New perspectives for fieldwork in ethnomusicology,* 2nd ed., edited by Gregory F. Barz and Timothy J. Cooley, 42–61. Oxford: Oxford University Press.

Roberts, Warren E. 1988. *Viewpoints on folklife: Looking at the overlooked.* Ann Arbor, MI: UMI Research Press.

Sartre, Jean-Paul. [1939] 1970. Intentionality: A fundamental idea of Husserl's philosophy. Trans. Joseph P. Fell. *Journal of the British Society for Phenomenology* 1(2):4–5.

Sawyer, R. Keith. 1996. Semiotics of improvisation: The pragmatics of musical and verbal performance. *Semiotica* 108(3/4):269–306.

———. 1997. Improvisational theater: An ethnotheory of conversational practice. In *Creativity in performance,* 171–93. Greenwich, CT: Ablex.

Schmidt, James. 1985. *Maurice Merleau-Ponty: Between phenomenology and structuralism.* New York: St. Martin's Press.

Schutz, Alfred. [1932] 1967. *The phenomenology of the social world.* Trans. George Walsh and Frederick Lehnert. Evanston: Northwestern University Press.

———. 1976. Fragments on the phenomenology of music. Ed. Fred Kersten. *Music and Man* 2:5–72.

Schutz, Alfred, and Thomas Luckmann. 1973. *Structures of the life-world.* Vol. 1. Trans. Richard M. Zaner and H. Tristram Engelhardt Jr. Evanston: Northwestern University Press.

Seitel, Peter. 1969. Proverbs: A social use of metaphor. *Genre* 2(2):143–61.

Starr, Larry, and Christopher Waterman. 2003. *American popular music: The rock years.* Oxford: Oxford University Press.

Stone, Ruth M. 1982. *Let the inside be sweet: The interpretation of music event among the Kpelle of Liberia*. Bloomington: Indiana University Press.
——. 1988. *Dried millet breaking: Time, words, and song in the Woi epic of the Kpelle*. Bloomington: Indiana University Press.
Sudnow, David. 1978. *Ways of the hand: The organization of improvised conduct*. Cambridge, MA: Harvard University Press.
Sugarman, Jane C. 1997. *Engendering song: Singing and subjectivity at Prespa Albanian weddings*. Chicago: University of Chicago Press.
Tenuta, Judy. 1987. *Buy this, pigs!* Elektra audiocassette 9 60746–4.
Throop, C. Jason. 2003. Articulating experience. *Anthropological Theory* 3(2):219–41.
Throop, C. Jason, and Keith M. Murphy. 2002. Bourdieu and phenomenology: A critical assessment. *Anthropological Theory* 2(2):185–207.
Titon, Jeff Todd. 1985. Stance, role, and identity in fieldwork among folk Baptists and Pentecostals. *American Music* 3(1):16–24.
——. 1988. *Powerhouse for God: Speech, chant, and song in an Appalachian Baptist church*. Austin: University of Texas Press.
——. 2008. Knowing fieldwork. In *Shadows in the field: New perspectives for fieldwork in ethnomusicology*, 2nd ed., edited by Gregory F. Barz and Timothy J. Cooley, 25–41. Oxford: Oxford University Press.
Todes, Samuel. [1990] 2001. *Body and world*. Cambridge, MA: Massachusetts Institute of Technology Press.
Walser, Robert. 1993. *Running with the Devil: Power, gender, and madness in heavy metal music*. Music/Culture series. Middletown, CT: Wesleyan University Press.
Webster, Anthony K. 2008. Running again, roasting again, touching again: On repetition, heightened affective expressivity, and the utility of the notion of linguaculture in Navajo and beyond. *Journal of American Folklore* 121(482):441–72.
Weinstein, Deena. 1993. Rock bands: Collective creativity. *Current Research on Occupations and Professions* 8:205–22.
——. 2000. *Heavy metal: A cultural sociology*. Reprint edition. Boulder: Da Capo Press.
Wolf, Richard K. 2006. The poetics of "Sufi" practice: Drumming, dancing, and complex agency at Madho Lāl Husain (and beyond). *American Ethnologist* 33(2):246–68.
Young, Katharine Galloway. 1987. *Taleworlds and storyrealms: The phenomenology of narrative*. Boston: Martinus Nijhoff.

Index

Body (*continued*)
behaviors, 85–87, 92–93; the musical
composition as set of embodied practices, 7; Todes on embodiment and
subjectivity, 11, 36, 112–14, 149n9
Body and World (Todes), 11, 112, 149nn 9,
10
Bourdieu, Pierre: anthropologists influ-
enced by, 138n7; on *habitus,* 146n5,
148n1; as influence on this study, 6;
Outline of a Theory of Practice, 65;
and phenomenology, 147n1; and prac-
tice theory, 6, 14, 97–99, 146n5, 147n1;
on the relationship of practice and
structure, 14, 97–99; on tempo, 65
Boxing, attention to other's stance in, 80
"Box Set" (Barenaked Ladies), 120
Brentano, Franz, 17
Brown, James, 145n14
Bucholtz, Mary, 139n8
Buckethead, 45
Bulgarian bagpipe music, 146n8
Butler, Judith, 145n12
Buy This, Pigs! (Tenuta), 48–49

Cage, John, 20
Calls to action in expressive culture, 121–
22
Cartesian Meditations (Husserl), 70, 71
Cash, Johnny, 120
Charisma, 119
Chess-by-mail example, 35–36
Chiasm, 57, 86, 146n1
Chopin piano piece example, 7–8
Chuck D, 120
"Cinderella" (Brothers Grimm), 98
Civil rights movement, 126, 133
Clash, the (band), 109
Collage, 106
Coltrane, John, 29, 123
Comedy: situation, 117–18, 127; stand-up,
48, 53, 66, 97, 102–3, 112, 116, 118
Composition: composer's grappling with,
12; facility in, 29; as intentional en-
gagement with a piece of music, 19;
mistaken attribution of, 75; as noetic
sub-mode, 19–20, 25; partial auton-
omy of, 10–11; seen as preexisting entity in Western music, 6–7, 8, 10, 141nn
13, 15; as spanning perception and
imagination, 19
Compositional stance: attempts to obscure
or eradicate, 22; audience member's

interpretation of, 15; defined, 10; ex-
ample of, 8–13
Composition class example, 9–10, 11–13,
32, 34–35, 59–60, 73, 74, 98, 114
"Composition Study 5," 9, 19, 32, 34–35,
59–60
Conceptual art, 22
Consciousness: as intentional, 17–18; re-
flexive self-consciousness, 42, 45, 89, 91,
92; stream of, 42. *See also* Intentionality
Consequences: consequentiality of ex-
pressive culture, 125–35; politics of
meaning and, 111
Context, 98
Contextualist critique, 2, 4, 137n2
"Corporate Veil, The" (*Law and Order*
episode), 67–68
Cowell, Simon, 120
Crying Game, The (film), 49
Csikszentmihalyi, Mihaly, 52
Csordas, Thomas J., 138n7, 142n26, 147n1
Cultural studies: Birmingham School, 105
Culture: attention affected by, xi; and
audience's grasp of performer's stance,
61–70; audience stance influenced by,
14; cultures of stance, 104–9; dialectic
of agency and, 25, 104; expressive behavior shaped by, 31–32; noetic sub-
modes as culturally specific, 19–20;
norms and models, 102; as organization of difference, 101–2; practice-
oriented constructions of, 102–3,
148n3; in relationship of text, experience, and meaning, xiii–xiv; stance
and, 100–104; stance as dependent on,
8, 23; and stance on the other, 74–75,
76–77; stance-prominent cultures, 106,
107–9, 148n6; subcultures, 104–6;
text-prominent cultures, 106–7, 108–9;
traditional view of, 100–101

Dance: awkward dancer example, 38
Danielsen, Anne, 145n14
Death metal, 122, 126, 128
De Certeau, Michel, 126
Del Negro, Giovanna P., 20, 77, 101, 102–3
Dennett, Daniel, 140n8
Depression, 44
Derrida, Jacques, 145n12
Des'ree, 122–23, 126, 128
Determination, 89
Didactic realism, 127
Digging-in-for-the-long-haul, 89, 90

Disinvoltura, 101
Dispositions: dispositional attitudes toward power, 131; valence, 44–45
Distorted guitar timbres, 62–64
Distraction, 40–43, 52
Domination, 100, 115–16, 126, 127, 132–33, 134
Dreyfus, Hubert, 36, 149n10
Dried Millet Breaking (Stone), 138n6, 145n15
Driven sound sources, 62, 63, 64
Dubbing, in improvisational theater, 21
Dundes, Alan, 98
Dylan, Bob, 98
Dynamics (in music), 7, 8, 141n11

Editing, 59, 68
Ensemble coordination, 78–80, 107
Epoché, 17, 18, 142nn 20, 21
Ethnography: ethnographic critiques of text-oriented folklore studies, 2; multisite, viii; participant observation, xii; phenomenology's applicability to, xviii–xix, 25–26; stance on the long scale and, 94. *See also* Fieldwork
Ethnomusicology: context as key concept in, 98; as disciplinary ground of this study, vii, xvi, 5; phenomenological research in, 137n6
Everybody Loves Raymond (television program), 117, 118, 124, 127
Expansive quality of meaning: and meaning contents, 45; stance and, 39–47; stance on the other and, 73; time and the dynamics of, 47–51
Experience: act character of, 18, 40–42; agency in, 51–52, 95; components of, 47; continuity within, 76; culture in relationship of text, meaning, and, xiii–xiv; in everyday talk, 17; foreground/background structure of, xiii, 33–34, 144n9; immediate experience of self, 142n17; as knowable, x–xii; phenomenological approach to, 17; production of expressive culture requires, 12; partial sharing of, xii, 25–26, 59–61, 70, 73, 74–77, 80–81; as social, 54, 139n7; and social practice, 97–98; structures of, xi–xv, 10, 25, 97; sustaining, 51–52, 95; temporal structure of, xiii, 47–51, 84–95; texts in, ix–x. *See also* Lived experience
Experimental Phenomenology (Ihde), 70

Expressive culture: complex relationships of subjects with, 4–5; consequentiality of, 125–35; defined, 137n1; experience as theoretical concept in study of, ix–x; foreground/background structure of experience and, xiii; formal elements seen as explaining meaning in, 1–5; as influence on social life of power, 134–35; and the large-scale social world, 95–96; and noetic sub-modes, 19–20, 25; political dynamics of activist, ideological, and stance-oriented, 125–29; politics and, xv–xvi, 25, 99; power and, 124–35; practice and, 98–99; stance-on-power in politics of, 116–21, 124. *See also* Comedy; Dance; Film; Literature; Music; Painting
Expressive-political nexus, 121–25
Extremes of experience, 61, 146n3

"Fables of Faubus" (Mingus), 124
Facet/facet-stance complex, 34
Facet stances, 32, 33, 34, 35, 103–4
Facility: in musical ideologies, 104; tempo as trace of, 66; as a type of stance quality, 28–29
Fair Housing Act (1968), 133, 150n15
Fales, Cornelia, 63
Faubus, Orval E., 124
Feld, Steven, 82, 138n6, 146n4, 150n14
Fields, Totie, 112
Fieldwork: attention to stance in, xv; examples from, xvii; phenomenology's application to, xviii–xix, 25–26, 94; Rice on phenomenology and, 138n6; stance on the long scale and, 94; Titon on phenomenology and, 138n6
Figure skating, 29, 101–2
Film: iteration in the reception of, 47–48; and mistaken attribution, 75; stance and complexity of production process of, 68–69
Flow, 52
Folklore studies: context as key concept in, 98; as disciplinary ground of this study, vii, xvi, 5; overlooked culture as object of study in, xii; relevance of phenomenology for, ix–xv
Folk revival, 118
"For a subject" qualities, 19, 142n24
Foreground/background structure of experience, xiii, 33–34, 107–108, 144n9. *See also* Experience; Phenomenology

Formal elements of expressive culture, seen as explaining meaning, 1–5
Foucault, Michel, 99–100
Free jazz, 79
Friedson, Steven, 138n6
Fry, Stephen, 24
Fugazi (band), 104
Funk music, 51
Future: experience and the negotiation of past and, 93–94; past and present constrain experiences of, 98–99; protentions of, 87–88, 89, 90, 91, 92, 93, 95; social context and expectations for, 94–95

Gadamer, Hans-Georg, 138n6
Gardening example, 41, 42
Garden path sentences, 48
Garrett, Brad, 112
Genre: in which stance is the focus, 111–12; text-prominent and stance-prominent cultures and the notion of, 108–9; timbre as sign of musical, 63–64
Gestalt, 15–16, 34, 44, 50, 60, 92, 93
"Giant Steps" (Coltrane), 123
Giddens, Anthony: on duality of structure and agency, 147n1; as influence on this study, 6; on power, 114–15, 150n11; on the relationship of practice and structure, 14, 97–99
Goffman, Erving, 116, 145n13, 149n7
Goldbergs, The (television program), 102–3
Gottfried, Gilbert, 46, 144n10
Granner, Nathan, 109
Grateful Dead, the (band), 145n14
Gravity, 112–13, 149n8
Greek tragedy, 49
Groove, xiii, 81–84, 150n14
Guitar exercises example, 85–87, 88–90, 91–93, 94

Hall, Kira, 139n8
Hanks, William F., 138n7, 141n13, 143n2, 145n11, 146nn 5, 7, 147n1
Happy Days (television program), 127–28
Hatecore, 121, 128
Heavy metal: audience attention to virtuosity in, 62; cultural shaping of awareness in, xi; death metal, 122, 126, 128; distorted guitar timbres in, 62–64; gender in pop metal, 110–11; hatecore, 121, 128; powerful stance in, 62–65; sweep picking in, 66–67; technically polished punk distinguished from, 104

Hebdige, Dick, 104–6, 108, 122, 126, 148n5
Hegemony, 130
Heidegger, Martin, 138n6
Hemming, Jan, 150n13
Herder, Johann Gottfried von, xvi
Hocket effect, 79–80
Holding-at-bay, 52
Hollywoodland (film), 119
Home Improvement (television program), 117, 127
"House of the Rising Sun" (Baez), 119
Human Body as Material Subject of the World, The (Todes), 149n9
Husserl, Edmund: anthropology and, 139n7; Bourdieu and, 148n1; Cartesian Meditations, 70, 71; in development of phenomenology, 16–17; on epoché, 17, 142n20; as influence on this study, xv, 5, 6; on intentionality, 16, 17–18, 30, 141n13, 143n4; on the living present, 48, 88; on noema, 18; on noesis, 18; on now-point, 49, 88; on protention, 87; on pseudo-organisms, 71; on retention, 49; on seeing as, 71; on seeing the other as a subject, 70, 71, 76; on time consciousness, 48, 87, 147n11
Hymes, Dell, 30, 101, 143n4
Hypothetical examples, discussed, xvii–xviii

Idealism, 18, 112, 113, 114, 142n21
Identity, as a type of stance quality, 30
Ideology: and expressive-political nexus, 121–25; ideologies of stance, 21–22, 109; political dynamics of activist, ideological, and stance-oriented expressive culture, 125–29
"I Don't Believe You" (Magnetic Fields), 45
Ihde, Don, 42, 70, 145n11, 147n11
Imagination: composing in, 9–10; as noetic mode, 18; partial autonomy of entities in, 11–12, 19; social and bodily ground of, 11–12; Todes's phenomenology of, 114
Improvisational theater, 20, 21, 25, 36–38
Impulsive sound sources, 62, 63
Individualism, 126–27
Industrial music, 84
Ingarden, Roman, 138n7, 141nn 13, 15, 16, 145nn 11, 13
Instant messaging, 58
Institutions constituted in practice, 132–33, 150n15

Intentionality: and act character of perception, 18–19, 30, 143n4; bodily chiasm as illustration of, 57–58; as ground of stance, 16–26; intentional objects, 141n13; structure given to experience by, 97; use in phenomenology defined, 17
Interpretation: definitions of, 140n9; in musical performance, 7–8, 140n9
Interpretative framework, 140n9
Interviews in fieldwork, ix, xii, xv, xix, 52, 94
Irony, 105, 106, 111
Irvine, Judith, 139n7, 143nn 2, 5
Iterability, 145n12
Iteration, 48, 50, 51, 52, 93, 104, 145n12

Jackson, Michael, 138n7
James-Lange theory, 44, 78
James, William, 52, 76
Javanese gamelan music, 8
Jazz: Coltrane, John, 29, 123; industrial music contrasted with, 84; Mingus, Charles, 124; mutual attention to each other's stance in small group, 78–79; negotiation of harmonic rhythm in, 79; participatory discrepancies in, 82–83; sharing of stance in, 73
Jillette, Penn, 144n10

Kant, Immanuel, 112, 114
Keil, Charles: influences on, 82; on participatory discrepancies, 81–84, 146n4, 150n14
Kinks, The (band), 119–20
Kockelman, Paul, 140n8, 144n6
Kohák, Erazim, 18–19, 142n20, 147n10
Kristeva, Julia, 105

Laughlin, Charles D., 138n7
Law and Order (television series), 67–68
Lévy-Bruhl, Lucien, 82
Liar, The (Fry), 24
Liberation movements: music of, 125–26; stance within, 130
Lipsitz, George, 133, 150n15
Listening: facility in, 29; as noetic submode, 19–20, 25; with open heart, 72, 73; to an other, 72–73; social nature of, 14–15
Literature: character development in, 49–50; interpretation and expression of stance in, 59. See also Novels

Lived experience: in analysis of expressive culture, 139n7; bringing texts into, ix, xii, xiv; iterative quality of, 48, 50, 51, 52; objectivity and, 17; phenomenology in study of, xviii; range of locations and modalities in which valences may appear in, 44–45; retrospection in, 48–50, 51, 52; stance as necessary feature of, 21–23; structures of stance in, 27–53. See also Experience
Lives, constitution of in time, 93–94. See also Lived experience
Living present, xiii, 43–44, 48–50, 88, 145n14
Luckmann, Thomas, 148n4
Lutz, Catherine, 139n7
Lydon, Johnny, 120

Machismo, 110–11, 121
Magnetic Fields (band), 45
Malmsteen, Yngwie, 66
Marx, Karl, 98, 148n2
Massage example, 56–57
Masson, André, 106, 108
McCartney, Paul, 2
McClary, Susan, xvi
Meaning: act character of experience and, 18; active valuation in bestowing, 28; audience stance in experience of, 14, 15; crosses borders between phenomena, 39–40, 52–53, 99; culture in relationship of experience, text, and, xiii–xiv; in expressive culture, formal elements seen as explaining, 1–5; interpretation of, vii–ix; and lives, 93–94; as product of texts in experience, ix–x; reification distorts interpretation of, 24; and semiotics, ix, 5, 105, 108, 139n7, 150n13; stance as pivotal factor in, xiv, 5, 25–26; temporal dynamics of, 47–51. See also Expansive quality of meaning
Melodic sequence, 67
Memory: limits on, 65; recalling the past, 76
Merleau-Ponty, Maurice: anthropologists influenced by, 138n7; Bourdieu and, 147n1; on chiasm, 57, 86, 146n1; Csordas and, 147n1; on embodiment and subjectivity, 11, 36, 44, 57, 86; as influence on this study, xv, 5, 6; on "palpating" an object of visual perception, 3, 57, 99; Phenomenology of Perception,

Merleau-Ponty, Maurice (*continued*)
57; secondary literature on, 146n1;
Todes influenced by, 112; *Visible and
the Invisible, The*, 57
Merriam, Alan, 98
Meta-stance, 32–33; dialectic of culture
and agency in, 103–4; on long time-
scales, 91–92; and quasi-texts, 107; in
stance-oriented research, 35, 108
Mingus, Charles, 124
Ministry, 84
Monroe, Bill, 148n6
Monty Python, 21
Mood, 44, 45–46, 147n13
Motor behaviors, stance on, 85–87, 92–93
Mozart, Wolfgang Amadeus, 109
Murder mysteries, xiii–xiv, 49, 69
Murphy, Keith M., 148n1
Music: aleatory, 22; as code, 61, 146n4;
examples in this study, xvi–xvii;
groove in, xiii, 81–84; industrial, 84; of
liberation movements, 125–26; politi-
cal singer-songwriters, 118–19; stance
illustrated by extended example from,
6–16. *See also* Composition; Ethnomu-
sicology; Folklore; Jazz; Rock music
Musical persona, 110

Nap example, 40–41, 42–43, 45, 144n9
Nettl, Bruno, 6
Newman, Stanley, 143n4
New musicology, xvi
Noema, 18; for-a-subject quality of, 19,
142n24; meta-stance on, 32; noesis
never completely dissolves into, 58;
total stance and, 33
Noesis, 18–21; for-a-subject quality of, 19;
modes of, 18; as never completely dis-
solving into noema, 58. *See also* Noetic
sub-modes
Noetic sub-modes, 19–21; comedy improvisation and, 38; as culturally specific, 19–
20; telling and listening to proverbs as,
30; and the understanding of expressive
practices, 25. *See also* Noesis
North Country (film), 127–28
Novels: character-driven, 50–51; rhythm
in, xiii, xiv. *See also* Murder mysteries
Now-point, 49, 88

Objects of attention: diversity of, 35–39;
as noema, 18; and stance as always
distinct, 38

"Old-time" music, 59
Openness-to-the-world, 52
Other, the: listening as listening to, 72–73;
seeing as a subject, 70–71, 73–76. *See
also* Stance-on-the-other
Outline of a Theory of Practice (Bourdieu), 65

Pacifism, 130
Painting: interpretation and expression of
stance in, 59; Pollock's abstract expressionism, 117–18
Parliament (band), 51
Participatory discrepancies (PDs), 81–84,
146n4, 150n14
Passeggiata, 20–21, 25, 99, 101
Past: experience and the negotiation of
future and, 93–94; recalling the, 76;
retention, 49, 88, 89, 90, 91, 92, 93, 95,
147n12; social context and experience
of, 94–95
Peanuts (animated cartoons), 31
Peirce, Charles Sanders, 5, 139n7
Perception: act character of, 18–19; the
body as agent of, 57, 86; in composing and performing, 13; as noetic
mode, 18; seeing as, 70–71; as social
practice, 147n1; Todes on practical,
112–14. *See also* Experience; Merleau-
Ponty; Todes
Performance: expansive character of
meaning and, 46–47; facility in, 29; as
intentional engagement with piece of
music, 19; meaning and formal details
of, 2–3; mistaken attribution of, 75;
mutual attention to the other's stance
in, 77–80; as noetic sub-mode, 19–20,
25; as space where power is enacted,
124. *See also* Performative stance
Performance studies: vii, ix, x, 100
Performative stance: attempts to obscure
or eradicate, 22; audience member's
perception of, 60–70, 147n9; defined,
8; differing attitudes toward, 22; example of, 6–8; genres in which it is
prominent, 112; meaning complicated
by, 110; stance-on-power in, 116–20;
features of a style contrasted with, 31
Personal examples, discussed, xvii–xviii
Persons: as inherently situated in a world,
114; mutually constitutive relationship
of world and, 19; potential coherence
of, 85, 93

Phenomenal tempo, 66–68, 69

Phenomenology, vii–xix; anthropology and 5, 138n7; applicability to ethnography, xviii–xix, 25–26; basic premises of, 16–21; ethnomusicology and, 137n6; living present, xiii, 48, 49, 88, 145n14; and mutually constitutive relationship of self and world, 19, 142n25; and structures of experience, xi, xii, xiv, 97

Phenomenology of Internal Time-Consciousness (Husserl), 147n11

Phenomenology of Perception (Merleau-Ponty), 57

Phenomenology of the Social World (Schutz), 147n11

Phish (band), 145n14

Platonism, 7

Player, The (film), 119

Plot, phenomenal density and, 68

Poise, 11, 113–14, 149nn 8, 10

Politics: expressive-political nexus, 121–25; and expressive culture, xv–xvi, 25, 99; "the personal is the political," 126; political dynamics of activist, ideological, and stance-oriented expressive culture, 125–29; of stance, 110–25; stance in politics of everyday life, 129–31; stance-on-power in explicitly political contexts, 116. *See also* Power

Pollock, Jackson, 117–18

Pope, Carol, 30

Popular culture: political significance ascribed to texts of, viii; stance and "scenes" of, 106; relevance of structures of experience for the study of, xi–xii

Power: consequentiality of expressive culture for, 125–35; dispositional attitudes toward, 131; hegemony, 130; issues in expressive culture, xv–xvi, 99; society as field of, 115, 150n12; twofold nature of, 114–15, 124, 150n11. *See also* Politics; Stance-on-power

Practice theory: on context, 98; as influence on this study, 6, 147n1; production and reception of expressive culture as practice, 14; on social practice, 97; stance and social practice, 54. *See also* Social practices

Protention, 87–88, 89, 90, 91, 92, 93, 95

Provenza, Paul, 144n10

Proverbs, 30–31, 143n5

Punk music: death metal and, 122; infacil-

ity in, 29, 104; stance-prominent culture of, 104–8, 127

Quasi-stances, 30, 31–32, 33, 38, 144n5

Quasi-texts, 38, 107, 108, 148n6

Reader response methodology, xii

Realism, 18, 142n25

"Rebel conservatives," 127

Reception: as active grappling with the things of the world, 4, 27; and groove, 82–84; reception-centered critique of textualism, 3, 4, 137n4; as social practice, 14; as used in this study, 137n5. *See also* Audience; Listening

Reflexive self-consciousness, 42, 45, 89, 91, 92

Reification: culture and, 20; traditional style terms and, 23–24

Religious ritual, stance in, 22

Resistance to domination, 100, 126, 133, 134

Retention, 49, 88, 89, 90, 91, 92, 93, 95, 147n12

Retrospection, 48–50, 51, 52, 53, 93, 104

"Revenge of the Double" (Buckethead), 45

"Reverse racism," 127

Rice, Timothy, 138n6, 146n8

Ricoeur, Paul, 138n6

Rites of Spring (band), 104

Roberts, Warren, xii

Rock music: instrumental guitar rock, 29; misjudging composition and performance in, 77. *See also* Heavy metal; Punk music

Romano, Ray, 116–17, 118, 124

Roth, David Lee, 110–11

Rubin's Goblet, 70

Running with the Devil (Walser), 62

St. Paul, Lou, 66

Sartre, Jean-Paul, xv, 142n22

Saussure, Ferdinand de, 150n13

Sawyer, R. Keith, 7, 21, 36–37, 146n8

Scalars, 150n13

Schutz, Alfred: anthropology and, 138n7; Bourdieu and, 148n1; ethnomusicology and, 138n6; as influence on this study, xv; on lived awareness of distant places and times, 93–94; on practice, 148n4; on provinces of meaning, 148n4; on temporality, 147n11

Seeger, Charles, 138n6

Seeing as, 70–71

Self-consciousness, reflexive, 42, 45, 89, 91, 92

Self-hypnosis, 45

Semiotics, ix, 5, 105, 108, 139n7, 150n13

Sensibility, 23, 24

Sensitivity, 55, 64

Settling-in-for-the-long-haul, 91

Shock-of-failed-control, 86, 87, 93

Shudder to Think (band), 104

Signifying practices, 105, 108

Singer-songwriters, 118–19

Situation comedy, 117–18, 127

Social practice: constitution of experience as, 97–98; differing domains of, 99–100; Hanks on language and, 146n5; political significance of, 99; practice-oriented constructions of culture, 102–3, 148n3; production and reception of expressive culture as, 14; stance and, 54, 98, 103–4. *See also* Practice theory

Stage fright, 119

Stage presence, 119

Stance: and act character of experience, 40–42; as agentive, 114; complexity of expression in media, 63; and culture, 100–104; as culture dependent, 23; cultures of stance, 104–9; definition of, 21; expansive quality of meaning and, 39–47; expressive features interpreted as traces of, 65; as factor in meaning, xiv, 5, 25–26, 110–11; faking, 147n9; formal fundamental dynamics of, 27–39; ideologies of, 21–22, 109; illustrated by extended example, 6–16; indirect relationships among, 34; intentionality as ground of, 16–26, 97; interpreting the stance of the other 54–70; and its expression, 54–70; in linguistics, 139n8; in long time-scales, 84–95; media of its expression distinguished from, 54–60; on motor behaviors, 85–87; multifacetedness of, 32–35; as necessary feature of all lived experience, 21–23; and objects of attention as always distinct, 38–39; politics of, 110–25; rehearsal and training for, 103; scholars interpreting, 69–70; social life of, 100–109; structures in lived experience, 27–53; temporal dimensions of, 47–51, 84–96; Titon's definition of, 138n6; Todes's definition of, 149n10; traditional style terms contrasted with,

24–25; varies by situation, 102. *See also* Audience stance (stance in practice of reception); Compositional stance; Performative stance; Stance-on-power; Stance-on-the-other; Stance qualities

Stance in practice of reception. *See* Audience stance (stance in practice of reception)

Stance-on-power, 111–21; among audience members, 120–21; among performers, 116–20; and decontextualized affect, 123; defined, 114–15; examples of, 115–16; in explicitly political contexts, 116; in the expressive-political nexus, 121–25; hegemony as complex of ensembles of, 130; and the political dynamics of activist, ideological, and stance-oriented expressive culture, 125–29; in politics of everyday life, 129–31; in politics of expressive culture, 116–21, 124; in social life in general, 131; social relations involved in producing expressive culture and, 119–20; stance qualities of, 115

Stance-on-the-other, 70–84; and culture, 74–75, 76–77; defined, 71; and expansive quality of meaning, 73; mutual, 77–81; and participatory discrepancies, 81–84; in punk music, 122; as quintessentially social, 72; stance-on-power among audiences, 120; stance qualities of, 71–72; variety of in everyday life, 129

Stance-on-the-other's-stance: defined, 71; and expansive quality of meaning, 73; mutual, 77–81; as quintessentially social, 72

Stance-prominent cultures, 106, 107–9, 148n6

Stance qualities, types of: affect as, 29; facility as, 28–29; identity as, 30; style as, 30; timbres of attention and action as, 29

Stand-up comedy, 48, 53, 66, 97, 102–3, 112, 116, 118

Stanley, Ralph, 148n6

Starr, Larry, 1–2

Stone, Ruth, 77, 137n2, 138n6, 145n15

Student recital example, 25, 34–35, 55, 59, 68, 70, 72, 73, 98

Style: compared with stance, 23–24, 143n4; Hymes's definition of, 143n4; as sedimented quasi-stances, 30, 31–32;

subcultures and, 105, 106; as a type of stance quality, 30

Subculture, 104–6

Sub-modes, noetic. *See* Noetic sub-modes

Sudnow, David, 7

Sweep picking, 66–67

Symphonic music, narrative structures in, 49, 145n14

Tel Quel semiotics, 105

Tempo, 65–68; negotiation in music performance, 78–79

Tenuta, Judy, 48–49

Text-prominent cultures, 106–7, 108–9

Texts: constitution of meaning of, xiv, 4; context and, 98; culture in relationship of experience, meaning, and, xiii–xiv; as emerging in practice, 99; in experience, ix–x; formal elements seen as explaining meaning in, 1–5. *See also* Quasi-texts

Theater, improvisational, 20, 21, 25, 36–38

Thoughts: dimensions of thinking, 144n9; embracing and resisting, 42; obsession, 40–41; valence of thought and valence of stance upon thought as distinct, 42–43, 144n9; valual quality of, 42

Throop, C. Jason, 138n7, 145n11, 148n1

Timbre: defined, 141n12; distorted guitar timbres, 62–64

Timbres of attention and action, as a type of stance quality, 29–30

Time: dynamics in expansive quality of meaning, 47–51; Husserl on consciousness of, 48, 87, 147n11; living present, xiii, 48, 49, 88, 145n14; now-point, 49, 88; phenomenological research on, 145n11; protention, 87–88; retention, 49, 88, 89, 90, 91, 92, 93, 95, 147n12; stance in long time-scales, 84–95. *See also* Tempo

Time and Free Will (Bergson), 147n11

Titon, Jeff Todd, 138n6

Todes, Samuel: *Body and World*, 11, 112, 149nn 9, 10; on embodiment and subjectivity, 36, 112–14, 149n9; as influence on this study, xv, 5, 6; on poise, 11, 113–14, 149nn 8, 10; on the social subject, 149n9

Total stance, 33–34, 35, 103–4

Trapeze artists, and stances, 80

Valual qualities: agency and, 95; as component of experience, 47; as connecting experiences across events, 88, 93; cultural knowledge in understanding, 61; defined, 137n2; of facet stances, 32; in experiences of long temporal scales, 90–92; range of locations and modalities in which valences may appear, 44–45; stance and, xiv, 5, 13, 21, 22, 30, 55; of thoughts, 42, 43; traditional style terms and, 23; valences cross borders between phenomena, 52–53; valences of stance on the other, 71–72; valence of thought and valence of stance upon thought as distinct, 42–43

Verbal Art as Performance (Bauman), 28

Virtuosity, 29, 62

Visible and the Invisible, The (Merleau-Ponty), 57

Voice, in music, 9, 141n14

Walser, Robert, xvi, 62, 137n4

Waterman, Christopher, 1–2

"Ways of Speaking" (Hymes), 143n4

Weinstein, Deena, 6–7, 137n4

White, Geoffrey, 139n7

Wilde, Oscar, 24

"Working at the Factory" (the Kinks), 119–20

Wrestling, 29

Yeats, William Butler, 39

"Yesterday" (the Beatles), 1–2

"You Gotta Be" (Des'ree), 122–23, 128

Young, Katharine Galloway, 141nn 15, 16, 145nn 11, 13

The Other Side of Nowhere:
Jazz, Improvisation, and Communities
in Dialogue
edited by Daniel Fischlin and Ajay
Heble

Empire of Dirt:
The Aesthetics and Rituals of British
"Indie" Music
by Wendy Fonarow

The 'Hood Comes First:
Race, Space, and Place in Rap and
Hip-Hop
by Murray Forman

Wired for Sound:
Engineering and Technologies in Sonic
Cultures
edited by Paul D. Greene
and Thomas Porcello

Sensational Knowledge:
Embodying Culture through Japanese
Dance
by Tomie Hahn

Voices in Bali:
Energies and Perceptions in Vocal Music
and Dance Theater
by Edward Herbst

Traveling Spirit Masters:
Moroccan Gnawa Trance and Music in
the Global Marketplace
by Deborah Kapchan

Symphonic Metamorphoses:
Subjectivity and Alienation in Mahler's
Re-Cycled Songs
by Raymond Knapp

Music and Technoculture
edited by René T. A. Lysloff
and Leslie C. Gay, Jr.

A Thousand Honey Creeks Later:
My Life in Music from Basie to
Motown—and Beyond
by Preston Love

Songs, Dreamings, and Ghosts:
The Wangga of North Australia
by Allan Marett

Phat Beats, Dope Rhymes:
Hip Hop Down Under Comin' Upper
by Ian Maxwell

Some Liked it Hot:
Jazz Women in Film and Television,
1928–1959
by Kristin A. McGee

Carriacou String Band Serenade:
Performing Identity in the Eastern
Caribbean
by Rebecca S. Miller

Global Noise:
Rap and Hip-Hop Outside the USA
edited by Tony Mitchell

Popular Music in Theory:
An Introduction
by Keith Negus

Upside Your Head!:
Rhythm and Blues on Central
Avenue
by Johnny Otis

Coming to You Wherever You Are:
MuchMusic, MTV, and Youth Identities
by Kip Pegley

Singing Archaeology:
Philip Glass's Akhnaten
by John Richardson

Black Noise:
Rap Music and Black Culture in Con-
temporary America
by Tricia Rose

The Book of Music and Nature:
An Anthology of Sounds, Words,
Thoughts
edited by David Rothenberg
and Marta Ulvaeus

ABOUT THE AUTHOR

Harris M. Berger is Associate Professor of Music and Associate Head in the Department of Performance Studies at Texas A&M University. He is the author of *Metal, Rock, and Jazz* (1999) and coauthor of *Identity and Everyday Life* (2004).